I0459562

THE BELGRAVE LEGACY

ZARA HOFFMAN

ZH
press

The Belgrave Legacy.
Copyright ©2016 by Zara Hoffman.

The Belgrave Legacy/Zara Hoffman — 1st ed.
ISBN 978-0-9864279-1-6

Book Cover Design ©2015 Jennifer Munswami, Rising Horse Creations
Title Font ©2015 Jennifer Munswami, Rising Horse Creations
Edited by Danielle Lincoln Hanna

For Grammy,
My guardian angel

For Mom,
My biggest supporter

part one

The world is full of magic things,
Patiently waiting for our senses to grow sharper.

W.B. YEATS

PROLOGUE

A POWERFUL SORCERESS WITH BLOOD LACED IN GOLD SEVENFOLD *shall determine the fate of the world.*

The ancient man's eyes scanned the scroll again. Fawn's destiny had been appointed at her birth, but the girl's mother had never spoken to her about it. He had done his best to conceal her identity from the Devil, but now the girl's powers had emerged, they formed a beacon which would attract the attention not only of Lucifer, but also of every other Supernatural in the world. Her existence would not remain a mystery from anyone, friend or foe, much longer. Unfortunately, the intensity of Fawn's powers had begun to shred the protective veil the month before.

Outside, metal clattered to the white marble floor, disrupting the silence. *He's early,* the man mused.

He waved a hand over the parchment, magically rolling it up. He snapped his fingers and the scroll disappeared in a puff of smoke, returning to its secret hiding place. Only when it was gone did he signal the guards to exit. Dusting off the lapels of his white suit, he stood and used his ivory cane for support as he walked up the marble stairs to his golden throne.

The doors burst open and a draft strong enough to pick any mortal off the ground howled through the hall. A young man strode in with his head held high. Insolence surrounded him like an ornate cloak. He had raven hair, eyes to match, and wore an immaculate black ensemble of a leather jacket, black t-shirt, and black jeans. His presence consumed light like a walking black hole. His black combat boots pounded the marble floor. It was the only sound in the hall and was loud enough to wake the dead.

The elder nodded in salutation. "Hello, Lucifer."

"Hello, Father," the fallen angel spat, his lips pursing like he had tasted something rancid. "Or should I call you by your official name?"

God rose and came to a halt mere inches away from the visitor, his cane forgotten at his throne. He stood tall, not in a menacing way, but his posture commanded respect. Even Lucifer had enough sense to retreat a few steps.

"I see you redecorated my old quarters," Lucifer said. "I don't like it. You should definitely fire your interior designer." He paused. "How long *did* you wait after banishing me before you erased any trace of my presence here? A month? A year? A decade? A century? Oh, wait. You started immediately and turned my fellow brothers against me by making me 'Angelic Enemy Number One.' Do you know what it's like being hunted by everyone you once called family?"

"Your rebellion required swift disciplinary action. You left me no choice." The walls seemed to waver as his deep voice rumbled through the hall. "I know why you're here and the answer is no."

Lucifer placed his hand over his heart, "How you judge me, Father. I am not going to demand anything. I'm not the spoiled youth I used to be. I swear I've changed."

"You're just as impertinent now as you were back then."

Lucifer straightened his spine. "Then I'll get right to business. Fawn Belgrave is the one, is she not? I hope she's careful." God could see the corrupt amusement lurking in his son's gaze. "All that power can be very tempting for someone as green as her. I'm sure you remember the last time a seventh generation witch got drunk on power..."

Morgan le Fay had destroyed Camelot. God had then rendered sixth generation witches infertile, but he knew the Chosen One would still be born. To his chagrin, there were things even he could not control.

"Do not trifle with me. Or do I need to remind you of the reason you were cast out in the first place?"

Lucifer's anger boiled beneath his calm veneer, but he kept his voice strong. "Let's make a bet. If Fawn abuses her power or sins as she learns magic, she becomes mine to exploit."

God frowned. *He* had declared it a sin to make deals with his son. There was now the potential for Fawn to be led astray, and he knew his son would stop at nothing to harness her power for evil. He would yield to this bargain to protect the world.

He could see Lucifer was growing impatient. The fallen angel's gaze roamed the grand hall, paying particular attention to the white marble throne in the center.

Lucifer's coal eyes ignited into smoldering red embers, finally settling into a fiery red. "I do believe we're talking about the fate of the world here. Do we have a deal?"

"If she remains pure, she will stay in my heavenly domain and you can never meddle in her affairs again."

"Agreed, but for the duration, I can send any temptations to persuade her and—so can you," Lucifer begrudgingly added. "We can speak to our own pawn but under no circumstances are we allowed access to the other's champion."

"If you are considering using the boy," God interrupted, "I will add that if he becomes pure, in any way, he will be freed from his contract with you." If he could save Caleb in this bargain, stripping Lucifer of his right-hand man, not only would he have redeemed one soul, but also saved countless others from his son's manipulations. "I will give you time to think this over. Know what you are getting into, my son."

Lucifer stiffened at the term of endearment and met his father with an expression of determination: "Deal."

They shook hands. A bolt of power passed between the two divine giants, strong enough to incinerate any lesser being, either angel, demon, or other monster. Thunder and lightning raged outside and the Earth was plunged into darkness for twenty-four hours.

CHAPTER 1

*N*O MEN WERE AT THE TABLE. WHAT THANKSGIVING *dinner didn't include the whole family? Fawn wondered. And what was she doing in her uncle's dining room, anyway? She only ever sat at the mahogany table once a year, and she inexplicably knew it was too soon for the holiday.*

Looking around, she realized she only recognized her mom and grandmother, but also felt like she'd seen the woman on her right before. She examined the woman more closely.

Evelyn? It was the venerated matriarch of the Belgrave family.

This had to be something from her imagination. It was impossible to eat a meal with dead relatives.

Scanning the faces again, she remembered the special silver album. It was traditional for each family witch to have a picture taken when her powers first emerged.

She was about to ask why they were assembled when her ginger ale began to ripple as if the table was shaking, but everything else remained completely still.

Suddenly, a man's face appeared in her drink. Her eyes widened in horror. She noticed his irises were black as coal and indistinguishable from his pupils, shining with sinister intent.

She backhanded the glass across the room, smashing it.

No one moved. Were they oblivious to what had just happened?

She froze when the same face stared back at her from the mirror hanging on the wall across from her. "You can't get rid of me." Flames flickered in his eyes, but then he surged forward. The man came out like Alice in the Lewis Carroll story.

When he was fully out of the mirror, she could see he wore an all-black version of James Bond's signature look complete with a dress shirt, tie, suit, and black Italian leather. Remembering the fictional character's motto: "Be polite, be courteous, show professionalism, and have a plan to kill everyone in the room," and hoped this man didn't emulate Bond in more than just his wardrobe.

The stranger stood on top of the cabinet, surveyed her relatives and chuckled. "A whole room of you and none of you could stop me. What a waste of talent. My father should have put better defenses in place to protect his precious champion." As he said the last words, he made eye contact with her, sending a shiver through her.

"What are you talking about?" she asked, searching for the door which normally led to her uncle's kitchen.

"Ah, he's left you in the dark. How unfortunate for you." He took another step forward. "And don't bother looking for an exit. I can assure you there isn't one."

Backing away, Fawn forgot to step around her chair. It fell backwards and clattered to the floor. Was she going to die like the kid who inspired A Nightmare on Elm Street had?

The man chuckled. "No, I have much bigger and better plans for you, Fawn Belgrave." A loud boom made her cover her ears and the menacing man looked up, glaring at the ceiling. "How inconvenient," he muttered.

The space began to rumble and the dining room started peeling away like old wallpaper, disappearing as gray wisps of smoke.

Fawn woke up to someone shaking her. She blinked multiple times until her eyes adjusted to the darkness after being in such a well-lit room, even if it had only been in her dream.

Her twin brother Alec loomed over her, his forehead crinkled with worry. "What just happened?"

Pressure in her head stamped out her senses as if a vice were squeezing her mind to the point where the pain was the only thing she could focus on. Black spots peppered her vision. "Don't yell. I have a migraine." Despite that fact, she grabbed her smartphone off the nightstand and, once her eyes adjusted to the offensive glare, read the digital numbers which declared it was past midnight. They were officially sixteen years old. A nightmare and a headache were *not* what she wanted as her first memories of the year.

Alec took the device from her hand. "Then you shouldn't be looking at screens."

She rolled her eyes, but knew he was right. As if to rub the point in, lighting flashed through the window, illuminating her purple wallpaper—a color she had chosen when she was ten. Alec had picked blue for his room. Fawn winced. The burst of exposure burned her eyes and even the distant rumble of thunder was too loud. She shivered, noticing her blanket had fallen to the floor while she slept. She pointed to it, in too much pain to retrieve it herself.

Alec grabbed the comforter and laid it over her. Though she was cradling her head in her hands, she could still feel his searching gaze penetrating the darkness.

She envied her brother, who remained unaffected by her pain. Their strange twin connection only meant they shared each other's emotions, not any physical conditions.

He motioned her to scoot over and the mattress sank under their combined weight as he settled next to her. They sat shoulder-to-shoulder on the double bed. "Tell me what happened."

"A man was stalking me..." Fawn trailed off. She had a history of psychic visions. Was this one, or just a terrifying figment of her imagination? "And how did you even know to come in here?"

"I was having a normal dream, when it suddenly fell away and a one-way mirror appeared. I was curious, so I checked it out. Just as quickly, I felt as if I was falling and woke up back in my room. I think someone didn't want me to see what was happening. I immediately came here to see if you were okay."

"I am—kind of," she amended when he pointed to her head and raised an eyebrow. "Have you ever seen my dreams before?"

"No. I was pushed into it, and then someone took me out." He paused. "I think we should tell Mom."

As if on cue, the door creaked open, revealing the silhouette of their mother, Stella. Despite the early hour, she wore her hair in a bun and sported a moon necklace, star earrings, and a triple-moon bracelet. They twinkled in the lightning flashes outside the window. Stella sat at the foot of the bed.

"Are you all right?"

Fawn shook her head. "I had a nightmare. And have a migraine."

"I saw her dream," Alec interjected. "That's never happened before. What's going on?"

"Fawn woke up in the middle of her transition. Halloween blurs the veil between the mystical and real worlds. Witches are responsible for keeping the balance during this window of time until the barrier is restored once again. Your birthday and the weakening of the veil triggered both of your powers."

Fawn had grown up with their family's magical history, but she never believed it was real.

Alec leaned back until his head touched the wall behind the bed. "Didn't you say only girls inherit the magic? Why am I affected?"

Stella took both her children's hands in her own. "Fawn is a very powerful witch because she's the seventh generation of our family. Some of her magic has rubbed off on you, Alec, through your twin bond. That is why you know each other's emotions." Stella turned her attention to her daughter. "Are you still frightened, honey?"

"I'm not as scared as before now that you're both here, but I've been better. And why was I having logical thoughts during the dream?"

"Your pain is caused by your magical powers transforming your DNA." Stella saw Fawn's eyes go wide with alarm. "Witches usually stay asleep while receiving their powers. Your body is pulsing with new, alien energy and it's trying to resist it. It's like growing pains."

"I thought I got over that when I first had my period," Fawn grumbled. Beside her, Alec gagged. She elbowed him in the ribs.

"As to your second question, magic allows us witches to maintain complete control over our faculties even while in the dream realm." She paused, clearly mulling something over in her mind. Stella waved a hand and sixteen candles appeared in a large circle on the floor. Then she instructed her children to sit in the center and hold hands.

"This is channeling. It's when witches tap into the energy around them. Ley lines are mystical energy trails which intersect throughout the world. Cleopatra's Needle marks a powerful convergence site."

Fawn nodded, understanding. She had read theories of why the major cities of the world all seemed to possess a special vitality. She had never believed studies claimed the basis was mystical energy, but when her mom said it, she did. A new thought occurred to her. "But what about Salem? Can't witches collect power from massacre sites?" At least, that's what she had seen happen in some television shows.

"Yes, but channeling magic so steeped in anger and pain can overwhelm one's personal magic. It's a dangerous method and one I advise you to avoid it at all costs unless it is a matter of life and death." A frown marred her usually peaceful expression. She took a deep breath and said more lightly, "Fawn, you're going to light these candles. This will bind your magic to you and help your pain go away. But first, here's a birthday present I think will help."

From out of nowhere, Stella produced a large, leather book. On the cover, a sun and a moon were embossed against a background of stars. "It's a Grimoire," she said, twisting the book in front of their eyes. "Every witch in our family, starting with Evelyn, has chronicled her magical experiences in it. Think of it as a witch's diary, if you will."

This was as old as the original Belgrave witch? Fawn was suddenly anxious about touching the book. Despite her worry, Fawn ran her hands over the cover.

Stella waved her hand over the cover, magically opening the book to a specific page before retaking her children's hands in hers. At the top, it read "Hope in the Dark."

"What does this do?"

"It's the spell to light a candle. Repeat after me: *Ignis et lux intus illuminat, hoc accende lucernam expellat tenebras.*"

She did and nothing happened. "Did I mispronounce the Latin?"

Her mother shook her head. "Spells are not just saying empty words. You need to visualize what you want to happen with a singular focus as you recite any incantation. Try again."

Fawn closed her eyes and imagined finding a beacon of light. A flame appeared and engulfed her, searing through her veins. It raced up her limbs toward her heart like bullets flying toward a target. She ground her teeth as the tendrils began to settle in her chest.

The burning subsided to a simmer and she felt the tingling warmth spread across her skin. Her headache slipped away, as if the light chased the shadows from her mind. Her skin started burning again. It was no longer comfortable and her heart felt as if it were on fire.

In an attempt to cool down, she imagined the current emanating from her palms and going into her brother and mother. Maybe if the three of them shared the burden it wouldn't hurt as much. She imagined her inner fire lighting the room in a single whoosh. She felt a breeze on her skin and sighed as it gradually faded to a soothing sensation...

"Fawn!" her mom shouted in alarm.

The light disappeared and her headache was back. Her eyes snapped open and she was surrounded by a thick cloud of smoke. She coughed and briefly worried how her room would look in the morning. She'd done all that within moments? She started to breathe harder. Guess it zapped more of her energy than she had thought.

"What happened?" she asked.

"You lit the whole room on fire," her mother answered, a grim expression in place.

"Damn, that was cool," Alec mumbled.

Stella leaned forward. "Fawn, did you visualize a lit *candle*?" The new witch hesitated and then shook her head. "You have to be specific in what you visualize. You're more powerful than I thought. When you channel someone, you have to—" Stella paused, the cost of speaking taking a toll on her.

Fawn was surprised. She thought she had done all the work. Had she also been channeling her mom and Alec without realizing it? Looking closer, Fawn realized her mother's normal glow had faded. And Alec looked like he was about to pass out. "Are you guys okay?"

Stella rose. "Good night and happy birthday. In the future, Fawn, it is important to remain aware of the people you channel. It can make or break them as well as the spell being cast." She kissed each of her children on the forehead and exited the room. Fawn noticed she walked slower than her regular, brisk pace.

Fawn heard the door to her mom's bedroom close. Alec left too. He stumbled once on his way out and another wave of guilt crashed over her as she reconsidered exactly how much she had unintentionally drained her family. *I am never doing this again*, she silently vowed.

A voice whispered in her mind: *Fawn*. Her forehead wrinkled in confusion. She glanced around the room. No one was there. She was now hearing voices in her head. Had she gone crazy?

No, my dear, you are perfectly sane.

Who are you?

Fawn was still searching for the voice when suddenly a young Evelyn appeared before her. She wore a floor-length gown. It looked as if it had been sewn from the night sky itself.

Her ancestor smiled. "You will. You have the gift and are special even among our kind. You are destined for great things, but until that time comes, you must be careful with your magic. He will come for you." Her voice was soft, but the warning was not lost on Fawn.

"Who? And how am I talking to you?" Fawn stood up and walked towards her ancestor. She stopped a foot away from the woman.

"As witches, our family can talk to the dead. It's one of many other talents." The hem of Evelyn's gown fluttered around her ankles in an invisible breeze.

Fawn stared at her. She seemed solid but Fawn did not want to test the theory. What if her touch made the woman disappear? "But I've never heard the dead before." She sometimes had psychic dreams and she shared a freaky twin connection, but she had never spoken to a ghost before.

"You didn't have the power, but now you are the most powerful witch in the world—a world you're destined to save."

"There has to be some mistake."

Her ancestor shook her head. Her image began to waver, like a hologram starting to fade.

Fawn scrambled to get her thoughts in line to ask the next question. "Evelyn—" but she was gone. Though she was still new to magic, Fawn could tell the connection had been broken.

The next morning, Fawn woke to the sound of her bedroom door slamming open.

Alec quickly appeared on the threshold and launched himself onto the bed, crushing her under his weight. "Happy birthday, baby sis!"

Fawn pulled the pillow out from underneath her head and whacked him with it. "Stop calling me that!" she huffed. "For God's sake, we're *twins*, Alec!"

He ignored her. "Hey! Seven minutes is a lot. Besides, we're sixteen now, so I'm going to have to protect you from all the guys who will be lining up to take you on a date."

Stella walked through the doorway and pulled two small wrapped boxes, one purple and the other blue, out from behind her back. The twins knew which was which.

Fawn stared at the objects in her mom's hands. "I thought I already got my gifts. You know, magic and a spell book that could fall apart the moment I open it."

"Well, yes. But I'm also giving you both charms—"

Alec interrupted, "I'm a guy. I don't wear jewelry."

"No one has to see it. Now listen. This is important. These charms are spelled to tap into the natural twin bond you two have and will allow you to know if either one of you are ever in danger." She pushed the purple box toward Fawn and the blue toward Alec.

They simultaneously ripped off the wrapping paper and Alec almost dropped his in the process. Turning to her own gift, she opened the box to reveal an oval opal pendant framed in silver on a silver chain.

Alec got one too, but it was smaller, therefore easier to hide underneath a t-shirt.

"These tap into the natural twin bond you two have and will allow you to know if either one of you are ever in danger." Stella explained. "Always wear this and make sure it is touching your skin. No pockets, sorry Alec."

They both put the necklaces on.

"Fawn, why don't you get dressed so you can take your picture for the album?" She hugged them both again before leaving.

Fawn groaned. The picture was bound to happen. She donned the purple dress she wore to her uncle's wedding and applied a little mascara and blush. Then she was in front of the camera alone, partaking in a family tradition she never understood, but couldn't quite bring herself to shrug off. She sighed in relief when her mother finally printed the chosen picture.

Fawn approached the coffee table with the lineage album. As she got closer, she heard a crowd of whispers. *Again?* she wondered. She gingerly opened the cover and a hundred people shouted at her with ear-splitting volume. *He is coming.*

Fawn inserted her photo and hurried back to her room. Once inside, she locked the door. *He?* It was more specific than what Evelyn had told her, but not by much. If the dead couldn't give her a straight answer, and her mother hadn't seen anything dangerous, she was sure no one—dead or alive—could tell her.

C ALEB HAD JUST RETURNED FROM A THREE-MONTH TRIP to England. He had been tasked with breaking the engagement of a nobleman's daughter. While the acting was not difficult, he found her rants grating. At least it was over.

A knock sounded. Caleb magically waved the door open to reveal Ivan standing with his arms crossed. He saw the infernal crimson light pouring into the stone courtyard behind Lucifer's Captain of the Guard. "He'd like to see you," the man tonelessly announced. "You've got another mission. I hear it's in Massachusetts this time."

"Tell him I'm too tired."

"You know I can't. Besides, do not act like you didn't enjoy yourself at least a little bit."

An image of the girl sprawled beneath him came to mind. Caleb swallowed his disgust and quickly shoved the memory away. He ignored Ivan's vulgar suggestion and pressed, "Can't or won't?"

"I would like to keep my esteemed and hard-earned position. Does that answer your question?"

"You're awful."

The guard shrugged. "They didn't call me Ivan the Terrible for nothing. There was truth in that reputation."

Caleb straightened his black t-shirt and his dark wash jeans before flipping him off. He spread his black wings and flew to the throne room.

Lucifer sat on a black iron throne, surrounded by flames and broken skeletons. He was still in his all-black suit, but had hung his jacket across the arm of the chair. Caleb folded his wings and stood as frozen as the rest of the room. One would think Hell was a fire pit—and it was in some places, especially when Lucifer got angry—but it was either hot or cold without anything between.

Caleb wrinkled his nose at the sulfuric stench wafting towards him. Lucifer needed to clean the place up—or at least move the corpses into a vault where no one could smell the rotting flesh. The drastic fluctuations in temperature only sped up the decaying process.

"I need you to befriend a witch," Lucifer decreed.

To do what? And how far would he have to go with the girl this time? When he had first started, seducing girls sounded like the best thing in the world, but after the first hundred assignments or so, it got tedious. Sure, he used to take delight in wooing them, or making them jealously fight over him, but now it was only a matter of business. It was boring.

He could only imagine his mother shaking her head at him. She had taught him intimacy was the most sacred earthly experience, and now it was just a commodity to him.

Caleb tried to keep his voice uninterested. "Why?"

"Because you're going to help me win a deal with my old man."

Caleb knew he had to do whatever Lucifer wanted because of their damned contract, but deliberately putting his head on the chopping block was not part of their deal. "There's no way I'm putting myself in the crossfire. It's *suicide*," Caleb insisted, dragging out the last word through clenched teeth.

"But you won't be. It's all part of the deal. He already knows you're involved." Lucifer announced as if that solved everything.

Caleb raised his chin in defiance, his violet eyes ablaze. "I want no part in it."

The infernos flared with Lucifer's anger and then shrank as a devious smile appeared. "Even for your freedom?"

Caleb hesitated before shaking his head, "I have nothing to go back to. My family died two hundred years ago—right after I made my deal with you." His eyes narrowed.

"I followed through on my promise: your mother's immortality in exchange for your eternal servitude—"

"You turned her into a statue!"

"Immortality! No one but angels can escape death."

"Then why didn't you turn her into an angel?"

"Because I couldn't!" Lucifer slammed his fists into the arms of his throne. "I can only create dark angels and demons thanks to my exalted *Father* in Heaven, who saw fit to limit me in yet another way, as if banishing me here weren't enough—and only then if they personally agree to a contract." He exhaled and the fires calmed until they were all but extinguished. "Now, about your assignment..."

Caleb breathed heavily, weighing his choices: do what Lucifer wanted in exchange for his freedom or... what? Nothing could get worse than it already was. "What would you have me do?"

A triumphant smile spread across Lucifer's hardened features. "Magic in itself is never good or evil. Your job is to corrupt her, or better yet, get her to agree to serve me. I'll leave it up to your imagination, but a broken heart can drive one over the edge."

Caleb nodded and began walking away, but Lucifer continued. "Your assignment won't begin until she's in college. Right now, she lives with a vigilant mother and an overprotective twin brother."

"No father?" Caleb interrupted.

"He died before she was born. You can go now."

Caleb nodded and took his leave. He was particularly anxious to get started, knowing this assignment could change his life.

A silver binder was waiting for him on his bed by the time he returned to his room. Caleb opened it immediately and began reading as he started formulating a plan of attack.

Wooing her would be the best course of action. He just had to meet her and personally assess what type of approach he would take. It would be best to start out as a jerk, and if she didn't like that persona, he could become the "misunderstood bad boy with a soft side" cliché literature had been propagating for centuries. He hadn't started it, but it had certainly made his job easier over the years. None of his assignments ever thought about the possibility of being ruined by a dark angel, but that was their mistake.

He pulled the picture of his family out from under his pillow. *We'll be reunited if it's the last thing I do,* he promised.

CHAPTER 2

FIVE YEARS LATER

L*IGHT FLASHED ACROSS THE INSIDE OF FAWN'S EYELIDS, tinting them red. She opened her eyes expecting to see sunlight flooding her room but instead, she was surrounded by a black void.*

She bumped into an invisible wall and she stumbled backwards. Pressing her hands to it, she tested its strength. Solid. Fawn groaned. This couldn't get any worse.

"But unpredictable events are the most interesting," a mystery voice countered from the darkness.

She whirled around and saw a person standing behind her. She tried to back away, wary of him and unsure of his intentions, but he followed her. Fawn squinted at him and saw he was around her age, but that was all she could discern in the darkness.

"Where do you think you're going? I just got here. It took me forever to enter this damn box, too."

If he wasn't responsible for trapping her, who was? She twisted away from him. Please don't hurt me.

Fawn heard him chuckling in her mind and she could feel goose bumps forming on her arms. His laugh seemed lighthearted and yet she feared there were very dark intentions hiding beneath the surface. Like a snake exhibit in a museum, it fascinated her, but inspired too much fear for her to follow her curiosity any closer.

"You have no reason to be afraid."

Fawn faced him. "And why should I trust you? I don't know you."

"But you will soon."

Fawn jerked away from him.

Without warning, the space started trembling. The darkness rippled, resembling heat waves on a hot summer day. Fawn frantically looked around, trying to locate the cause of the disturbance, but she could not find it. The stranger was doing a better job of composing himself, but he was still frowning. Did he know what was happening?

Suddenly she was floating in the air, rapidly ascending into the black unknown. Naturally, she tried to fight it. Fawn imagined herself rooted to the ground, but it didn't help. The pull was impossible to resist and without thinking, she grabbed his hand. He looked up at her, just as surprised at her action as she was. She stared at him, hoping to see his face, but it was mostly hidden in shadow. At the last moment, she saw a distinctive feature. His eyes shone a piercing violet as he smiled at her one last time before she was yanked away.

She woke up to a blaring noise. It sounded like someone was blowing a horn in her ear. Fawn slammed her hand on top of the alarm clock.

Slowly, she sat up and pulled her knees to her chest. She had not had a strange dream since she got her magical powers five years ago, on her sixteenth birthday. And now, on her twenty-first birthday, not only was she required to attend all of her college classes, but she also had a meeting with some ass who got his kicks at her expense.

Her thoughts were cut off when the door opened and Ivy, her best friend and now college roommate, launched herself onto the bed.

"Ow!" Fawn yelped as the bed jostled, hitting her head on the wall.

"Sorry. I just wanted to wish you happy birthday!"

"Thanks for that." Fawn threw aside the sheets and walked over to the dresser. She passed Ivy and pulled out a graphic t-shirt she had made back in eighth grade with a phoenix crawling up the side. She cringed as she readjusted the cold silver of her opal necklace laying against her warm chest under the fabric, but she didn't let that slow her down. Next came a pair of dark-wash jeans and black ankle boots.

"I'm going to grab breakfast. I'll see you in class." She grabbed her coat, phone, and keys before swinging her messenger bag across her torso. With one last glance into her room, the memory of the dream still in her head, she turned out the light and closed her bedroom door.

When she was in line to buy her usual bagel and cup of tea, she felt as though she were being watched. She turned, searching for the culprit in the open student center, but didn't see anyone. Paranoia urged her to walk faster than her already brisk, New-Yorker pace.

As she was sitting down in her first class, her phone beeped. She pulled it out and saw a message from her old friend Dylan. *Happy birthday!* it read. *You need to come visit us in NOLA soon.*

She smiled and typed, *Thanks, and that sounds awesome. Maybe this summer?*

The sound of someone sitting next to her made her look up. To her surprise, it wasn't Ivy, but a guy who looked very familiar. Even weirder, her best friend took a seat behind them without an argument.

The stranger followed her gaze. "Oh, I'm sorry. Did you want to sit together?"

"No, it's fine," Ivy said, surprising Fawn. Normally her friend would have insisted otherwise.

He turned back to her and she noticed his strange eye color. One she had seen just that morning. It couldn't be—

"My name is Caleb. It's nice to meet you."

She mentally chastised herself for staring and quickly replied, "Likewise. I'm Fawn."

He answered in her head like he had in her dream. *Yes, I know.*

Her spine straightened as if preparing for an attack.

No need to get defensive, he continued. *I'm not your enemy.*

She wavered and let her muscles relax, but still stayed alert. *Did he know who was?* she wondered, remembering Evelyn's old warning.

The Devil, Caleb answered.

"And you know that how?" she whispered, not wanting Ivy to overhear their strange conversation.

"It's common knowledge in the Supernatural world," he replied at the same volume. "You're quite famous."

"What are you talking about?" How did he know she was a witch? She hadn't done magic since the night she received her powers.

Before he could answer, the professor walked in and they were forced to stop talking. Fawn hoped he wouldn't continue the conversation in her head. She wouldn't be able to ask any of her questions if he did.

Luckily, he didn't. She wasn't sure if he had heard her wish, or if they were just on the same wavelength. But she did feel his gaze on her throughout the period. By the time the class finished, Fawn was ready to jump out of her own skin. Fortunately for her, her resolve was stronger than her instinct to tell him to stop. Instead, she silently suffered the discomfort and acted as if he weren't there.

After the lecture, Fawn bolted, walking swiftly away from the English building—and from Caleb.

Later that night, she found him waiting outside the dark room where she had photography class. "What are you doing here?"

"I believe we got off on the wrong foot this morning and I wanted to remedy that." He held out his hand. "I'm Caleb Pearce."

She hesitantly accepted the gesture and said, "I'm just about to go get dinner. Why don't you walk with me?"

They started off in silence, but after a few moments, Caleb whispered, "To answer your question from before we were so rudely interrupted, I know you're more than human because I am too. We're not the only ones."

Fawn inhaled sharply before recovering. "What are you saying?"

"It's not for me to say who else is Supernatural."

Fawn let out a frustrated sigh and tugged the elastic out of her hair, causing brown waves to engulf her for a few moments before she started combing it back with her fingers. "So what are you?"

"An angel."

Fawn's step faltered and his hand was instantly on her arm, steadying her. Her mother had said witches weren't the only supernatural beings on earth. Surprisingly, most of the ones in literature were based on reality. But what was one doing sitting across from her? "What are you doing here? With me?"

"You're an important person. I'm here to watch over you."

She could hear her heart beating hard and no doubt he could too. "I don't believe it. I have a guardian angel."

He mirrored her and said, "You should."

Before she could reply, he had disappeared from her side. Fawn heard Evelyn's voice in her head: *Brace yourself, child. It's starting.*

A WEEK LATER, CALEB HIT HIS HEAD AGAINST THE headboard. The dull ache quickly disappeared, one of the perks of being an angel.

He had known his target for a full seven days, and he had absolutely nothing to show for it. Whenever they were in a group, she would be civil, but he needed to get closer if he was ever going to succeed. Every time he tried to talk to her privately, she would find some way to avoid the interaction though he couldn't figure out why. What type of person—who knew the Devil was coming after them—tried to ditch their guardian angel?

Granted, the last part had been a lie, but she didn't know that. And she seemed to be an intelligent person with enough sense to hopefully listen to someone saying she was in danger, or at least to her instinct for self-preservation. He shook his head. It didn't matter whether she wanted to save herself. What mattered was she wasn't *talking* to him. To make matters worse, Lucifer demanded daily reports. The man was more anxious than a mother on her daughter's wedding day. Caleb had started bullshitting information just to keep him off his back because the alternative—admitting he was clueless—was not an option. Luckily, Lucifer was too distracted to catch him.

Speak of the Devil, and he shall appear.

One knock was all the warning Caleb received before Lucifer was sitting at his desk. "You didn't report tonight."

"I was tired."

"I don't pay you to be tired."

"You don't *pay* me, period."

Lucifer let out a sharp laugh before his features resumed their serious expression. "You know I'm not a patient man, Caleb. I need to know this situation is being handled with the utmost care by the best person. And if you pull another stunt like tonight, I may be forced to question whether that person is still you."

"It is," Caleb snapped. "You gave this mission to me because you know I'm the best at blending into modern times."

"I would watch your tone. You're not released from your contract with me yet." With that, he disappeared in a puff of red smoke.

Caleb let out a long sigh. Damn, he hated it here in Hell.

Fawn slammed her laptop closed. The latest Social Psychology assignment was driving her crazy and no one in the class was online except Caleb. She stared at the green circle next to his name and muttered a curse before clicking on his name.

It had been a week since she last let herself stay in his presence more than a few minutes. He may be her angel, but being near him made her brain go fuzzy and if the Devil really *was* coming after her, that wasn't a good thing. But God help her, she needed help on this homework.

Can you help me with the latest Psych assignment? she typed. She stared at the screen and wondered if she should have started with a politer greeting. She had all but given him the silent treatment since she found out he was her guardian angel, and suddenly contacting him out of the blue probably wasn't the best plan of action.

His reply was immediate. *Yes. Where are you having trouble?*

She sighed in relief. At least he didn't seem to find her rude. Or maybe it was because he was her guardian angel and *couldn't* get mad at her? She shook her head. It didn't matter *why*, what mattered was he wasn't pissed and open to helping her.

Explaining how people could have gone along with Hitler's plan to annihilate the Jews. Maybe she was naïve, but even with the research on conformity, compliance, and obedience, she couldn't understand how so many people idly or joyously watched as a culture was being systematically destroyed and buried in mass graves.

The chat box indicated Caleb was typing, but it had been showing that for the past five minutes. Too anxious for his reply, she messaged him again. *Want to meet at the library so we go over this in person?*

He still hadn't finished his response. Why was he taking so long?

Fawn shook her head. Why was she overanalyzing everything? *You're acting like you have a crush on him*, she reprimanded herself. *He's not even a normal college guy!* God, she was acting like an absolute idiot. Her phone buzzed.

Be there in five. Do you want some tea?

His offer sent a flurry of butterflies through her. She was thankful they weren't face to face because she was sure she was blushing. *Yes, please*, she replied. She packed her bag and left to meet her angel.

CHAPTER 3

CALEB WAITED AT AN EMPTY TABLE IN THE back. He had been surprised when she had reached out. If he thought God would help him, he would have guessed it was an act of divine intervention. Which was utterly ridiculous given his mission was to corrupt Fawn and make God *lose* in his bet against Lucifer.

He heard the library doors open and saw her searching for him.

Where is he? He heard her thought loud and clear as if she were projecting it specifically to him. He knew she wasn't. She didn't even know he could read her mind.

Not wanting her to take the opportunity to lose her nerve and walk back out, he quickly sent her a text. She glanced down at her phone and her gaze snapped up to his.

He smiled and held up a hot cup of tea. "Get it while it's hot," he mouthed at her. "You like oolong, right?"

She nodded and hesitated in moving toward him for only a moment before needlessly readjusting her shoulder bag, gripping the strap with enough strength to turn her knuckles white. He suppressed a chuckle. She probably didn't even realize she was doing it. He magically pulled out the chair beside him and pushed the hot beverage toward her. She immediately took a long sip and sighed, but stayed standing.

"You should have worn gloves," he lightly admonished. "Wouldn't want you to get frostbite now. What would I do without you in class?"

She rolled her eyes, and he saw her aura flare with orange annoyance before settling into a calmer blue.

"I've grown up in the North East my whole life. The cold isn't anything new."

"Still," he quietly objected. He felt as though he were chastising his little sister like he used to back when they had all been together as a happy family. He shook his head. Comparing Fawn to his sister was a bad idea. "You have them for a reason."

She softened at his tone and answered honestly. "I always forget to put them on before I go outside. By the time I remember, my hands are already too cold for it to matter." She took a sip of the tea and sighed.

He watched her light pink aura expand with contentment.

She said, "Thanks for this, by the way." She raised the paper cup in a silent salute to him. "And for agreeing to meet with me."

"It's my pleasure," he replied, not missing how her cheeks turned matched her aura at his words, especially the last one. He smiled.

For some reason, he could also feel residuals of her emotion as if they were his own, as if he were inextricably and inexplicably connected to her emotional state.

But rather than drape his arm over her chair like he would for any other assignment, he kept his elbows resting on the table. He figured going from "guardian angel" to "romantic interest" with one of the most commonly known signs of a male showing interest in a female might give her whip lash and scare her off for good.

She looked down at his hands. *Where is his paper?* he heard her wonder. He saw confusion settle over her features. "You didn't bring your assignment?"

He leaned back and crossed his legs, settling in for the upcoming show. "I didn't do it."

"What?" Her voice was loud enough for a few of the people at the surrounding tables to look over, some with annoyance, others with confusion or pure curiosity. "Then how can you help me?"

He smiled at her disbelief and patted the seat next to him, urging her to finally sit down. Once she settled, he said, "I know enough to help you without needing to complete it myself. I'm an angel, remember? I've been around for a while. And there's always the internet."

Fawn's aura confirmed her lasting skepticism, but she remained silent on her reservations. Instead, she pulled out her laptop and folder, withdrawing a sheet of paper riddled with marks in highlighter and green pen. She was clearly getting down to business.

"If I end up not being helpful," he added, feeling a bit as though he were a desperate used car salesman saying anything he could to keep his customer, "I'll buy you an apologetic dinner. That way, you won't have wasted your time. How's that?"

She looked as if she was going to refuse when her aura suddenly switched from gray to the pale green of gratitude. She turned to face him head-on and said, "Okay." He caught a twinkle in here eye right before she added, "I could use a free meal."

He laughed. "Overconfident, I see. We'll see if you'll even be getting one. I fully intend to surpass your expectations of my helpfulness."

AFTER TWO HOURS OF GOING BACK AND FORTH over her proposed paper, she was finally done with the assignment. She leaned back and closed her eyes, grateful to have it over with.

Somehow, Caleb had anticipated all of her questions before she said them. If she hadn't known magic was real, she would have written it off to coincidence, but maybe angels could read minds? She hoped not. Otherwise, he would have heard her embarrassing, inner monologue.

She had long since finished her tea and now that she wasn't locked into work mode, she realized how hungry she was. Her stomach growled, a clear indication that if she didn't ingest food soon, she'd become hangry and she'd be mortified if she let anyone—let alone Caleb—see her that way.

He must have felt the same because he said, "Want to leave this place and go find something to eat?"

Like an idiot, she said, "I thought you were only offering a meal as compensation," instead of just accepting.

What was *wrong* with her tonight? She usually was never this suspicious or seemingly ungrateful, especially to her guardian angel who—her original discomfort aside—had done nothing but help her. He *was* her guardian angel, and it wasn't fair of her to make his job

THE BELGRAVE LEGACY

harder. It was his job to hover and she resolved to be more cooperative in the future.

He smiled good naturedly, thankfully unaffected by her rude behavior. "Consider it an apology for bailing on your dinner invitation a few days ago. I was unexpectedly needed at headquarters."

She finished packing up her materials and rose from her seat. "Is that what you angels call Heaven?"

"Technically, there are many names, but given it is the main place of business for guardian angels besides earth, I call it that." He held his hand out to her. "Want to avoid the cold this time?"

"How?"

He gently took her hand in his. "You may feel a bit weird for a moment. Remember to breathe normally. And don't let go."

He gave no further explanation before Fawn felt all her muscles tensing so tight as if her body were trying to collapse in on itself. A moment later, her feet hit solid ground and she stumbled a step forward, Caleb's hand steadying her.

"What was that?" Her head still felt like it was spinning. She bent over and tried to center herself.

"Magical travel. Much faster than any other transportation. You'll get used to the dizzy feeling after you've done it a few times. I promise it'll go away soon."

"Uh huh," she said skeptically. Like she'd ever be repeating *that* experience. Not likely.

He patted her back. "Come on. It's better to walk it off. Besides, there's a good restaurant around the corner. You like Thai, right?"

"It's one of my favorites," she said. "But I assume you probably already knew that." Guardian angels knew everything, right?

"Always polite to check." He held the door open for her and they were immediately seated at an empty table away from the outside chill.

He pulled out her seat and draped her coat over the back. Fawn straightened her spine, his proximity causing a tingle to dance over her skin. Why did he always have this effect on her? What made it worse was he didn't even seem to notice.

"I've never been here, but I hear good things. You can get whatever you want. I'm treating."

25

"Does that make this a date?"

His eyebrows rose and Fawn wanted to smack herself. *Way to let me down, mental filter.*

"I would like it to be, but I didn't want you to feel like I was rushing into things too quickly. It's entirely up to you, Fawn. It would be remiss of me to put my wants above yours."

"I would, too, but I'm sorry. I'm not normally that forward. We've only known each other for a few days. Maybe this *should* be just a dinner between..." she gestured between them, but couldn't find an accurate description for their bizarre relationship.

"Friends?"

Her gaze locked with his in surprise. "Are we?"

"I may be your angel, but I hope you can eventually also view me, at the very least, as someone you can confide in."

What was she supposed to say to that? She cleared her throat. "I would like that."

"Then this is a simple dinner between friends." He gave a reassuring smile. "Let's not think about anything else tonight."

Fawn nodded and was grateful when the waiter chose that moment to approach their table.

CALEB WATCHED FAWN CAREFULLY. SHE WAS SO UNLIKE the other girls throughout the years, even ones he met from his small town back when he was still human. She was incredibly intelligent, straight forward, but simultaneously shy and innocent, and something else he couldn't name.

She had surprised him by broaching the subject of a possible romantic relationship. In the past five hours, she had initiated contact and allowed him to make more headway than in the past five *days*. Caleb had no idea what was making her so agreeable, but whatever it was, he hoped it continued until he was done with his mission.

"I would ask you what your major is, but since I already know..."

She smiled. "Yeah, the psychology bug bit me. I think I got it from my mom."

"What do you enjoy doing in your free time?"

"Nothing in particular. I haven't found a passion yet."

"You will eventually."

"Sometimes I doubt that. Most of my other friends already know what they want to do with their lives and I just... don't."

The disappointment in her voice and aura urged Caleb to reach out to her and take her hand across the table. He was surprised to feel real emotion over her indecision. He mentally shook it off. "I'm positive you'll do great things."

She gave a small, weak smile. "Thank you, Caleb."

It was the first time she had called him by name and he felt a shiver run down his spine. "You're welcome," he answered. And he meant it.

"I feel like we've been talking about me the whole time. Tell me more about you."

He opened his arms. "I'm an open book."

"How did you become an angel?"

"You could say I was picked for the job when I was still a human." It was a stretch, but she didn't know that.

"So much for being an open book," she quipped, leaning back as disappointment and feigned disinterest transformed her body language.

"I'm willing to share anything else, but we aren't allowed to share the specifics of our creation. Otherwise all sorts would be clamoring for the chance to become like us, or worse, attempt to transform themselves and rival those selected by God himself."

He saw her sit up straighter. "Like Lucifer's army?"

"Those were fallen angels who were originally in God's service," Caleb corrected. He hesitated, unsure of whether he should go on. "But yes, the Devil does sometimes create dark angels to do his bidding."

"Do you run into them often?"

Caleb detected a hint of concern and nodded solemnly. "They often roam the Earth pretending to be humans and stir up trouble. When they stay invisible, they whisper bad thoughts and feelings into unsuspecting victims' ears and minds.

"Even if someone's guardian angel is around?" He heard her mentally add, *That's ballsy.*

"We are not permitted to engage in combat unless we receive direct orders to." Caleb almost laughed at how easily he was impersonating a light angel and how many times he had engaged in fights over the years. "We can't violently defend our charges against words or change anyone's behavior. Only tend to our charges and try to persuade them against the poisonous words of demons. The only time we can take *action* is if there is a bodily threat to the person we are protecting."

"Does that get frustrating?"

"What do you mean?"

"Well, I know when I read and characters do stupid things, I sometimes want to smack them with their own books. I think I'd lose patience very easily if I were in your position. How do you do it?"

"I'm sure a lot of us originally felt that way. I certainly didn't believe I could do what was expected of me when I first started." He smiled at the half-truth. "It gets better with time and lots and lots of practice."

"What's eternity like?"

"There's always something new, but seeing the cycle of fads is also interesting. When I was a human, I never imagined I'd ever get the chance to see society truly move forward. It's amazing, really."

"Does it ever get lonely?"

He tilted his head as he considered her question. "At times," he quietly admitted. "Losing people to time is never an easy thing to accept, but when your own life is extended and theirs aren't—" he paused. "They say time heals all, but it doesn't quite account for the fact that new wounds are constantly being formed." He saw Fawn watching him with sympathy and cleared his throat. "How's your meal?" He noticed she had barely touched it, probably because she was spending so much time questioning him.

She looked down at her plate and said, "It's really good." As if this were a reminder to herself, she took another bite, licking her lips in the process before she took a sip of her water.

It was only a small gesture, but it woke something in him, making him want to pull her in and kiss her. He shook his head. *Strange.* He couldn't remember the last time he felt *true* desire for a girl, much less one of his assignments.

They ate the rest of the meal in comfortable silence, and every so often he would catch her watching him out of the corner of his eye.

He never let her know he knew, not wanting to embarrass her, and let her look her fill.

At the end of dinner, he paid the check, pulled out her chair, and walked her back to the dorm after she expressed her dislike of magic travel. He had lightly teased her about it, but relented. He wanted to make a good impression, not make her resent him.

At her dorm, he took her hands in his and said, "Goodnight, Fawn."

"Goodnight, Caleb. Thank you for everything tonight."

"My pleasure. I hope we will repeat the experience." He turned and began walking away. He could feel her gaze on him and looked back, waving once, before using magic travel to return to his home in Hell.

He went straight to the throne room and said, "She's hooked."

Lucifer smiled. "I would expect nothing less." His expression turned serious. "Tonight you're going to start training with Bernael."

"Why? She won't be able to do black magic yet. She barely even knows *magic*, period. How do you expect her to do anything when she doesn't even know the basics?"

Lucifer leaned forward. "Because he's going to teach you a crash course on magic so you can act the sage with Fawn when you start teaching her."

Caleb opened his mouth to ask more questions, but the Devil waved his hand and he found himself in the courtyard across from the intimidating demon whose red eyes blazed with dark glee.

"Ready to begin?"

CHAPTER 4

FAWN DIDN'T SEE CALEB FOR THE NEXT TWO days. At first, she thought nothing of it. But when the second day came and went without any sign of him, she had to admit she missed him. Logically, she knew his absence disappointed her more than it should have, but that didn't change how she felt.

Ever since their non-date, she hadn't experienced the ominous feeling she had when they first met and decided she enjoyed being around him more than she did avoiding him. And not just because he could protect her, but his sometimes-cocky-sometimes-sweet attitude had somehow gotten underneath her skin in the twenty-four hours she had known him.

But the warning still puzzled her. Why had Evelyn given it that first day, and what was she talking about? And if she really *was* in danger, why wasn't Caleb at her side? Was he busy dealing with the threat now in a preemptive attack? She was so confused as to how he could protect her if he wasn't allowed to fight unless he was under strict orders. All guardian angels should have a license to protect their charge by all means necessary. What did she know about angelic politics?

After a third day without his company, her mood dropped even further. She called off lunch with Ivy and instead took a nap in hopes of boosting her energy and mood in time for her next class. Fawn was surprised when she saw Caleb waiting outside her building after her last class. She felt her pulse pick up and the hair on the back of her neck stand on end in anticipation. She pulled the key out of her pocket and slid it into the lock and attempted to contain her excitement. "You're back."

He laughed. "That I am. Did you miss me?"

She didn't answer, earning another chuckle from him.

"It's all right, you don't need to tell me. And if I may confide a secret, I'm glad to be back in your company. It can get quite boring with my other colleagues."

"Really? How?"

"They don't talk about interesting things, always preferring to reminisce on the past. And for beings so close to the modern world at all times, one would think they would be more interested in current events. I wasn't even *alive* for most of their conversation topics. It makes me feel like quite the black sheep among them."

She patted his arm. "Poor you," she cooed, fighting a smile. "You have my sympathies, though I can't rightly say I pity your situation."

"Was my story not miserable enough for you?"

She shook her head. "What are we doing tonight? I assume you have a plan."

Caleb's expression lost the majority of its levity as he got down to business. "We're starting your first magic lesson tonight." He started walking toward the center of campus and she quickened her pace to match his.

"Wait, what? That's an awful idea. Don't you know what happened the night I got my magic?"

He nodded and continued moving. "You're the most powerful witch on the planet and I'm your protector. While I'm very good at what I do, it's best if you're prepared to defend yourself."

"You make it sound like the whole world is coming after me."

"The Supernatural community has been waiting to learn your identity for centuries. They all want a piece of you, for better or worse, and we can't let that happen." He sighed. "I don't mean to frighten you, but it's important you know the threat you're facing. Lucifer is not easily beaten. You need to be prepared for every possible outcome."

"Okay, but that could take a while. I haven't used my abilities for four years. And where are you walking to so fast? As much as I love it here, there isn't anywhere *nearly* interesting enough for me to run to like you are."

He chuckled. "This is unusually slow for me. You see, we angels usually travel at the speed of light. Can you imagine what it's like for me when I need to walk even slower when there are other students around who *don't* know I'm Supernatural?"

She shook her head.

"To answer your question: we're going to the Great Lawn."

"My first spell was out of control. If I make a mistake here, people could get hurt!"

"You're going to start channeling and learn how to be in touch with nature," he calmly explained. He held his arm out and she felt her stomach clench with anxiety. "Shall we?"

"Is our magic the same?"

He shook his head. "I can't do spells. The Creator is very careful about what privileges we get since Lucifer's rebellion."

"Oh. Then how can you teach me?"

"I may not be allowed to do this magic myself, but as your guardian, I have access to *knowledge* about it. If I didn't, I would be ill-prepared to protect you."

She stared up at the cloudy sky. Standing beneath the shadow of the trees in the middle of the courtyard did little to calm Fawn's nerves.

"You'll do fine." He quickly squeezed her shoulder.

Fawn fought the impulse to rub the spot. It was tingling, and she didn't know if that was good or bad. She stared down at their hands. If she moved slightly, they would be touching.

He grabbed her hand and laced their fingers together. She could feel her skin heating up and tried to pull away, but he held on tight. She would *not* hurt him. Her blue eyes met his purple ones, pleading for him to let go.

"If it gets to be too much for either one of us, we'll stop."

"What if I can't?" The tears were now freely rolling down her face.

"I have complete faith in you." He wiped her cheeks with the back of his right hand. "Just focus on breathing."

With each inhalation, she felt the warmth spread inside her, pulsing through her veins, and every time she exhaled, her palms briefly heated up before releasing the energy into Caleb. Out of nowhere, a light breeze came and lifted her hair off her shoulders, and her eyes flew open.

"That breeze you feel?" Fawn nodded, captivated by his words and actions. "You made that. I said you could do this." He placed a hand underneath her chin, tilting her head up so she was staring into his eyes. "Do you believe me now?"

She swallowed. "I do."

"Ready to try something else?" he asked.

She nodded.

"Part the clouds and bring out the sun."

"Won't people notice?"

"Yes, but humans—as much as they want there to be magical solutions to all their problems—refuse to believe in magic, and therefore write miracles off to coincidence or yet-to-be-explained science." He smiled. "There's no worry of being discovered."

She nodded. "How do I do it?"

"Say this until the sun appears. And remember to keep an image in your mind of what you want the end goal to be. *Veniat sol, lumen tuum. Tenebras et de orbe clara.*"

Rather than close her eyes this time, she stared up at a particularly dark cloud and began silently chanting the incantation as she imagined the sun's rays bursting through the dark mass. She only got through three repetitions before her imagination was realized. Fawn spun around and laughed when she took in Caleb's awed expression. "How did I do?"

"Fantastically, and you know it."

She beamed almost as brightly as the morning star.

THAT NIGHT, CALEB HAD MORE THAN ENOUGH *REAL* information to report without needing to resort to lies.

While he hadn't been at Fawn's college the past few days, he also hadn't returned to Hell. He had needed some time alone to analyze why Fawn was not only more fascinating than his past assignments, but also how she made him *feel* for her. And he couldn't do that type of musing with Lucifer lurking over his shoulder. It's not like he was in love with her or anything, but the last time someone was able to inspire true emotion in him, he had been a naïve human.

Lucifer had probably burned the ceiling of the throne room at his disobedience, especially after his last warning, but he would get over it. Or Caleb hoped he would eventually.

He didn't even want to imagine his final months on the King of Hell's bad side. He had heard other horror stories being whispered in the palace corridors whenever Lucifer was busy with a meeting, but no one ever dared to fully explain the depth of the Devil's wrath.

Caleb took a deep breath, steeling himself against whatever waited for him, and pushed open the double doors.

"You've been missing in action," Lucifer's voice boomed through the throne room. "You promised you wouldn't repeat the mistake. And yet... here we are again. You *know* how I get when I'm displeased."

"But I'm back now and she fully believes I'm her guardian angel. And I've given her a magic lesson, though I still don't understand why you want me to train her. It's like arming your enemy."

"If you do your job correctly, she'll be an ally."

Caleb gave a stiff nod.

"A little birdy told me she is starting to fall for you, but you haven't taken advantage of it yet. Are you going soft?"

"No, sir. And your spy didn't tell you that every time she mentions a romantic relationship between us, she immediately shuts down afterwards. If I actually acted on her unfiltered comments, I'd scare her off. I know what I'm doing."

"Perhaps I should have Asmodeus visit her..."

No way in Heaven. Caleb would do everything in his power to avoid Fawn meeting the demon of lust—and his hellish mentor back when he first began. He forced his tone to stay casual. "It would be a waste of everyone's time."

Lucifer's gaze sharpened. "Are you growing attached to her?"

"Of course not," Caleb scoffed. "Don't be ridiculous. She's just another girl to be seduced." He unfurled his wings, giving them a single shake to relieve his growing anxiety. "If that's all, I'd like to go now."

The Devil made a snort of disbelief. "Just stay focused and do your job. Deliver her to me, and I'll keep up my end of the bargain."

"As long as it's not like our last deal," Caleb muttered.

Fawn was glad to see Caleb in class the next day. Although she knew he didn't need to attend, it was strangely reassuring to see him during the day and not just during their routine nighttime magic lessons.

Ivy kept insisting there was something more going on between them, and though she consistently told her she was wrong, Fawn was starting to wonder the same herself. She had initially wanted to tell her best friend he was her guardian angel, but Caleb had recommended keeping that fact a secret—for security reasons, he had said, though she couldn't understand why her best friend would pose a threat.

"It's nothing against her character. It's just a precaution we need to take with everyone," he had assured her.

They had proceeded to another lesson about channeling before moving on to some simple incantations for levitation. Luckily, they hadn't done anything breakable or *that* would have been a mess she didn't know how to magically clean up.

"The reason it keeps shaking is because your focus isn't stable," Caleb said. "Which is probably because you're so nervous." He walked behind her and ran his hands down her arms until he was holding her hands, guiding them toward the floor. "Put it down for a moment."

She sighed, feeling tingles running up and down her arms, and lowered the pillow back onto the floor. "Am I doing *that* bad?"

"No," he insisted. "But let's try something else. Close your eyes and think of a candle flame."

How am I supposed to focus when you're holding my hands? "The last time I tried this, I set my room on fire."

He chuckled. "You're a lot better now than you were back then."

She closed her eyes and whispered the words she had somehow committed to memory: "*Ignis et lux intus illuminat, hoc accende lucernam expellat tenebras.*"

"I'm going to make one change given there is no candle here. *Ignis et lux intus illuminat ostende te me.* Do you need me to repeat it?"

She shook her head and silently made the adjustment.

Fawn heard Caleb's voice at her ear and felt the vibrations of his speech roll through her. "And now open your eyes."

She did. Hovering in front of her was a small, but vibrant flame. She made it disappear and spun around. "I just *levitated* a flame I created out of thin air."

He smiled at her. "You're more powerful than you know."

CHAPTER 5

"How's my little witch doing?" Lucifer didn't even bother looking at Caleb as he asked from atop his black throne.

Caleb bristled at the question. He didn't like the idea of Lucifer owning Fawn, or her even being someone to be owned, period. What was wrong with him?

Lucifer had a faint smirk on his lips, and Caleb was suddenly worried it was too obvious he genuinely liked Fawn.

He dug his fingernails into his palms to check his frustration. He then carefully concealed his annoyance by banishing it to the recesses of his mind and answered, "Fine. She's getting better by the day."

"I'm glad to hear it. Just remember to stay focused rather than daydreaming of your future."

"I don't daydream."

"You didn't when you had no future but this one, but now you do, it's only natural you would think about what you will do once you're no longer in my service." Lucifer raised an eyebrow in a silent challenge for Caleb to contradict what he had just said. When Caleb didn't, he added, "Keep up the good work."

Caleb was stunned. Never in his more than two-hundred years of service to Lucifer had he been complimented for his work. "Will do, sir." With nothing left to say, he took his leave and returned to his bedroom.

In the privacy of his own room, he began contemplating what to do next with Fawn. There were times he almost forgot she was a mission, which was extremely dangerous, and now was certainly not the time to make a misstep.

However, she hadn't mentioned again or made any Freudian slip referring to the possibility of them entering a romantic relationship. He had, however, felt her physical reaction to him during their last magic lesson and it encouraged him to believe her secret wish hadn't changed.

But how to broach the subject without scaring her off still puzzled him. He needed to pull her out of her shell and make it seem as though it were her idea for them to move forward—but how? Or perhaps he should take charge?

Caleb hit one of the wooden bedposts. A loud crack sliced through the air as it splintered. Still frustrated, he fell onto his bed and threw an arm over his eyes, groaning in frustration. What was wrong with him? Normally he had Plans A, B, and C in place before he ever met his assignment and would build more back-up strategies spanning to the end of the alphabet. He was known for being prepared, and yet with Fawn Belgrave, he barely had a single, complete plan of attack to fall back on when he found himself faltering—which now seemed to be all the time.

He sighed, trying to calm himself down, but he never felt more out of control in his life, save the situation which sent him to Hell in the first place. He had never been so uncertain as how to best handle any of the girls he had been previously assigned, and yet for his most important one ever, he was acting like an inexperienced schoolboy.

Determined to shake his uncharacteristic doubt, he sat up just as quickly and pulled out his family photo. He would complete the mission as any other and move on from this damned existence to one of simple, divine peace in the company of his family in Heaven.

WHEN FAWN SAW HIM AGAIN, SHE WAS EXCITED to get to work. "What are we doing today?" she asked before he could greet her. "No hello?"

She rolled her eyes. "Tell me what I'm getting into tonight."

"We're going to transition toward traditional magic. You're special and can do a lot of things without written incantations, but you'll still learn most magic from your Grimoire." Magically it appeared in his outstretched hand. He moved closer. "Don't be nervous," he added when she eyed the tome with barely hidden terror.

"I'm just beginning to use my magic after a five-year hiatus. How am I supposed to know how to do a giant book of spells?"

"With practice. And don't worry, it's like the other magic you've already done. You visualize what you want to happen. You feel it in your mind, body, and soul as if it's already happened. That's the basis of all magic." He paused. "Some more complicated types of magic have rituals attached, and for those, the steps are written in your Grimoire, but you're not ready for something like that yet."

Fawn took a deep breath, trying to calm her frustration. "This is just so embarrassing. I've been hearing stories about my family's mystical legacy since I was old enough to understand sentences, but I always thought they were just stories. I wish I had paid more attention."

"Stay in the present, Fawn," he said in an even tone.

The reminder calmed her again. She closed her eyes and tried to picture a pen in her hand. When she looked, nothing had happened. "I don't understand this. Why can't I make a pen appear?"

"It's okay. Not everything is the same. It takes a lot of repetition. Your first spell from here is a transformation spell that presents a different image, based on what someone wants to see."

"I don't think I can do this."

In an instant, she felt his hand underneath her chin, tilting her head upward to meet his smoldering gaze. "What did I say about you selling yourself short?"

Fawn could hear her heart pounding and didn't know if it was from the adrenaline of practicing magic, or having him so near her. Realizing he was still waiting for her answer, she took a deep breath of air. "It hurts my magical abilities?" she whispered, answering his question.

He nodded and let her go. "Exactly. If you don't believe in your power, your channels become clogged and it is harder to execute spells as easily and accurately as it normally would be. It's imperative you're confident while doing spells."

"If I screw this up, what happens?"

"Nothing. There aren't any nasty half-baked consequences."

Fawn nodded once again and started turning the pages until she found the spell Caleb had just described to her. "Will people see what I want them to?"

"Yes. Only the caster can control the spell."

"All right." Fawn stood and walked over her book shelf and picked her well-used copy of *Pride and Prejudice* from the collection. Returning to Caleb, she looked to him for approval.

He nodded in approval. "Recite the words written in the grimoire and imagine every page of Jane Austen's book, even the cover if you want, as blank canvasses for your mind to project onto. Visualize what you want and it'll transform into that, then clear the image so it reverts back to its original state. Ready?"

She read the words off the page once. "*Ostende mihi voluntas quidem cordis mei, oculus aspicientis.*" Then she closed her eyes and repeated them as she erased the cover and the pages of the romance novel. Then she imagined the book of her grandparents' love letters she had heard described so many times by both her mother and grandma. She started with the cover, with an image of her newly married grandparents when they were in their early twenties. She had seen a small copy of it enough times to remember it in perfect detail. For the pages, she had to imagine more, and hoped her mental description was accurate enough to manifest what she wanted.

She opened her eyes and his eyes shifted to the book in her hands. On the cover was the image of her grandparents. Excited by that small victory, she immediately opened the book. On the first page was a letter written on old stained paper. Fawn smiled nostalgically and started reading them. Even as she felt Caleb's body warmth at her back, she was too absorbed in the letters to feel her usual nervousness at his close proximity. When she was done, she imagined wiping the book and the pages shimmered, transforming back to normal.

"What was that?" Caleb asked, his voice oddly tight. He seemed to be as caught up in the letters as she was.

Fawn rose to put the book away. "A precious family heirloom we can't seem to find. I think it's in storage somewhere."

She saw Caleb's eyes clear as he returned to the present. "Congratulations, Fawn Belgrave. You have completed your first Grimoire spell."

CALEB WATCHED THE SMILE SPREAD ACROSS FAWN'S FACE and felt her happiness seeping into him. He couldn't explain it, but it was as if her aura expanded so wide as to encompass him with not only its physical reach, but also its emotional influence.

It had never happened before with any of the previous girls he had worked with and it made him wonder. Was it because she was a witch?

She must have noticed his confusion because her aura quickly changed to a confused gray. "What's wrong?"

He shook his head. "Nothing. I mean it," he added when her aura didn't change. "You truly are a natural at this. You just have to remember to keep calm when trying new things."

"I can try, but I'm a perfectionist at heart."

"Don't let that spoil the good thing you have going here."

She brushed off his comment and said, "What else can I do?"

"You want to do more?" *What else can I teach her?* He hadn't planned going beyond this lesson tonight.

She nodded. "I think the magic is giving me a high."

"Then perhaps it would be better for you to slowly come down now rather than build up for a more severe crash later."

She looked disappointed, but didn't argue.

He internally sighed in relief. Well, that fixed one problem. "Goodbye, Fawn. I'll see you tomorrow."

"Bye, Caleb."

FAWN WAS BEGINNING TO DOUBT THE NATURE OF her relationship with Caleb. A solid week had passed since he had started teaching her magic and she felt closer to him than ever.

Yes, he watched over her and had become a special sort of friend to her, but there were times he would look at her, say something, or briefly touch her in a way that made her wonder again about their mutually expressed desire to go on a date.

He hadn't brought it up again since, and though she was all for women asking men out, she couldn't muster the courage to do so with Caleb. And that small fact aggravated her almost as much as not knowing where he stood on the subject.

Unable to stay in her own head, she finally asked Ivy her thoughts. Unsurprisingly, her friend suggested if she was unwilling to ask him out, she should at least ask him if he felt anything remotely romantic towards her.

When they met each other again the next day in Abnormal Psychology, Ivy very obviously said, "Ask him," just as Caleb approached them.

He greeted them both with a smile and replied, "Who and what is being asked of me?"

"Nothing," Fawn quickly answered, casting a quelling glare towards her best friend.

Caleb glanced between the two and laughed. "Now my curiosity is piqued, but I shall give you the benefit of the doubt and not pry."

Fawn forced an embarrassed smile and tried to ignore the bizarre giddiness she felt at his teasing, praying her expression didn't give away her inner thoughts.

Though he didn't bring it up again during the class, Fawn caught him staring at her with an amused expression more than once during the period. And when she did, he would raise a questioning eyebrow and she'd quickly look away again.

She got a text from Ivy. *Stop eye-fucking each other and get a room!* Fawn's eyes flew up to her friend's in the row behind her and an uncontrollable blush detonated across her cheeks as she turned away from Caleb.

At the end of class, Ivy yet again urged her friend, this time silently, to ask Caleb about their relationship before Ivy took off. As they left the building, Fawn could practically sense him buzzing with anticipation and finally said, "Alright, I know you're dying to ask. I—" She took a deep breath, "We mentioned maybe going on a date last week—or, not *going* on a date, but maybe... I don't know. I was wondering if you were still interested in something like that?" She cut herself off and prayed he wouldn't laugh at her.

He smiled and a small chuckle escaped from him, but his words were as surprising as they were reassuring. "I was considering asking you the same thing tonight, but it seems you've beat me to it."

"Is that a *yes*?" she hedged, wanting him to answer explicitly.

He nodded. "Absolutely. In fact, I would like nothing better."

She couldn't help the smile that appeared.

"Perhaps we can do something tonight after our lesson."

"What are you thinking of?"

"I could cook for you and we can watch a movie at my place, or we can do something else if you prefer."

"Your suggestion sounds lovely."

"Then it's settled." He hugged her. "I'll see you tonight for our lesson at our usual time at my place. I'll text you the address."

She beamed at him. "I'm looking forward to it."

CALEB SMILED BACK, ENJOYING THE INEXPLICABLE DIRECT LINK between their minds even when he wasn't actively prying. He had yet to tell her he was able to listen to hers whenever he wished, but it was an advantage he was not ready to give up.

"In the meantime, I believe we also have time for a quick lunch together before your next class. I hope you won't mind indulging me a bit longer with your company. You can tell me what movies you like so I can have a good selection for you."

Her eyes flared with small alarm. "Oh, you don't have to buy anything new for me. I'm sure there will be something interesting on Netflix for us to find."

"I want you to be happy, and I'll gladly shell out a few dollars to ensure that happens tonight."

She blushed and he added, "You can let me know later during our lesson. Now, about food."

"For tonight?"

He shook his head. "I think I'll keep that a surprise, but I was talking of now. I want to make sure you don't accidentally skip lunch like you used to last year."

"You say it like I did that intentionally. It's not my fault I had a class and a lot of work that kept me too busy to go to the dining hall."

"There were other options." He held out his arm. "Eat with me?"

She nodded and he took the moment to dip into her mind and heard her initial excitement and then, *I should tell Ivy.*

"If you prefer not to, there's no pressure. I'll be seeing you later today anyway and would not wish to monopolize your time. Just be sure to take care of yourself."

She smiled. "I would like to see Ivy, but thank you for the invitation."

"Yes, of course," he quickly supplied. "May I say hi first?"

The question clearly took her off guard, but she said, "Sure."

T HEY FOUND IVY SITTING WITH A DATE. FAWN drew up short and Caleb stopped right behind her, so close she could feel his body heat at her back, threatening to engulf her.

Her friend stood up and hugged her tightly, cutting off Fawn's ability to draw breath. Though Ivy was shorter than her, her friend's strength more than made up for her lack of height.

Fawn whispered back, "I didn't realize we weren't meeting alone."

"Oh, I can send him away. He's just a hookup from last night."

She hid a smile. "Yes, I remember you two coming in."

Ivy blushed but made no move to hide it. They both knew she had the more voracious sexual appetite between the two of them.

Fawn didn't exactly approve of the almost-nightly rotation of hook-ups coming through their dorm, but as long as her friend was happy and safe, who was she to judge?

Ivy turned to her date and said, "My friend and I need some girl time. Could you give us some privacy? I'll text you later."

Instead of being offended like Fawn expected him to be, he rose as if in a trance and left them without a word or complaint. Fawn stared at his retreating back for a moment before turning her incredulous eyes to her friend.

Ivy shrugged and said, "He's not really one for words."

Strange, he wouldn't stop yammering last night. Maybe it was just the alcohol talking, she reasoned.

"I see you also brought a surprise plus one."

Fawn turned to Caleb and he took a step forward. "Just wanted to say Fawn and I will be going on a date tonight. I understand good friends like to be kept apprised of such social arrangements."

Ivy turned her huge eyes on her friend. "Really?" Ivy asked in an extra sweet tone. "This is the first time I've heard about it."

Fawn silently thought, *Great, now I'll have to fend off her Spanish Inquisition.* "We *just* made the plan."

Her friend nodded. "Uh huh. I want details. Now."

Caleb cleared his throat, drawing Fawn's attention. "I'll see you tonight, then." He moved forward and hugged her before releasing her and walking away. She and Ivy watched him go.

Fawn turned to see her friend wearing an intense expression. "Spill."

"Can I get something to eat first?"

Her friend shook her head. "Dish now, food later."

Fawn rolled her eyes. "Well, I took your advice and finally asked if he wanted to go out with me and he said yes."

"I knew he would. He'd be an idiot to turn you down."

"Can I finish?"

Her friend waved her on. "Proceed."

"I'm going over to his apartment after our tutoring session." The lie still felt strange, but less so than it originally did. It had been Caleb's idea to call their regular meetings that to dissuade any suspicion her friend might form. "And he's going to make me dinner before we watch a movie."

"That sounds amazing. You're going to have such a great time. And let's be real, movie-time is just code for second base."

"He has to get past first before I can even consider something past that. Anyway, I wanted to ask for your advice because I have no idea what to wear tonight."

"Of course I'll help you, silly! Now, let's get something to eat."

Once they had their food, Fawn asked the other question on her mind. "Am I wrong to be going out with him?"

"What do you mean?"

"Well, he is my tutor." She wanted so badly to say he was her guardian angel, but respected his wish to keep the true nature of their relationship a secret even if it hurt to do so. "Am I letting him take advantage of me?" She felt awful for doubting Caleb, but she couldn't help what she felt.

Ivy shook her head. "I don't think so. You're both consenting adults. If you both like each other, I wouldn't worry. But just because you want a relationship now, doesn't mean you can't change your mind."

CHAPTER 6

AT THE END OF HER LAST CLASS THAT day, Fawn was texting Ivy when she bumped into someone, her phone falling to the ground. She looked up, about to tell off the idiot for walking into her, but the reproach died on her lips. A dark-haired guy smiled apologetically and handed it back.

She swallowed and pocketed the device. "Thanks," she mumbled.

"You shouldn't text and walk at the same time."

Fawn nodded, unsure how to reply, feeling more flustered by how intently he was watching her. She finally settled on "Sorry," after a beat and addressed his feet rather than his face. Doing so would have required her to strain her neck in looking up at his tall stature.

He held out his hand and said, "I'm Viktor. I apologize if I was harsh just now. My family has raised me to always be vigilant. We live in dark and troubled times, yes?"

She detected an Eastern European, perhaps Russian, accent and took his offered hand in her own and shook it. "Yes, I suppose so. My name is Fawn."

She was surprised by his hard grip and even more so by the fact that he held on for so long. She was about to ask him to lighten up when he released her. He didn't walk away immediately and Fawn lingered, unsure if leaving now would be rude.

His peculiar behavior was making her second guess all her actions.

But Viktor unnerved her more than her angel ever did. When she could no longer stand the awkward silence, she took a step back and said, "It was nice meeting you," before walking away.

She could feel the stranger's gaze on her and she shivered, as if experiencing a draft. It wasn't a pleasant one, like the one she sometimes felt around Caleb, but one that made her paranoia kick in, spurring her to walk faster to her dorm. She kept her gaze forward, unwilling to look at the shadows which were beginning to creep across the ground as the sun dipped behind the trees.

She hoped Caleb was watching her, keeping her safe, even if he wasn't by her side. She had no idea why Viktor had given her such a bad feeling. Even as she made her way further from their spot of their collision, it didn't lesson her gut instinct that something was wrong.

When she shut the door to their suite, she was relieved to find Ivy waiting in her room. "I need to dress quickly. He should be here soon. Help me pick something out?" Realistically, she knew he wouldn't be there *immediately*, but the strange interaction outside had made her jittery, and now she wanted to get ready in double-time and have Caleb take her mind off it.

Ivy noticed her agitation. "Are you all right? You seem a bit... hyper."

"I'm fine," she answered, not pausing in taking off her top and pants. "I just had a funny meeting with a stranger. Don't really know what it was about him, but he seemed weird."

Ivy stared at her for a moment, trying to decipher a deeper meaning in her words.

Fawn waved her off. "I'm telling you, it's nothing. Now help me get ready for this date."

If anyone had told her even a year ago she would now be preparing to go on a date with her guardian angel after he tutored her in magic, she would have laughed them out of the room. And yet, sometimes real life was stranger than fiction.

"You should go with something casual, but flirty." Her friend strode to the closet and pulled out a pair of dark blue jeans and another black pair and hung them on the knob.

"It's not *that* cold out yet, so you could probably get away with a blouse," Ivy added, still deep in the closet, so her words came out muffled. "It shows your arms, and classily hints at what's underneath without being too revealing. And it's closer to your normal clothes, so it doesn't *look* like it was picked specifically for your special time together. You should probably wear red. Guys always like red." She finally emerged, holding three red blouses as options. "What do you think?"

Fawn picked the blue jeans from the closet's small handle and lay them on her bed. She pointed to a flowing, sleeveless, almost sheer, and low-cut top. "Not that one. It screams sex and this is just dinner."

"It's never *just* anything, these days," Ivy scoffed, but put it back. "Want me to keep looking for others?"

"No. I like this one." Fawn picked the silk halter top connected with a gold chain.

Ivy whistled. "I'm impressed. I thought you'd pick the second-to-last one," she said, referring to the most traditional one, which was fully buttoned up from her clavicle down to its hem. "I'm sure he'll love it."

They heard a knock on the door and Fawn shooed her friend out. "Be nice to him. Don't scare him off."

"I promise I'll be the perfect host." Ivy winked and then left, leaving Fawn alone in her room, staring at the closed door.

She strained her hearing to monitor their conversation.

"Hello, Ivy. Is Fawn still getting ready?"

"Yeah, she'll be ready in a few moments. Feel free to sit. Can I get you something to drink?"

Fawn smothered a laugh at just how much her roommate was getting into her hostess character.

"Just some water, please."

Nothing else was said and she didn't want to keep him waiting too long. Sighing, Fawn quickly changed clothes, brushed her hair, and dabbed on a small amount of lip gloss.

One last glance in the mirror and she was ready. *Relax*, she scolded herself. *It's another normal magic lesson.*

When she opened the door, she saw Caleb. Dressed up, he looked as though he belonged to a different era, one where gentleman took as much pride in their appearance as the women and where chivalry was the expected mode of behavior, not the outlier.

He took her in, scanning her head to toe and his surprised expression was worth it. She smiled. "Hi, Caleb. Ready?"

He smiled. "Yep. You look gorgeous, by the way."

"Thank you." Fawn held the door of her room open, and saw Ivy give an approving nod before she followed him inside.

Caleb felt like an idiot. He hadn't been able to say "Hello" after seeing Fawn dressed up. She was always beautiful, and there was certainly no ugly duckling transformation, but he was still blown away by her appearance. The blame was totally on him.

She turned to face him, smiling. "What are we doing tonight?"

"Eager, aren't you?"

"I can't help it if I like learning."

"You should never apologize for that. Since you're ahead in my plan, we have time to do something you've been wanting to learn."

She looked up at him in surprise. "Like what?"

"You mean you haven't been privately creating a wish list of things to learn with your magic? I find that hard to believe."

"Well, what would qualify?"

He peeked into her mind and said, "I could teach you to read tarot." He waved his hand and a dark purple velvet draw-string bag appeared.

She reached for it, but he pulled back. "What are you doing?"

"Promise me you'll be as patient with yourself as I have been with your magic inferiority complex."

"I wouldn't go that far." She tried to take the bag, but he switched it into his other hand. She sighed and conceded, "Fine."

He handed the bag to her. "That wasn't so hard, was it?"

She rolled her eyes and started shuffling the cards. When she was done, she spread them out in an arc in front of her.

"Have you done this before?"

She shook her head. "No, but I've just watched my mom do it a bunch of times." She let her hand hover over the cards. She closed her eyes and moved her hand across the floor until she suddenly halted.

He watched her open her eyes and, without looking at the card, place it vertically closer to her before restarting the process. In full, she drew six cards. Curious as to what spread she had chosen, he opened the Grimoire and smiled when he saw she had unknowingly just created the True Love spread.

He watched Fawn turn over the first card, which represented her, revealing the Empress. *I could have guessed that given how important I am*, he heard her think. When she didn't say anything out loud, he pretended to not have read her mind and asked, "Well?"

She startled and looked over her shoulder at him. "It's supposed to be me. It says I'm powerful and apparently fertile." She rolled her eyes at the last part. "Clearly their priorities of women's attributes needed some work back then."

Before he could reply, she had moved onto the second card which represented her partner in the relationship. A quick peek into her mind revealed it was *him* and he held his breath as she flipped the image over. It was the Knight of Cups. He exhaled in relief. Even her magic saw him as her "knight in shining armor."

"That's you," she said before flipping the third card which was the Two of Cups. "That's us," she briefly added before moving onto the next reveal. Their relationship strength was apparently the Ace of Cups.

Fawn didn't verbally say anything, but he heard her think, *We're in the honeymoon stage... does that mean there will be a drop soon?* It was a natural question, but if she was so easily doubting their relationship, he needed to up his game when it came to romancing her.

She more hesitantly flipped over the fifth card, which revealed their relationship weakness and Caleb felt as though he had been punched in the stomach when he saw it was the Emperor. Fawn's expression morphed into a frown, but even as he strained to listen to her thoughts, there was nothing for him to hear. She seemed too stunned to even process it.

"Final card?" he prompted. "Maybe the full picture will explain all the parts."

She seemed to mentally shake herself and flipped the last card with a new sense of urgency. It was the Lovers. He heard Fawn sigh in relief and suppressed a smile. Her reaction had been the same as his.

"See? We're destined for happiness together."

She turned toward him. "You knew what all these said?"

He nodded. "I see you did too." Pink spread over her cheeks. "Are you ready for our date?"

Fawn felt her heart rate pick up and nodded quickly. She called out to Ivy, "We're going. See you later."

Her friend came into the main room. "Have fun! Don't do anything I wouldn't."

Fawn rolled her eyes. "Like that limits anything."

Ivy shrugged, a satisfied smile in place.

Caleb held the door open for Fawn and she walked through.

"Tell me more about yourself," she asked him as they walked down the main path which cut through campus.

"And if I wanted to talk about you?" he parried.

"You're my angel, don't you know everything about me already?"

"Most, but I'm not omniscient. Only God has that privilege."

She didn't know how to reply.

He seemed to take her silence as acquiescence and continued, "I had a hard time picking a film. I personally pegged you for a rom-com girl, but I also know you have a surprising dark streak."

"Only in books and movies," she clarified, feeling uncomfortable that her *guardian angel* had just called her dark.

"Of course. I'll let you pick when we get to that stage."

He smiled and the strangest hope fluttered through her—that they'd be preoccupied and *wouldn't* need to pick a movie at all.

"This is me," he said, gesturing to one of the newer housing options reserved for seniors.

A small flare of jealousy went through her, but she quickly squashed it. He was an angel. He probably had a few perks on earth.

"Are you coming?" he asked, breaking into her thoughts.

She realized she had been standing still ogling the building and started. "Yes. Sorry, got distracted."

"No problem." He opened the door for her and placed his hand on the small of her back as she passed him.

The first thing Fawn noticed about Caleb's apartment was it was so clean. She wasn't sure what she had expected, but something out of an interior design catalog hadn't even crossed her imagination.

Dark wooden panels covered the floor and made up the furniture populating the apartment. And there was more open space than she thought was able to fit into such a small building. The entry way opened into a large living room with a flat screen, sleek couch, and glass coffee table in the center. Connected to it was a kitchen separated by a granite and wood counter.

"Do you like it here?" Caleb asked, drawing her gaze toward him and away from the furniture.

"Yes. I'm really impressed." Fawn undid her coat.

Caleb helped her out of the garment and hung it up. "Thank you. Would you like something to drink?"

"Water, please."

He entered his spacious kitchen and withdrew a crystal cup from one of the wooden cabinets. He handed her a full glass. He had pushed his sleeves up his forearms and began pulling cooking supplies out of the cabinet.

"You're making dinner by hand?"

"I could do it magically, but I thought this was a better way to connect. After all, how often do college students get to enjoy home-cooked meals?"

"Not often enough," she sighed. "What are you making?"

"Italian. Linguine puttanesca."

"Where did you learn to cook?"

"My mother taught me. And then I picked up a few more things over the years. But you can tell me how good I actually am."

"I'm sure you excel at it like everything else." The conversation lulled and Fawn watched in silence as he quickly made the meal. He chopped the vegetables so quickly she wondered if he was using his angel speed to help him along or if he was just that good.

He dropped the pasta into the pot and set the timer. Then he turned his attention back on her. She noticed he hadn't even broken a sweat despite all his movement.

"More water?" he offered, gesturing to her empty glass.

She had completely forgotten about it and nodded.

"What is Ivy doing tonight?"

Fawn shrugged. "Probably on another date."

"With the gentleman from lunch?"

"I don't know. I can never tell how long they'll interest her."

Caleb seemed to be amused by the information.

"What?" she asked.

He shook his head. "You'll learn eventually." Before she could ask him to elaborate, he added, "Want to pick what we're watching later as we wait?" He led her into the living room.

She sat on the couch and surveyed the spread before her. He clearly hadn't listened to her request about saving money. There were at least six different DVDs. She separated them into categories and waited for a mood to strike.

Fawn looked up at him. "What are you thinking?"

He shook his head. "It's your choice."

She stared back down at the table and picked one.

He took it from her hand and chuckled. "I wasn't expecting this one. You do know it's a horror film, right?"

"I heard it wasn't that scary. And even if it is, don't guys like that? So they can hold us or some other misogynistic reason?"

"You're right. Though I will only hold you if you ask."

The timer beeped and they made their way back over to the kitchen. Soon they were sitting and eating.

Fawn took a bite and sighed. "This is amazing. How are you not a chef in your free time?"

"Don't have any."

"Do you miss being able to relax? Having your own life?"

Her words brought an amused expression to his lips. "My life ended over two hundred years ago. My existence, however, is now centered on taking care of you."

"Just remember, all work and no play makes Jack a dull boy."

"You did *not* just imply I'm insane. And did you call me a *boy*?"

She shrugged. "If the shoe fits..."

He crossed his arms and smirked. "I assure you it doesn't."

Fawn coughed at his innuendo and the bite she had just swallowed went down the wrong pipe. She guzzled the water in her glass until the discomfort disappeared and quickly finished eating, too embarrassed to look up at him again. From the corner of her eye, she saw him watching her with thinly veiled amusement and scowled at him, to which he merely smiled.

When she was done eating, he cleared her plate, refilled her glass, and offered her a stick of Toblerone chocolate. "Your favorite."

"Thank you." She ripped the strip off to open the package and proceeded to unwrap the tin foil and methodically broke the chocolate into even pieces, licking her fingers each time some of it melted.

"Can I have some?" he asked.

She hesitated, and felt guilty for being so greedy.

"I suppose you can have it," he said when she didn't reply. She nodded and continued to bring the treat to her lips. "And then I can just kiss off the excess."

It slipped from her fingers and fell towards the floor. "I cannot believe you just said that."

Using his supernatural speed, Caleb caught the sugary morsel and popped it into his mouth. He was crouching in front of her and their faces were only a few inches apart. He licked his lips and smiled. "Now I understand why you didn't want to share."

Her breathing became so loud she was sure she sounded like an aircraft carrier. "You were joking?"

"About?"

"Kissing me?"

"I would never joke about something so important." His right hand reached across the counter and came up to cup her face.

Fawn stiffened before relaxing and leaning into his palm. Her lips parted ever so slightly and a blush rapidly spread across her face. She stared at his mouth. He smiled at her and her eyes flew back up to his. Her face heated at being caught.

"The offer is still on the table. If you want me to kiss you, all you need to do is ask."

She snapped out of the trance and quickly removed his hand from her cheek. "I think—" she glanced at the living room. "I'm ready to watch the movie now."

Once he joined her, she felt his magnetism's pull multiply with their close proximity, even more so than during the strange almost-kiss they had just shared. For the first few minutes, she ignored his gaze.

Her efforts, however, were thwarted once the first ghost appeared. She had known it was coming due to the trailers, but *seeing* the whole ghost still startled her.

And it only went downhill from there because to her shame, she moved closer to him during a particularly scary scene.

He looked down at her and raised an eyebrow in silent inquiry.

She nodded and he wrapped his arm around her shoulder, bringing her closer to his side. By the end of the movie, she was as close to him as humanly possible while keeping clothes on.

"Are you okay?" he asked her, a smile in his voice.

She sat up, putting some distance between them. "Yeah. Though I'm not really sure what I was thinking. I know how I get with things like this."

"There's nothing wrong with trying something new," he comforted.

For some reason, her mind jumped to kissing him. *That* would be something new to experience. Next thing she knew, she was leaning towards him and he towards her.

Stop! a chorus trumpeted in her mind. She didn't know all the voices, but she did recognize Evelyn's among the group. Fawn hesitated. *Continue*, another group of ancestors, including her grandmother, urged her. What was she supposed to do?

She pulled back and he gave her a quizzical look.

"I—I'm sorry. I think I should go," she said.

He stood up and, using angel speed, retrieved her coat. "Of course. I'm sorry if I've made you uncomfortable."

"It's not you." She smiled at him. "I'll see you tomorrow?"

He nodded and she left.

CHAPTER 7

CALEB TAPPED THE QUILL AGAINST THE SILVER BINDER about Fawn. Normally, he would only write down a few notes and then wing it, but she still had him second-guessing himself.

Her unexpected departure at the end of their date had certainly thrown him for a loop and it puzzled him more now than it had in the moment. His own shock at the turn of events had prevented him from realizing how confused he was until some time had passed.

But he wasn't totally clueless. At least, not any more than Fawn was. His quick glimpse into her mind that night had revealed she was as confused as he was. The revelation comforted him only slightly because confused or not, he needed to find out why she had bailed before he could proceed on the romantic front.

That evening, Caleb waited at the dorm for Fawn to come back from her last class and decided he would act in accordance to how she reacted to him. He hated being uncertain, but he couldn't afford to make any errors with her, so he would tread carefully until she gave him the green light to move into more interesting ground.

When Fawn saw him, she appeared surprised, but pleased at his presence. Her yellow aura, which doubled in size once she recognized him, urged him to smile at her. She bit her lip, probably to contain her own smile, and inclined her head before walking into the dorm. If she were anyone else, he would have said the small gesture was an intentional flirting maneuver, but he knew better with her. She was too innocent to even notice what she was doing, and that fact made her all the more endearing.

He followed her, propping the door open before it could close. Not that a locked door would have kept him out. When they stopped outside her door as she fished her keys out of her bag, he leaned on the wall and asked, "What would you like to do, tonight?"

He noticed her hand shake slightly as she fit the key into the lock. So, she was nervous. He checked her aura. No, he had made a mistake. She was excited. Now *that* he could work with. After all, it only took a little muddling of perception to fool someone into believing fear or excitement was sexual arousal.

She didn't look up as she unlocked her door. "Does it have to be related to magic?"

Caleb wondered if she had more—pleasurable—alternatives in mind. He checked, and to his disappointment, her non-magic idea for an activity was watching another movie. He had the urge to chastise her unimaginativeness, but instead replied, "Perhaps it would be best to stay on track tonight."

"Okay," she acquiesced, finally pushing the door in and flipping on the light.

Her quick abandonment of her more romantic ideas gave him pause. Was her attraction to him so weak that it took nothing more than one breath to dissuade her from pursuing her desires? And why did he care? He was skilled enough to make her change her mind—so why wasn't he doing just that?

She pulled him out of his reverie, surprising him with her next words, "Could you teach me how to conceal my aura?"

He raised his eyebrows, grateful she still wasn't facing him as she unpacked her schoolbag. It would seem she had been busy since their last meeting. "Absolutely." It's not like he could refuse without raising her suspicions. "What made you think of it?"

"Some of my ancestors advised me it would be the wise thing to do."

Meddling ghosts, he silently cursed. He checked her mind for her reaction and said, "I'm sure you were frightened."

She froze. "You can read my thoughts and emotions?"

He nodded, forcing himself to not feel guilty over the fact. It was strange. He had never felt he was violating his other assignments' privacy when he used their auras and more to his advantage, yet with Fawn, it often felt as though he were a shameful thief stealing precious jewels from an unguarded window display. It was too easy, and more importantly... it felt *wrong*.

Unaware of his inner turmoil, Fawn sat up as curiosity shot through her. She scooted so close to him he could smell the faint scent of vanilla and coconut wafting off her skin. "Does that mean I can read yours?"

She seemed way too excited by the possibility and it made him feel slightly ill as a new fear took root in his mind. *What if—?* he cut himself off. No, it wasn't possible. If she had heard *any* of his thoughts through their relationship, she would have sent him packing long ago.

Caleb immediately shook his head, feeling only slightly guilty as he watched the orange excitement disappear from her aura. "Mortal and angelic thoughts run on different frequencies. Only divine beings can transcend the 'language barrier,' if you will."

She crossed her arms. "That's not fair." Now she looked annoyed in addition to disappointed.

He smiled, hoping to divert her, before he became serious again. "Close your eyes and think of something, anything will do." He waited a moment, giving her time. "Are you doing it?"

"You can't tell?"

"I'm giving you some privacy."

"A bit late to be the gentleman, don't you think?"

"Don't patronize me or I won't teach you after all."

A few moments passed before Fawn said, "I thought of something."

"Focus on the details, bring it alive like you did with the fire, but do not try to strain yourself. Mind conversations do not require as much energy because they are not in the physical realm. Understand?

"I do."

In that moment, a picture of a beautiful woman entered Caleb's mind along with an overwhelming sense of love and admiration. "Who is she?" he asked.

"My grandma." Fawn's voice was barely a whisper. She clearly missed her.

Caleb could feel his tear ducts beginning to water. Damn, she was better at this than she realized. She was emitting all her emotions onto him. Time to reel it in. "Good job, Fawn. Now you know how to communicate through a mind link, I am going to teach you how to hide your thoughts. This is more difficult, so don't be discouraged if you don't immediately succeed. Ready?" She nodded. "I want you to now pretend you can't feel your emotions. You're not getting rid of them, just pushing them into a corner."

Fawn nodded. Caleb winced when he saw pink and yellow encase her. Why did he feel guilty at her easy trust? He shook himself. "Begin."

She closed her eyes again. Her aura flickered around her, but just as quickly disappeared. "Did I do it?"

"I'm not sure... I can still feel your emotions."

"How is that possible?"

He had no idea—and he didn't like not knowing.

F AWN STARED AT CALEB AND WISHED SHE COULD hear his thoughts. Suddenly, she heard his voice in the back of her head saying, *why didn't this work?*

"I can hear your thoughts!" she exclaimed.

His eyes snapped to hers instantly. "What did you just say?" He didn't seem half as pleased as she was and she suddenly felt guilty for invading his privacy—even if he had done it to her first.

"I'm sorry. I promise I won't try and listen again."

He nodded, but the tension in his body didn't leave.

It was a bad time for Ivy to walk in on them. She paused in the threshold, taking in the scene. "Sorry, didn't know you had company. I'll be out of your hair soon. I just need to get ready to see Erik."

"The guy you were with yesterday at lunch?"

Ivy nodded then disappeared into the bathroom. Moments later, she left.

Caleb turned to her and said, "I believe we have done enough work for today. I am needed elsewhere, but if you need me for any reason, just call out my name three times and I'll be by your side."

"Okay." It came out softly and she had the oddest feeling he was saying goodbye. "Wait, could you tell me where you were the past few days? I don't mean to pry, but I was worried about you. Is everything okay up there?"

He nodded. "Of course. But with you learning magic now, the entire Supernatural community is now abuzz about your identity and abilities. I've been trying to put people off from asking too many questions, but some people are particularly persistent in their curiosity. I appreciate your concern for me, but I assure you, I can take care of myself. If I couldn't do that, I would be an awful guardian angel."

"The next time you leave for an extended time, could you just let me know? Your departure was a little sudden last time."

He nodded and turned to leave.

"Will I see you again tomorrow?" she added.

His posture finally relaxed and he gave an easy smile. "Of course. We can work more with the Grimoire." Then he was gone.

When Ivy came back a few hours later, she'd brought no one with her.

Fawn sat next to her on the couch and said, "You've always been good at reading guys... Could you tell me what Caleb thinks about me?"

"He's definitely attracted to you. But he's confused about it too. Maybe just give him some time to think it all through."

"How are you sure?" And how could she gain the same conviction?

Her friend sighed. "Because... I just know."

Fawn had the sense that her friend was hiding something and grew curious. "How?"

Her friend shook her head. "It's one of a siren's powers."

Fawn wasn't sure she heard correctly. "A siren?"

"We can sense love and lust. It's how we find prey."

"We? You're one of them?"

Her friend flinched and Fawn realized her mistake. "I'm sorry, Ivy. You know I didn't mean it like that. I'm just a little surprised here. How long have you been keeping this from me?"

"Since forever? But before you get super mad, I didn't actually grow into my abilities until puberty. It's one of the reasons I hid it from you earlier, and why I always have a date. Men *literally* can't resist me."

Fawn sat back as she absorbed everything. "I have a siren for a best friend... It's like I'm living in *Twilight*."

Ivy sighed. "I still fantasize about getting it on with a werewolf. Can you imagine how savage they must be when they finally—"

Fawn slapped her hands over her ears. "Stop it, Ivy! Don't corrupt me any more than you already have. I beg you."

Her friend laughed. "We're in college now. It's natural for people to sleep together."

"You said 'prey'... you don't lure people to their deaths, do you?"

"No, of course not! Sirens thrive off of sexual energy and it's kind of addicting, so the more we have of it, the more we need. No one is hurt in the process."

"Isn't that what succubae do?"

Ivy rolled her eyes. "Succubae don't exist."

Fawn's eyebrows slammed together. "What do you mean?"

"Remember how supposedly Hathor and Isis were originally one goddess, but the Egyptians worried she was too powerful, so they split her in two?" Ivy didn't wait for Fawn's answer. "People don't want to think sirens can hunt out of water, so they created the *idea* of succubae, but they never really existed." Ivy sighed.

"Caleb knew about you instantly."

Ivy leaned forward. "Really?"

"He's an angel, that's how he knew. He's my guardian angel." She hoped he wouldn't be mad at her for revealing that, but she didn't feel right keeping that a secret from Ivy anymore, especially after she had shared such an important thing. "He told me someone close to me was keeping a secret, but I never guessed it'd be you. Why didn't you ever tell me? You knew about my magic."

"I would have told you if I could, but my mom forbade me because if the word got out, it could make us a target to Hunters."

"Hunters?"

"Paranormally gifted humans who are dedicated to the extermination of the Supernatural. It's pretty hypocritical if you ask me."

"How horrible."

"My family was attacked by them a few decades ago. That's why my mom moved us to America."

"I never would've guessed."

"That was kind of the point."

Fawn hugged her friend. "I promise to keep your secret."

"Thank you," Ivy said, the relief clear in her voice.

"You sound surprised," Fawn said. "Did you really doubt that I wouldn't share your nature with other people?"

"No, of course not." She paused before admitting, "Well, I thought you might at least tell Alec..."

"If you don't want me to, I won't say a word."

Ivy pulled her into another hug. After a moment, she said, "Okay, let's move onto to something happier. Pizza and movie night?"

Fawn laughed. "I don't see why not."

CHAPTER 8

CALEB IMMEDIATELY KNEW SOMETHING WAS WRONG WHEN HE met Fawn in class the next day. Searching the lecture hall, he couldn't find anyone who posed a threat. That knowledge, however, did not assuage his anxiety, and for the next hour, he could not allow himself to relax.

Fawn must have noticed his alertness because at one point when the professor wasn't paying attention, she turned to him and whispered, "Is everything all right?"

He subtly shook his head.

"What's wrong?"

"I'm not sure, but stay close to me when we leave. I feel danger lurking, but can't seem to pinpoint its source."

"What does that mean?"

"That they may not be in here, but surrounding the building." He noticed her aura turning a darker, worried gray and added, "Don't worry. You're safe with me." It was a lie, but the idea of people coming after Fawn didn't sit well with him. "Fawn," he said, when she didn't answer, making her look him in the eye. "I don't want you worrying about anything, okay?"

She nodded stiffly, but he could hear her thoughts whirling with as many conspiracy theories as he had in his own head. What in Heaven's name was Lucifer playing at by sending people after them?

And why didn't he know it was happening? Did he send them to spy on him?

When they left the lecture together, with his arm around her waist to protect her, he had only a moment to use his angel speed to evade the demon flying at them.

He released Fawn and pushed her behind him. He turned around and recognized the three goons who were currently circling them.

I need you to stay focused on protecting yourself, okay? Caleb told Fawn. *I'm immortal, so don't worry about me.*

It wasn't the total truth. Technically, dark angels could be killed, but he knew the two attackers to be less skilled in combat than him. But he couldn't explain that to her, and he didn't feel the need to needlessly give her more to worry about.

But I—

Promise me you'll save yourself. They stared at each other, neither willing to yield. *Fawn—*

Fine, she mentally snapped.

They pulled away from each other. Caleb saw two large men coming at them from both sides. Quickly turning so he and Fawn were back to back, he eyed the demons with distrust.

"The Chosen One and her angel bitch. You look good on a leash, boy," one of them sneered.

Fight back, Caleb pressed into Fawn's mind. Thankfully hiding one's aura didn't limit mental communication.

I don't know how, she shot back.

Don't over think it. Hopefully it would come to her naturally like all the other magic had so far. "I see you're still doing Lucifer's dirty work." Caleb hadn't run into a Black Eyed Being since he first became a dark angel. He shivered. He certainly hadn't missed their creepy presence.

The creature he taunted pounced, but Caleb was prepared. He blocked and punched the monster in the throat before driving a fist into its stomach. His attacker hunched over in pain. He heard Fawn battling the other two and swiftly threw a right hook to the one closer to him. Caught off guard, the demon swayed before regaining his balance and shifting his fury to the angel.

The one Fawn was fighting jerked away from her with a violent curse before bursting into flames. Caleb saw the human skin burn off, revealing scaly, demonic forms with soulless black eyes.

"Now you see me..." he taunted, suddenly disappearing into the air, "Now you don't."

The other two followed suit and Caleb realized they were leaving him alone when Fawn fell to the floor and curled up in a protective ball. Caleb moved closer to her, fighting above her, protecting her with his body. Suddenly he felt the air become still around him. Three catatonically still bodies appeared, hovering in mid-air, and burst into white flames. The flames subsided, leaving no trace of their assailants.

He heaved a sigh of relief and instinctively pulled Fawn in for a hug. *Had he been a moment slower*, he thought, *they would both probably be dead.*

She pulled back and looked up at him. "What just happened?"

F AWN COULD HEAR HER HEART BEAT PUMPING FASTER and louder than she ever had before. It sounded like a crowded train station. She hadn't been able to fully comprehend the danger Caleb had often told her about, but now she understood why he was so cautious.

"You saved my life," she said on an exhale as the adrenaline began to leave her body.

"I protected you, but *you're* the one who saved *us.*"

She nodded, too dazed to argue with him over the semantics.

His eyes narrowed as he scanned her body. "Are you okay?"

She examined him with equal intensity. "Are you?"

"You should sit down." He picked her up in his arms and instantly they were back in her bedroom.

Oddly enough, she didn't experience any of the discomfort she had the first time he had used magic travel to transport both of them. *I guess he was right*, she privately thought, being sure to keep her mental barrier up so his ego wouldn't grow any larger.

He lay her down on the bed gently and sat beside her, gently pushing down on her shoulder when she tried to sit up.

"This is unnecessary," she complained. "And you haven't told me whether you're okay."

"Answer me first." His tone brooked no argument. "You had two, and then *three* of them attacking you at once. You may feel differently, but by any account, I have failed miserably in my duties."

"No you haven't. I'm tired, but otherwise, I swear I'm *fine*."

He didn't seem to trust her answer, but didn't push it any further.

She sat up and took his hands in hers. "Now you."

"Fawn, I can assure you I am completely fine. Definitely more 'fine' than you, that's for certain. We angels are a very sturdy sort. It takes a lot more to hurt us." He winked, but she had a feeling he wasn't feeling as lighthearted as he was acting.

Now the adrenaline had subsided, she remembered her earlier confusion. "They acted like they knew you."

She had meant it to come out as a question, but she wasn't sorry it hadn't. It was a fact, after all.

Caleb sighed. "That's because they do."

She pushed herself up into a sitting position without any interference from him this time.

"Back when I first became an angel," he explained at her silent urging, "I had the unpleasant experience of coming across a group of Black Eyed Beings while I was on one of my first missions."

"What were they doing?"

"Slowly draining a family of their life force. They had posed as a homeless family and were invited into their prey's house."

"Okay... so they're normally passive, parasitic creatures. Why were they attacking us—me—so violently?"

"Well, those three certainly had a grudge against me after I banished them back to Hell. But I wouldn't be surprised if they were sent up here as mercenaries by Lucifer."

Fawn sucked in a sharp breath. So her instincts had been right. "How did they find us?"

"We're not exactly well hidden," Caleb said quietly. "You aren't prepared to cloak yourself like many witches do to avoid detection."

"When can you teach me?"

"Patience. Believe me, I'll teach you that as soon as you're ready." He leaned closer and kissed her forehead. "You should rest. You're perfectly safe now."

As if the words were a sleeping spell, Fawn felt her eyelids drooping and soon she was carried off into dreamland.

CALEB BURST THROUGH THE DOORS TO LUCIFER'S THRONE room and shouted, "What in Heaven's name was that about?"

At his tone, the guards took a step forward, brandishing their spears to protect the King of Hell. Caleb took a deep breath and more calmly added, "You could have given me a head's up before you sicced those creeps on us."

Lucifer waved the guards away. "And spoil the genuineness of your valiant efforts to save her? I wouldn't dream of it."

"They didn't seem to get the message that they weren't *actually* supposed to kill us."

The Devil rolled his eyes. "Stop complaining, Caleb. It's unbecoming. Besides, you're still alive, aren't you?"

Caleb realized he wouldn't get anything else out of his employer and nodded. "You're correct. I apologize for being so unprofessional."

Lucifer levelled him with a stern stare. "As long as it doesn't happen again. You're dismissed."

Caleb took his leave and began cursing himself to high Heaven as he paced his room. How had he not realized *of course* the Devil knew about—and most likely ordered—the lethal attack? And he hadn't been warned. He stopped short. *Lucifer doesn't trust me anymore.*

The revelation felt like a brick had been dropped into his stomach. He pulled his family photo out from under his pillow and stared at his sister, his father, and then finally his mother. What would they think of him now? For the first time since he started his involuntary servitude, he allowed the shame of his line of work to wash over him.

But I still have to finish this mission.

FAWN NOTICED CALEB WAS EXTRA TIRED THE NEXT day. He didn't make any quips like he usually did, and his purple eyes were duller than she had ever seen them.

"Is something wrong?" she asked.

"No." He didn't elaborate.

Fawn cleared her throat. "Would you go on another date with me?"

He turned to her, but didn't seem to see her until his eyes cleared, returning them to their regular vibrant hue. "Of course. That sounds like a wonderful idea. What film would you like to see?"

Fawn didn't answer immediately, wondering what had triggered the change in him. "What do you want to watch? I don't mind as long as it's not horror."

They settled on watching the latest Marvel movie and magically transported to the theater. As they filed into the auditorium, Fawn felt someone watching her and craned her neck to look behind her. Her gaze finally rested on the guy she had bumped into outside of class a few days before. He didn't even try to hide he was watching her.

"What's wrong?" Caleb asked, placing his hand on hers.

She quickly turned back around and momentarily stared at the sweet and unexpected gesture. "I just thought I saw someone I knew."

Caleb leaned closer and whispered, "Casually point him out to me."

She did, and her angel stiffened in his seat. "It would be best if you avoided him, Fawn."

CHAPTER 9

HER CELLPHONE RANG. FAWN PUT DOWN HER HAIRBRUSH and answered the call. "Hello, Mom."

"Hi, dear. Evelyn just visited me, and I felt you panic through my necklace yesterday. Did something happen?"

"Yes. I was attacked by a group of..." What had Caleb called them? "Black Eyed Beings."

"Fawn! Why didn't you tell me?"

"It's okay, Mom. Caleb and I fought them off."

"Who's that?"

"He's my guardian angel."

There was a pause on the other end. "I'm glad you're safe, and if he is your guardian, then I feel better. But please be careful. The last time Evelyn visited me was when you were born. Her warning should not be ignored. I would like to give him a Reading as soon as possible."

"Well, I've been learning magic with his help. And a few days ago I did a reading. We're meant to be together Mom."

Stella's tone softened on the other side. "I would still feel better if he had another Reading. You can do it if you like, but I would like to be conferenced in either through the phone or Skype."

"Okay," Fawn agreed. "What spread?"

"I believe the simple four-card one will do. Let me know when you plan to Read him, and stay safe."

"I will. Love you, Mom."

"Love you, too."

The line disconnected and she walked out of the bathroom. "What was that about?" Ivy asked.

"I'm not completely sure," Fawn answered. She shook her head. "She wants me to give Caleb another Reading. And soon."

Ivy's eyebrows shot up. "Must be important, then."

"I guess so." Fawn quickly added, "Now I just have to tell Caleb about the Reading. I hope he doesn't get offended."

"I doubt it."

"Here's hoping."

When she came back to the dorm later that night, she was confused when she didn't see him. Turning on the light in her room, she found Caleb sitting on her bed.

"You nearly gave me a heart attack!"

He flashed a mischievous grin. "I know."

She sat down beside him. "My mom wants to you to have a tarot reading over the phone soon."

"We can call her now if you like."

She smiled "Okay. Thank you for not being offended. You know mothers, always overprotective."

He just smiled. "It's to be expected. Give me a moment, okay?" He ducked into the bathroom before Fawn could answer.

CALEB WANTED TO DISAPPEAR. HE HAD NEVER BEEN so nervous before, and his conflicting thoughts were wreaking havoc on his mind as he stared at the reflection of his wet face in the mirror. He had hoped the cold water would make him more alert, but to no avail. When two minutes had passed, he forced himself to appear calm and rejoined Fawn on her bed. His anxiety never abated as Fawn dialed her mother.

Fawn pulled her legs to her chest. "I have Caleb here." Fawn put her cell down on the coffee table and put the call on speaker.

"It's nice to meet you Caleb, though I understand the circumstances are a little strange."

"It's no problem at all, Mrs. Belgrave."

"Please call me Stella."

"Apologies."

"No need. I'd like to start now. Fawn, proceed when you're ready."

Caleb turned in surprise to Fawn. He watched Fawn spread the cards in an arc like she had the last time and swallowed his nervousness.

"Can I try something?" she asked.

He hesitated and Stella said, "What were you thinking?"

"What if I channeled Caleb and let the cards spread themselves?"

Her mother slowly answered, "I don't know if it can be done, but you can try."

She held out her hands to him. Their eyes met and she smiled at him. On full contact, the heat increased until Caleb was sure he would have third degree burns once he let go. He clenched his jaw and concentrated on projecting an innocent aura.

Stella spoke. "Caleb, to make this easier on Fawn, please open your mind to me and focus on yourself. Think of who you are, your values, what defines you." Closing his eyes, he imagined the outermost mental barrier receding, but his dark intentions were safely locked away. He pictured himself with his family, back when he was still pure, and heard Fawn gasp as his aura blossomed around him.

A few moments passed, and then he heard a card move. And then another, and two more. He opened his eyes and saw Fawn staring at the four cards. In unison, they flipped over revealing their images.

"What is the first card?" Stella asked through the speaker.

"The Fool. Naiveté."

Caleb had a feeling Lucifer was laughing his ass off.

"And the second?" her mother asked.

"The Magician. That's power, skill, and concentration, right?"

Stella quickly affirmed it was.

This time, Fawn declared the third, future card without prompting. "The Future is The Hermit. Loneliness?" He could tell it was less a question on meaning but of confusion on her end.

He frowned. He had never been and would never become a recluse in his life.

"And the outcome is The Lovers again." Fawn blushed as she said the words and Caleb almost sent a 'thank you' prayer skywards.

"You can stop channeling now, Fawn," Stella said.

Fawn dropped his hands and he immediately, and inexplicably, missed the physical connection.

She gasped too and he wondered if she felt the same or if she was just put out by exerting her magic for so long. "I'm okay," she mouthed at him.

"Are you sure?" he replied in the same manner.

She nodded. "Positive."

Stella continued, "All your cards were from the Major Arcana, Caleb, which means you have a powerful role in Fawn's life. It seems I was mistaken about you. I apologize for not trusting you."

Fawn ended the call before grabbing Caleb's hand, beaming up at him. After she closed the bedroom door behind them, Fawn lay down on her bed and watched him take his usual seat at the desk. "Why did you get the Fool?"

"I had a rough start in life. My family was very poor, and after my father died, I became responsible for putting food on the table. We were doing okay, but when my sister got cholera, we didn't have enough money to save her. After she died, my mother also got sick, and I scraped together some money to get medicine. We only had enough to buy for one of us."

It was a minor lie, but one none the less. He paused and stared at the ceiling in a trance. He was duping her, but he couldn't help but think about how he had never told so much of the truth to someone else before. *Time for the clincher*, he thought. "Despite her protests, I gave it to her and I died."

He made sure his voice cracked at the end and saw Fawn wince. "After I became an angel, I learned she had died. The medicine hadn't saved her."

Caleb lowered his eyes to Fawn's face, waiting to see her reaction.

She silently stared up at him as the words sunk in. "I'm...so sorry. If I'd known, I wouldn't have asked." She reached out to rub his arm, but he moved away. He wouldn't look at her, and sounded so defeated when he said, "It's okay."

"Do you see them now?" she asked in a small voice. "Do you see them while you're in Heaven?"

He shook his head, and felt Fawn's hope deflate. He stood up. "I should go now."

"Caleb?" she asked, her voice unusually small. "I know this is really bad timing on my part, but... are we together?"

He knelt down so they were eye-level and took her hands in his, reveling in the warmth that engulfed him yet again. "Emotions don't always run on timelines. As to your question, I would very much like us to be, but I don't want to pressure you."

She stared at their interlinked fingers before looking up at him. "I want us to be too, but I don't want you to get in trouble."

He smiled at her. "Believe me, I wouldn't be. Fawn. If you want us to become official, I would be extremely happy and honored to be your boyfriend."

"I would like that." She also added, "Would you be my date to the Halloween party next week?"

"Then it's settled. I will gladly take you to the ball. Until then, girlfriend." He gently dropped another kiss on her forehead, and then he was gone.

CHAPTER 10

A WEEK LATER, FAWN STARED IN AWE AT HER reflection in the bathroom mirror. She had never considered herself an overly vain person, but given she rarely dressed in anything besides concealing tops and jeans, she had almost forgotten how nice she could look when she bothered to put some work into her appearance besides brushing her hair and teeth.

Something her mother continually asked her to do, especially as she grew older. "You're so beautiful and you always hide it." And she was right, but Fawn never *intentionally* hid herself. In fact, most of her tops were very form-fitting, as were her pants, but she understood what Stella meant by her motherly criticism.

Tonight, her hair was currently pinned up in an elegant bun and her eye shadow was mainly natural colors with highlights of purple. She had wanted to go with a more natural palette, but Ivy had insisted on the extra pop of color. "It emphasizes your blue eyes," her friend had insisted. She thought she looked as though she had lost a fight with a fairy, and since Ivy had been the one wielding the eyelash wand, she supposed she had.

Her eye shadow not only contrasted with her eyes, but also matched the dress she wore: a beautiful plum dress with a corseted top and gold trimming. Fawn twirled in a full circle, enjoying the way the fabric fluttered around her ankles. But what if Caleb didn't like her outfit? The thought stopped her in her tracks and she suddenly worried he would think she was trying too hard.

Her thoughts were cut off when the man—angel—himself appeared in the doorway. She turned to fully take him in without her own reflection blocking his. He wore a tux, and his mask was black and silver, a perfect complement to her white and gold mask. His cologne was a musky cucumber which smelled wonderful.

He walked forward until he stood right in front of her. "You look stunning, love," he murmured, trailing his hands up her bare arms.

She suppressed a shiver and briefly regretted not wearing gloves to hide such a reaction, but decided she would much rather feel his touch than not to. "You don't look so bad yourself. Had I known you looked this good in a suit, I would have made you always wear one."

Caleb chuckled and produced a gold heart pendant on a chain from his inner jacket pocket. "A gift for you." She turned around, and he secured the necklace over her opal one.

She touched the pendant. "It's beautiful. Thank you."

"My pleasure." He offered her his arm. "Shall we go?"

When they reached the gym where party was taking place, Caleb held his arm out for Fawn. They glided onto the center of the dance floor beneath the black and white chandeliers. Fawn laid her cheek against his shoulder and closed her eyes. She felt him stroking her hair. When he eventually stopped, she lifted her head and blushed.

Ten songs later, Fawn's feet were hurting. While the silver heels were pretty, they were only comfortable for the first few minutes, and that didn't account for dancing. "Can we leave soon?" she asked.

Caleb nodded. When the song ended, they left the dance floor. When they reached her dorm, he asked, "Do you want me to come in?"

She blushed and some red seeped into her aura, but realizing her mistake, she quickly snapped it back in.

"It's okay if you say yes," he encouraged, his eyes twinkling.

She thought for a moment. "Yes."

CALEB SHUT THE DOOR BEHIND THEM. HE HEARD the lock click in place, but Fawn didn't notice. She sat in her chair, peeled off her adhesive mask, and put it on her nightstand. Next to go were her heels.

After placing them in the closet, she stood in front of the mirror and unclasped Caleb's necklace which covered her opal pendant. She laid it on her desk. She took out her silver earrings, and they glistened in the light when she placed them next to the necklace.

He stood behind her and placed his hands on her waist. They trailed up her back, tracing her spine, eliciting a shiver from her. When he grasped the clasp to her opal necklace she moved away. "You're going to sleep with it on?" he asked, even though he knew they wouldn't be sleeping anytime soon, especially if they kept going at this rate.

"I can't take it off."

"What do you mean?"

"It links me to my mom and brother. I was told never to take it off."

That could be a problem. If it amplified her link to her family, they might feel her lust and then they'd be found out. He needed privacy to do the job right. But now she was an independent college girl, miles away from home. Her family wouldn't be able to stop them, even if the twin connection held. Time to change topics. "Want to help me get more comfortable, too?"

Tentatively, Fawn reached around to the back of his head and tugged at the tail of the ribbon, undoing the bow, and his mask came off. She caught it and put it next to hers. Returning to stand in front of him, she deftly undid his tie and lifted it over his head. Next, she went after his shirt buttons, undoing them from top to bottom before she stepped back.

"What? You're not going to take my shirt off?" he teased.

"No, Caleb," she answered with wavering conviction. He could see the want in her eyes.

"Can I at least kiss you?"

She nodded and in a moment, his lips descended on hers and he was rewarded with Fawn's encouraging sigh. He pulled her closer until their bodies were pressed together as closely as possible. When he heard her gasp, he pulled back to give her time to catch her breath and gazed into her eyes. "You are so beautiful," he murmured before placing another sweet kiss on her lips.

He grunted when he felt her fingers tentatively playing with his hair.

As they kissed, Caleb tugged gently on the pins holding Fawn's hair in the bun. After he removed all of them, he ran his fingers through her hair and he kissed her jaw until he reached her ear.

Fawn turned and buried her face in the hollow of his neck as she breathed him in. For a while, they stood still, merely holding each other.

Then she slowly lifted her mouth to his ear and whispered, "Will you make love to me?"

He held her face in his hands. "Are you sure?" They had finally kissed the day after they had started 'officially dating,' and done even more since, but this seemed fast even to him. She was giving him her virginity without any forethought... But why did he care? Wasn't that his goal? "We've only been together for a short time, love. I'd hate for you to later regret this decision."

It had never bothered him to deflower his past assignments. Why did the prospect of taking *Fawn Belgrave's* virginity under false pretenses sour his conscience?

"Yes, I'm sure." she breathed, raising her hand to his jaw, drawing his attention back to her. "I can't explain it, but this feels right. I feel like even though I only recently met you that I've known you longer. Does that make sense?" She didn't wait for him to answer. "I know what I'm doing and I want to be with you tonight."

Any qualms he had disappeared and Caleb shrugged off his shirt, then unzipped the back of her dress. "And you'll have me forever," he replied, even though he knew that was impossible. She stepped out and looked expectantly at him, suddenly too shy to make another move. Taking the initiative, Caleb swept her up in his arms and walked them to the bed where he gently laid her down. "If you change your mind, tell me to stop."

"I know what I want. I love you, Caleb."

Her words made him freeze. He looked up at her, eyes wide.

She was blushing. "I—I'm sorry. I shouldn't have said anything. Just forget it." She tried to sit up, pushing him away.

He caught her hand before she could fully climb off the bed. "No. Don't go." She wouldn't face him, and suddenly seemed to shrink before him as her confidence waned. "Of course I love you, Fawn. You just surprised me." He squeezed her hand. "Look at me."

She finally turned to look at him, her keen eyes suddenly clear as she examined him. "Do you mean it?"

"I would never lie to you about this." And he wasn't lying and that both confused and terrified him.

She joined him on the bed again. The fit of their bodies felt surprisingly right.

"What are you doing to me?" he murmured into the base of her neck before pressing another kiss to her heated skin.

Fawn sighed. "I could ask the same thing."

Their conversation ended there.

When midnight struck, Caleb was staring at the white ceiling while gently stroking Fawn's face. He smiled, remembering the way she wrapped around him as they had sex—made love. She loved him, which meant his mission would soon be over, if his success continued.

Her feelings weren't one-sided, which led to his final epiphany of the night: he didn't want to leave her when this was over.

It was already affecting him. The more he spent time with her, the harder it was to leave her each night and return to Hell. It was as if an invisible tether had formed between them. The unnamed connection made him feel happier and more complete than he had ever felt since his family fell apart.

But what could he do but betray her? He had to finish the assignment in order to reunite with his family. Becoming attached wasn't in the plan, and now that he thought about it, he didn't even know how it could ever work. Once Fawn learned of his deception, she would hate him for sure, and rightfully so.

He was pulled from his reverie when he felt her tremble in her sleep. He pulled her closer, hoping to soothe whatever nightmare plagued her. She stilled, blissfully unaware of the treacherous waters that lay ahead.

When he felt a tear fall on his chest, he stroked her hair and murmured, "It's okay." He didn't know what was happening between them, but he knew he needed to figure it out soon.

CHAPTER 11

FAWN WOKE IN THE DARK TO A BURNING sensation on her chest. It took her a moment to realize, through her sleepy haze, it was caused by her opal pendant.

Fawn grabbed the pendant to take it off when she suddenly heard her mother and brother speaking.

"We've been kidnapped. Be careful. Something evil is brewing."

Now deeply frightened, she let the stone go and turned to ask Caleb what he thought it meant, but his side of her bed was empty. Throwing on a robe, Fawn began walking around the suite and realized Ivy hadn't returned last night. *She's probably on a fling*, she thought.

Her necklace burned her again, as if reminding her of the problem at hand. Alone and afraid, she sat on the couch and put her head in her hands. What was happening, and how could she help her family?

And where was Caleb? She wanted to talk to him, but had no idea where he had gone. He hadn't left a note or hinted last night he would be ducking out. Then she remembered what Caleb had once told her and summoned him by repeating his name three times. She did so and a small gust of wind hit her and she looked up to see Caleb land on the floor.

Before he could ask what was wrong, she ran to him and hugged him with all her might. "Something is wrong with my family. They said they've been kidnapped. I don't know what to do..." She started hyperventilating and squeezed her eyes shut.

Caleb led her to the couch. "Start from the beginning, love. You're not making much sense and I can't figure out a way to help you unless you tell me everything."

"I woke up to my chest burning—it was my necklace," she added when she saw his eyes widen in horror. "I tried to take it off, but when I touched it, my mom and brother who told me they had been kidnapped. I tried to find you, but you weren't here, and neither was Ivy. I'm sorry for calling you back here. I hope I didn't pull you from anything important, but I was panicking and didn't know who else to talk to. As much as I love Ivy, you have more experience with the Supernatural world than she does."

He wiped her hair out of her eyes, and offered her a box of tissues.

A flash of red light appeared in the center of the room. It faded to reveal Lucifer wearing black jeans, t-shirt, and biker boots. He looked like he belonged in the cast of Greece, but still looked as handsome as he did when he had worn the James Bond suit in her dream on her sixteenth birthday. "I see you're still playing house. I would have thought you'd already be with united with your family again, Caleb."

"You know him?" Fawn gasped. "That's the man I saw in my dream when I turned sixteen."

Before he could answer, Lucifer answered. "Of course he does. He works for me." He snapped his fingers. "Where are my manners? I'm Lucifer. Pleasure to meet you."

She recoiled and said, "That's not possible. He's my guardian angel. He would never associate himself with you." She turned to Caleb and asked, "Right?"

"What are you doing here?" he demanded, ignoring her question.

"I'm just stopping by to see if Fawn wants to get her mother and brother back. From the amount of tissues, I would say she does. Family is by far the most important bond—wouldn't you say?"

Caleb refused to be baited. "She's not making any deals with you."

Lucifer jerked his chin toward Fawn. "Why don't we let her decide? Miss Belgrave, you're an intelligent young woman who is capable of making your own decisions. What do you say?"

Caleb moved in front of Fawn, facing her and blocking her sight of Lucifer, as if he could shield her from the Devil's manipulative influence. "Don't do it," he warned.

"It's my family we're talking about here. I need to save them."

"We'll find a different way."

"Is there one?"

He hesitated. "I don't know," he admitted when she stared at him in anticipation.

"Well, before you make me the bad guy," Lucifer said, "why don't you take a moment to evaluate your charming angel first?"

"What are you talking about?" Fawn asked again. She addressed Caleb, "You never answered how you know each other."

Lucifer continued mercilessly. "He disappears without explanation for extended periods of time and didn't want you to tell anyone close to you about him being your angel. Like you said yourself, they *are* your family. Didn't that rule make you a little suspicious?"

Fawn shook her head, unwilling to listen to his poisonous words. "I don't believe you."

Lucifer chuckled before turning to his pawn. "It seems like your lies have been more effective than I thought." He addressed Fawn again. "And do you believe he loves you?"

"Yes, of course" she snapped.

"My dear, Caleb has been spying on you for me the whole time. He's not your guardian angel, but a dark angel I've sent to seduce you."

"You're lying."

Lucifer snapped his fingers, and a pained cry pierced the air as Caleb fell to his knees while his wings were forcibly unfurled in their black, infernal glory.

"Now do you see?" the Devil demanded.

"So it's true?" Fawn said, half speaking to herself. "It was all a lie?"

"Fawn—" Caleb reached for her but she backed away.

He tried to hold her again, but she willed him away from her. Suddenly, he was pinned to the wall, his wings sprawled open. His expression was one of surprise, mirroring her own feeling at her unexpected spell. She hadn't even intended anything specific, yet she couldn't say she was dissatisfied with what had happened.

"Give me a chance to explain," he begged her with the pathetic voice of a wounded animal.

"I gave you a chance. I trusted you! And you used it against me! You've forgotten what family is. What trust is." She jabbed a finger into his chest. "You aren't capable of love, Caleb."

He opened his mouth, and another blast of power hit him.

"I'm not done," she warned. "If you loved me at all, you wouldn't have gone through with it."

"I do love you!" he protested.

She ignored him and continued, "But you have no idea how sorry I am—that I ever loved you." Her voice cracked at the end.

"No! Fawn! You don't know what you're saying."

"Do you know what the saddest part is, Caleb?" She didn't wait for him to answer. "The saddest part is I would've gone on loving you until the day I died, even if you made up a bogus excuse to leave once you were done with me. That's how much I loved you."

She turned away and snapped at Lucifer, "Give me back my family."

The Devil smiled and said, "Gladly—for a price, of course."

"Name it, I'll pay it."

"Don't—" Fawn shot Caleb a look that could freeze Hell and burn Heaven at the same time.

"I return your family and you become my queen."

"Deal."

"No!" Caleb shouted from his temporary prison as they disappeared in a burst of red light.

*D*AMN! *DAMN! DAMN!* CALEB COULDN'T EVEN CARE HE was probably lessening his chances of reaching Heaven by cursing, but honestly that was no longer a priority—Fawn's happiness had miraculously taken first place. And he'd lost her.

Looking at the scorch mark on the floor made him feel as though he'd been branded himself. And while the mark hadn't been physically imprinted on him, hew knew he would never forget it for as long as he lived. Which, now that he was essentially fired from Lucifer's ranks, could be any time now. There had never been a termination clause in his contract with the Devil, but he doubted there was a severence package that allowed him to keep his angelic powers. Now that they had brought him to this point, he wasn't sure he even wanted to keep them. They were just another reminder of what he'd lost with Fawn.

What have you done? he demanded of himself. Unable to control his rage at himself, he punched the wall, leaving a gaping hole. He kept going, barely registering each time his fist made impact.

"No need to throw a tantrum."

"Oh, great! Now is not the time—" Caleb turned around and froze. An old man in a white suit and matching beard stood before him and he knew it had to be none other than God. If he hadn't known he was damned, Caleb would have assumed he had died and gone to Heaven. Never in a million years had he ever expected to meet the Creator.

God looked around the room. "Where is Fawn?"

Caleb's eyebrows furrowed. Wasn't God supposed to be omniscient? "Lucifer dragged her to Hell to become his queen."

"Go after her, Caleb."

"I can't. Not after what I did. She hates me too much, and who blames her?"

"Then unfortunately, I cannot let you see your family in Heaven."

"Why not!" Wow, he sounded like a spoiled brat who was denied a new toy. "Forgive me."

God nodded. "Because you still have work to do. She's your soulmate and you must gain her forgiveness."

"I've already been in Hell for two hundred years, and now my perfect other half hates me. Don't you think I've suffered enough?"

"I bargained for your soul when I made the deal with Lucifer to cleanse you by having you near Fawn," God continued, ignoring him. "Who better to purify you than your own soulmate?"

"I doubt she would let me within a hundred feet of her."

God sighed. "It's hard for her to reconcile that you loved her and simultaneously betrayed her."

Caleb couldn't deal with hearing that right now. He was already dancing along the cliff of sanity and even the slightest push would toss him over the edge. He swallowed. The thought of being rejected by Fawn again hurt too much. The only thing worse was the thought of hurting her again.

"It won't be easy, but you will succeed."

"How do you know for sure?"

"The prophecy isn't only about her. It's about your shared love. Lucifer only knows the first part. He does not know it continues to say: *Love misled shall betray her and destruction shall reign until forgiveness won.* You will save each other."

Caleb nodded. He sincerely hoped so.

part two

Love isn't a decision. It's a feeling.
If we could decide who we loved,
It would be much simpler,
But much less magical.

TREY PARKER

CHAPTER 12

H ER SURROUNDINGS FINALLY STOPPED SPINNING AND FAWN ONCE again
felt a solid floor beneath her feet. She swayed a little, dizzy from
the disorienting travel, but Lucifer caught her around the waist. Fawn
wanted to spit in his face for touching her, but she remembered her
deal: she was to become his queen for eternity. Although it was only
to save her family, Fawn had enough self-preservation to know piss-
ing off the devil was not the smartest move.

He brought her body close to his, their faces within inches of each
other, and flashed a dazzling white smile. *If he tries to kiss me*, Fawn
began thinking, *I'm going to puke.*

Luckily, he pulled away. "I'm hurt you're relieved I didn't kiss you,"
Lucifer said, but he was still smiling, so Fawn knew he was teasing.
And then she got mad when he continued, "Is Caleb the only one
allowed to kiss you?"

Her eyes narrowed. "I want proof my family is safe."

"Of course. I'm a man of my word."

"You won't mind if I request something more substantial than
your verbal promise," she said extra sweetly.

He chuckled and waved his hand in front of them, opening a visual
portal into her childhood apartment.

She saw her mom walk into the kitchen and start making a smooth-
ie. "And my brother?" she asked.

Lucifer wiped the air again and a scene of her brother sleeping peacefully in his dorm room replaced the one of her mother. The portal dissolved into thin air. "You're mine now, Fawn."

His words made her shiver, and not in the good way. "Why don't you take me on a tour? I can't live here if I don't know where anything is," she said, resorting to the protection of sarcasm.

The Devil laughed and it echoed through the black slate hall. "I like you. On the outside you're the ice queen, but there's a fire in your heart my Father will never understand. You and I are not that different."

"Yes we are," she snapped. "I have a heart. You don't."

"Maybe you'll change your mind. In the meantime, if you would come this way..." Lucifer took her hand with surprising gentleness and led her through two black iron doors. "I'll show you the throne room."

She saw two black iron thrones seated among piles of bones and fire pits. A fire gem was embedded in the top of each throne. Next, he showed her the Great Hall and Great Ballroom. Fawn didn't say much on the tour until he revealed the Great Library with thousands and thousands of books.

Fawn was dumbstruck. When did he have time to read? "Are there nine circles of Hell, or is that just another myth?"

Lucifer came to stand behind her. "Ah yes, Dante's *Inferno.* There are different levels, yes, but they are not limited to a number. It just goes to show how small human thinking is concerning things beyond their understanding. In reality, there are general Hells as well as personal ones within each level. As long as sinners exist, the number will keep increasing. It is truly infinite."

Fawn nodded and continued to scan the shelves. She saw many original copies of famous books about making deals with the Devil—she expected that—but on another side were romantic classics and some of her modern favorites. "How accurate was *Paradise Lost?*"

"Ninety-eight percent, though I suppose that's because I told the story to Milton. He was merely my scribe."

"You spoke in epic verse?"

Lucifer shook his head. "That was his artistic expression. I didn't mind as long as my side was being told."

"Should I start calling you Satan?"

He frowned. "As you're soon to be my queen, calling me 'The Adversary' isn't quite appropriate."

"And the Messiah? He was really the son of God?"

"You sound doubtful."

"The story always rubbed me as too coincidental."

"He is, though he's not the only one. *That* one part of my story appalled Milton so much, he didn't put it in."

"You're God's son?"

"His first born. I was supposed to inherit Heaven."

"Is that why you're so mad at God? Because you got kicked out?"

"If you were denied your birthright to some usurper, wouldn't you be angry?"

"I never thought about it. I suppose..."

She continued walking through the shelves and noticed a special display where a single book stood on a black marble alter.

Fawn turned to Lucifer. "The Bible? Really?"

"I did not put it there. You could say it was a homecoming gift left by my Father. Try as I might, I can't move it. And believe me, I've tried everything." He paused, recollecting himself. "This is all yours. I don't come here anymore." He led Fawn up an elegant flight of stairs and through more corridors. As they walked, she realized that although this was a castle, its layout was more complicated than any earthly one and its floorplan could take her centuries to memorize.

Lucifer guided her down a corridor which ended in a perpendicular hallway with a set of black iron double doors at both ends. There was a plaque next to each of the entrances. One said his name in graceful red calligraphy engraved into the black marble and the other said her name. Lucifer made a left toward her room without glancing at his own. Two guards stood outside her door. They pulled open the doors.

The room was decorated with dark purple couches, matching curtains, and a black iron coffee table. A desk and an armchair sat in the corner. "Your sitting room." Lucifer guided Fawn to the left. He opened two doors revealing a room-sized walk-in closet.

In it were what seemed to be countless dresses, high heels, hair ornaments, and jewelry. There were also pants, blouses, and sweaters.

Fawn knew which side of the closet she'd go for, but maybe being queen in Hell required fancier attire. In the back of the room stood a black and silver wardrobe.

Fawn was immediately curious and began walking toward it, but Lucifer led her away, "Not until your coronation, dear." He closed the closet doors and they walked through the sitting room and another set of double doors.

A huge canopy with dark purple curtains and silver detailing hung over an ornate queen-sized bed with a quilt matching the curtains. Two maids were just folding down the bed. They quickly finished and were about to leave when Lucifer said "Wait." They stood still. Lucifer brought Fawn forward. "This is your queen-to-be. Fawn, these are your lady's maids, Selene and Alicia." Then he turned to the maids once again and said, "Please leave us."

Fawn watched them bow and leave and wondered if their job was to just do housecleaning or also to keep an eye on her. Fawn turned back to the room and noticed there were two large windows on either side of the bed with their curtains drawn. Fawn went over to the windows wondering what the view would be in Hell. Fawn half expected to be seeing a gallows or a guillotine set up, but instead saw the black marble courtyard and servants quickly passing through.

Fawn felt compelled to say something about the tour. "It's beautiful, but it's still a cage. I don't want to be here."

He leaned in dangerously close and menacingly whispered, "You don't have a choice." He left her without another word.

Fawn took a long hot shower in the huge bathroom which rivaled any five-star hotel she had ever seen. She dried herself off and put on the silk robe her maids had laid out before crawling into the giant bed. Once under the covers, she began to weep. When Lucifer came for dinner, dressed in an admiral blue suit, her appetite was gone and she told him she just wanted to be alone.

From that point on, Fawn stayed cooped up in her opulent suite. The only time she ventured outside her room was to go to the Great Library to pick out a new book, which she would then enchant to read aloud to her. Sometimes she would run into the guards and servants, but most left her to herself.

She refused to see Lucifer again, despite his relentless efforts which involved a stream of extravagant gifts she didn't want and increasingly forceful requests. She did have to wonder why he didn't force her—he was the King of Hell, after all—but she didn't dwell on it too much for fear of manifesting that very scenario, and only talked to Selene and Alicia when she got particularly lonely.

A few weeks later, Fawn was sitting at her desk, feeling utterly bored. She'd read every book which had been placed on her designated shelf in the Great Library and didn't know what to do now that her one source of entertainment had been exhausted. Staring out her window at the red courtyard had also quickly grown tiresome.

Suddenly, a sharp pain manifested in her chest. Fawn looked down expecting to see a bloodied wound staining her cream gown, but there was none. *Was it voodoo?* she wondered. Caleb wouldn't try and harm her, would he?

Her head was growing heavier with every passing second. She imagined the pain fading away. Nothing happened. If anything, it magnified to the point where she thought she'd prefer being burned alive to this current torture.

Slowly, Fawn got up from her seat and lay down on the ground, praying for the searing sensations to go away. She was staring at the ceiling when her vision became spotty. This wasn't like any migraine she'd had before, so what was it? Her memories of Caleb were assaulting her mind so quickly and powerfully that she couldn't shut them out fast enough. Her first dream of him when she hated his cocky attitude and he promised they'd meet soon. Her surprise when she found out he was the new student at her college. Her unease when she had to sit next to him in European Literature. She wanted to laugh at her stupidity for disregarding her gut reaction to him, but her jaw was too clenched to get a sound out.

Their first date, her first magic lesson with him, their first make-out session. All the memories kept playing like movies before her very eyes, but she didn't want to see them. She felt like a voyeur peering at her own life and it sickened her. In a final attempt, she imagined silence and wiped her mind, pretending to suck all the memories into a magic vault and locking them in.

A few moments passed. The physical pain was still as strong as ever, but her mind was at peace. She opened her eyes and sighed. And then everything came back and hit her at full force. Fawn cried out as if someone kicked her in the gut. She held out her hands as if to ward off the images as she convulsed against the carpeted floor.

At the last moment, her door burst open and Fawn saw Caleb enter the room. He knelt next to her and said something, but she blacked out before she could comprehend what it was.

When she came to her senses again, she was alone in her room and couldn't tell if he had really been with her or if it had been a fever dream. She was still puzzling through it when the doors suddenly opened revealing a pissed off Lucifer.

"This is ridiculous, Fawn. You are to be my queen and yet I can't get you to dine with me. I won't take no for an answer this time. I have given you space in hopes that you would begin to settle in, but it has gone on long enough." His eyes shifted from red to black, and he added more calmly. "Get dressed. I expect you in my suite in ten minutes. Do not keep me waiting." He left without another word.

She wanted to curse at him for putting her in such a difficult position, but decided it was best not to argue. Opening her closet, she found a fiery red silk dress. It had a low neckline, a cutout back, and a flowing skirt. Not something she would normally wear, but ever since arriving in Hell, she hadn't felt like herself. She needed to grin and bear it, she decided, as she donned the gown. She put on gold earrings and matching bangles to complete the outfit.

Her opal necklace was still on. She almost took it off, but then remembered her mother had told her to always wear it. She made sure to open her twin link and moved into her sitting room.

There was a knock. Fawn magically opened the doors, revealing Selene and Alicia. The latter held a velvet blue box. "We're here to give you this, Miss." They placed it on the desk in front of her. "It's not your official crown. You won't get that until your coronation, but Lucifer wanted you to begin feeling like his queen immediately."

His queen, Fawn thought. *A possession.* She had already known it before, but it still bothered her she was essentially his property. She frowned in the mirror, touching the crown.

She almost wanted to cry, thinking of her mom and Alec. Did they even know she was missing? Did they appreciate her sacrifice and know how much she loved them? She could feel tears threatening to spill and quickly wiped them away.

"Is something wrong, Miss?" asked Alicia. "Have I upset you?"

She turned to her and smiled, "No, but please, call me Fawn. And after I become queen, I still want you to call me by my first name. I don't want to be called a title. Is that understood?"

"But Miss," Selene interrupted, "the King commanded us to address you so, miss. We cannot disobey the King."

Fawn smiled for the first time since seeing the Library. "I'll handle the King." Selene and Alicia looked at each other, back at her, and left her suite quickly.

As she walked past the guards, they didn't try to stop her. Lucifer must have told them to let her pass and she was glad for it. Otherwise she may have been likely to yell at them to alleviate her frustration.

When she entered Lucifer's suite, she was surprised to see his room was furnished with surprising warmth compared to the rest of the cold black and silver which decorated the rest of the castle. Candle light illuminated the burgundy drapes, couch, and a dark cherry wood table.

"You look ravishing," he complimented, taking her hand and kissing it before leading her into his bedroom.

She internally recoiled, but forced herself not to stumble or stall as she followed his direction. Tonight, he wore a garnet-colored suit, matching tie, and a black tie and shoes.

A small table for two was set up at the foot of his bed with a single candle between them. He poured two glasses of red wine from a silver decanter and offered her one. "To our long and happy future."

She braced herself and surveyed the room with suspicion.

He must have noticed because he took a sip and sighed. "I promise I haven't poisoned it."

She decided to eat the steak and vegetables on her plate first, but after a while she grew thirsty and gave into the temptation of the mysterious drink. She saw him smile, causing her stomach to immediately knot up. "What did you do to me?"

"I did nothing. You, however, just drank pomegranate wine. It's my favorite domestic delicacy. I do love the taste, but my favorite aspect of it has to be it binds whoever consumes it to my realm. Now you can't leave me, no matter what you do."

"You Persephonied me?" Without waiting for an answer, she threw the wine in his face.

With an unsettling deadly calm, he wiped his face with his napkin. "I doubt she would appreciate the bastardization of her name, but yes." She expected an outburst in retaliation, but he merely continued eating.

They ate the rest of the meal in silence, silently fuming at her own stupidity. Why hadn't she trusted her instincts? Though, in light of recent events, not even those were foolproof.

INSTEAD OF FILLING HIM WITH HOPE, CALEB'S NEW mission gave him only dread. He found Ivy in a café.

She stood when he walked up to her table, ready for battle.

"You can relax. I just want to talk to you."

Ivy crossed her arms and looked at him like he had just told her the sky was purple instead of blue. "Just like you love my friend, but still betrayed her? Yeah, I don't think I'll be relaxing any time soon." At his surprised expression, she rolled her eyes. "Alec told me everything once he and Stella made touchdown on Earth again after being abducted by the freaking Devil, who I now know is your *boss*."

"Not anymore," Caleb snapped, needing to defend himself. He took a deep breath and added, "I understand you're angry with me for hurting Fawn, but I need you to listen."

"Why should I? Do you know how much I've had to deal with? I had to tell my best friend's family I didn't pick up on your shady character—much to my shame—and I don't know how to help my best friend." Ivy's eyes narrowed much like Fawn's did when she was upset. "I looked like an idiot because of you! And Alec blames me—as he should. You don't know how much I hated being on the other end when he told me what happened." She let out a frustrated cry and he felt pity for her, though he doubted she would want to hear that. "This is all *your* fault!"

He took the verbal abuse without complaint. When her breathing had steadied, he said, "Speaking of her family, do you think you could call them for me? I need them to hear what I have to say."

"Why would I ever agree to do something to help you out? If I haven't already made myself *abundantly clear*, I don't like you. And I'd go as far to say 'I hate you,' and I don't use that word lightly, asshole."

"Could you give me a break, Ivy? I'm here trying to make amends with your best friend and maybe even try to save her from Hell." The siren finally fell silent. "Fawn is hurt because I was stupid—"

"Isn't that the truth?"

"I thought you were going to let me make my case."

"Those words never left my mouth, pretty boy."

He sighed. She clearly wasn't going to listen unless he cut straight to the point. "Fawn is suffering because of the soulmate bond."

Ivy closed the distance between them and glared up at him.

Despite her small stature, he fought the urge to take a step back. Right now, the small siren looked like she could commit murder—more specifically, his.

"Say that again."

He started to, but she interrupted him.

"Swear on your mother's grave, and look me in the eye as you repeat yourself. You better not lie to me. You can't play around with something as serious as soulmates."

He sighed and met her gaze straight on. "I swear on my mother's grave, Fawn Belgrave is my soulmate and in pain because she is denying our connection."

Ivy took a step back and whispered, "Shit."

"Will you do this for Fawn?"

"I'd do anything for her and her family. She's practically my sister."

Caleb nodded in thanks.

"Which means," Ivy continued, "if you hurt her again, I will hunt you down and castrate you."

Caleb backed away from the fierce siren. "I understand. She's lucky to have you as a friend."

Ivy stared him down for a few more moments before nodding and picking up her phone.

It barely rang once before Alec picked up. "Ivy! Tell me you found some insight into how we can help Fawn."

"Calm down," she said into the phone. "I do have news, but I don't know how much you'll like it." She paused. "Caleb is asking to speak to you and Stella."

"The asshole is with you?"

Caleb grabbed the phone from Ivy. "I apologize for my past actions. Truly, I am sorry."

The phone was silent for a while then Stella said, "Hello?" Her voice came through the speaker. "Caleb, you wished to speak to me?"

He repeated the news he had just told Ivy.

Silence met his announcement.

Ivy took the phone from him and said, "I don't completely trust Caleb, but when he and Fawn were together, I always saw a true bond of affection. He seemed to change the longer they were to-gether. Despite his betrayal, he was—and is—genuinely in love with Fawn. I don't think he's lying to us now. I made him swear on his dead mother's grave when he told me."

Caleb took the phone back and repeated his question, "Will you help me, Stella? Alec?"

"Of course we will," Alec grumbled. "I don't like you, but I'll help save my sister."

Caleb heard Stella murmur her own assent.

CHAPTER 13

WHEN FAWN WOKE THE NEXT MORNING, SHE SAW Lucifer standing at the foot of her bed. He was back in his James Bond outfit and looked more severe and menacing than he had the past few times she had seen him. This was the Lucifer she had met when she was sixteen in her dream. "Your coronation is this afternoon. Shower first. Selene and Alicia are waiting for you in your sitting room."

His tone was as imperious as it was agitated and she wondered what had happened to change his plan. "I thought it wasn't until next week."

"Plans change, dear."

"What happened?" she demanded. "I have a right to know."

He rolled his shoulder, the action reminding her of a predator gearing up to attack if provoked further. "Just some people attempting to meddle in preventing our upcoming union."

"Wait, am I *marrying* you?"

"Why of course. Every king is married to his queen."

"How is that even possible for you? Isn't marriage a God-sanctioned institution? Is there a Hell-equivalent?"

"It doesn't matter. Stop stalling, Miss Belgrave, and get ready. You will find I am not a patient man." He left and she groaned, too tired to push the point further. No point in making a worse enemy of him when she was stuck with him.

Stepping into the shower, she internally raged as the hot water pounded against her and the tiles below. When she reentered the bedroom, another silk robe was folded on the bed. Fawn quickly put it on.

Fawn dismissed Selene and Alicia and stared at the black and silver wardrobe in the center of the room. She waved her arm and it opened, revealing her dress from the masquerade ball.

She walked up to it and felt the fabric, feeling warmth run through her. Magic. Lucifer had enchanted it. Is this what she was supposed to be guarding herself from? What was she supposed to do?

"I could give you a hint."

"Dazzle me." Fawn turned around to a beautiful blonde woman in a gold dress. "Who are you?"

"My name is Helen Anne Pearce, and I'm Caleb's mother."

"You've got to be kidding me."

"I'm quite serious."

Fawn sobered quickly when she realized that the woman was, in fact, not joking. "How are you here?"

"My son is in a lot of pain too, you know. But of course, he's too proud to admit it to you. Right now he's very fragile and he doesn't want you to completely break his hope for the two of you."

"You seem nice, but what your son did is unforgivable."

"I know what he did to you is unforgivable. But he was an exemplary man, always rising to meet difficult expectations."

Fawn shook her head. She didn't want to hear more about Caleb. "You offered me a hint."

"That dress isn't from Lucifer. It's from God. It's meant to protect you from Lucifer's influence."

Fawn made an unladylike snort.

"Have you felt different during your time here?"

Fawn cocked her head to the side and thought about it. "I felt more confident, fiery. Angrier, too. Although I'm sure you can understand why."

Helen ignored her last statement. "Do you normally feel like that?"

"I'm not perpetually in a bad mood if that's what you're asking. Ever since I found out the truth about your son I've been a bit on edge. So yes, he got to me. He broke my heart. I hope he has a nice life, death, existence or whatever it is. You can tell him that." Fawn exhaled angrily and steadied her breathing. This wasn't fair. She was taking out her anger on his mother—it certainly wasn't her fault. She turned back to Helen and whispered, "I'm not mad at you. I'm sorry, I shouldn't blame you for his crimes."

She nodded. "Your personality has changed because your clothing has been enchanted to bring out different emotions—good or bad. You weren't fully yourself. This dress today was originally spelled by Lucifer to make you demure so you'd be agreeable and do almost anything he said today, which would have meant disaster for you and the Earth. Thankfully, God fixed it without him knowing." She paused before continuing, "As to Caleb's sins, you're his salvation. He needs you as much as you need him."

"Bringing up being his savior right before I become queen of the damned is a little ironic don't you think?" Fawn started pacing. "And why didn't he use that in his lie? If he'd done that, maybe I would've tried to help him before he duped me. But no, he didn't mention me being his savior because it's probably just another lie!" She stopped pacing and yelled at the ceiling, "When are you guys going to get I don't take orders! I hate being a damn puppet. I have—had—a life. A family!" Fawn started choking on her tears.

Helen patted her on the back and Fawn looked back at the dress before turning to Caleb's mother. "Is it safe to wear?"

Helen nodded.

"I'm trusting you, but so help me God, if you're lying I'll forever curse you and your son," Fawn promised, emphasizing each word.

Helen nodded again and Fawn moved to put on the dress. When she turned back, Caleb's mother was gone.

She changed into the purple ball gown in peace, called Selene and Alicia back into her closet, and they proceeded to weave diamonds into her hair as they braided it into a tight bun on top of her head. When they were finally done, Fawn walked to the throne room flanked by the two guards who were normally posted outside her suite.

Personally, she'd rather have gone alone, but Lucifer had ordered them to escort her everywhere today, and this was certainly no exception. Ten feet away from the throne room, Fawn heard yelling and something crash.

Fawn stopped walking in the hall and turned to the guards, dismissing them. At first they refused, insisting no one unexpected must enter, but she wouldn't take no for an answer. When she couldn't convince them verbally to let her pass, she closed her eyes. Without the distraction of vision, she amplified her hearing and listened.

"I won her fair and square, Father! Stop interfering, and accept you lost our bet."

Another man snorted. "I would hardly consider your tactics 'playing by the rules,' Lucifer. You broke the deal the moment you had direct contact with her. I believe that was the only rule. Her soul belongs in Heaven, and yet here she is, trapped by your contract."

"She made a deal with me, remember? Or are you finally going senile after all these centuries? She will stay here as my queen for all eternity."

Fawn had heard enough and snapped back to her normal hearing. Time to knock some sense into the hot-blooded males who were arguing over her future.

The guards were still being stubborn and she finally willed them to leave. A few moments later, they caved, bowed, and did as she asked. She turned her attention to the pair guarding the massive doors and willed them to allow her entry. Once their large, iron spears were parted, she waltzed past and held her hands out, bursting the doors open with a bang.

Lucifer and a white-haired man in a white suit were standing about a foot away from each other, their powerful voices still ringing in the rafters. The guest carried an ivory walking stick with a gold handle shaped like a lion's head. She finished her inspection and knew who stood before her. This man was the almighty God of Heaven and Earth—yet another man who'd forsaken her, leaving her to face a terrible fate alone. Beside him stood a determined-looking Caleb.

Fawn fought her instinct to run and instead strode forward, her anger trailing behind her like a bridal train. She stopped in between the divine beings and turned to the Creator.

"Fawn," He greeted.

She nodded in acknowledgement. "It's probably customary to curtsy, but please forgive me if I forgo the formality, just this once." She didn't want to show respect to the man who had sat back as her life had literally plummeted into Hell.

"I completely understand. It's nice to meet you, Miss Belgrave."

Lucifer's hand clasped around Fawn's wrist and tried to pull her back, but she stood firm. She had some questions for God, and she wasn't moving until they were answered.

"Why didn't you help me?"

"I was watching you the whole time," he assured her.

"That's not an answer," Fawn snapped, and a nearby window shattered. "Why did I have to go through that all alone?" She couldn't help the tears threatening to flood her eyes, nor could she control how her voice cracked at the end.

"If I had helped you directly, it would have influenced your choices. I could not take the chance. You are destined to save the world."

"How? Why me?"

"I didn't decide. The Septemgeminus Prophecy states you will save the world from darkness."

"Some kind of warning would've been nice."

"Who do you think sent your ancestors?"

"They didn't help, though, now did they? I got played despite their multiple vague warnings of, 'He's coming.' It wasn't even a helpful hint." But she wasn't mad at her dead relatives. It wasn't their fault they had been forbidden to help their own kin by the so-called benevolent Creator. "Do you know how broad that one pronoun is? It could've meant you, Lucifer, Caleb, or the entire male population of humans and Supernaturals alike. How was I supposed to know it was your estranged son who just *happens* to be the Devil? It's not like I could read minds at the time, and certainly not either of yours."

"If I told you what was coming," God started, "it would have altered your destiny with dire consequences."

"Oh, so it's not that you *couldn't* tell me what was really happening, it was your *decision* to leave me in the dark. Thank you so much for clearing that up. I really did find it hard to believe that *you* were bound to some higher law."

"I was protecting you."

"Well you did a fantastic job. Bravo." She scoffed. "You don't care about me. All you care about is your bottom line: my destiny as the world's savior which I don't even want! If you don't want Lucifer taking over the Earth, why don't *you* stop him? Why do I have to be involved as some twisted trophy?" She marched closer to him. "And if you're expecting me to end him, I have news for you: I am not the girl qualified for the job. I am not an assassin who will do your dirty work. I am a college girl who happens to have magic powers I don't even want."

"Fawn," Caleb interrupted, his voice stern.

She pointed at him. "You don't get to talk to me."

He didn't argue, but she saw sadness darken his expression. She looked away before she could start feeling pity for him.

"Granted, maybe the vague warning *was* accurate, after all," Fawn said, returning to her previous topic. "You all screwed me over in the end, so maybe I should just swear off men altogether."

"Caleb is your soulmate, Fawn. Your stubbornness is hurting him, too."

"It's not *my* fault I never want to see him again. That was his doing. Which you knew was going to happen because all you do is keep your head buried in a book or scroll or whatever lets you meddle in people's lives. You could have stopped him, but you didn't so now I need to protect myself."

"You are better off together. You complete each other and without the two of you united, not only are you both in danger, but so is the entire world."

"Maybe I don't care about saving the world." She took a deep breath and spoke softer. "Maybe I just want to live my life in peace and forget all of this!"

Her gaze fell on Caleb again and maintained eye contact with him as he slowly approached her, stopping a mere foot away.

An inexplicable ache appeared in her head and chest. She saw him wince out of the corner of her eye. *Was he feeling it too?* God had said he was affected, but she hadn't believed it. They stared at each other for a moment, but then she turned her head. She heard him sigh.

"Isn't her anger magnificent?" Lucifer noted to his father. "You wouldn't know what to do with that."

Fawn's aura shot deadly rays as she marched up to the King of the Damned. "Don't you dare act like you're innocent in this situation!"

He put up both hands and backed away in surrender, a smug smile in place as he continued to watch her.

"Fawn, I just wanted to save my family," Caleb whispered.

"You're worse than anyone else here."

"How can you say that?"

"*They* didn't lie straight to my face or break my heart. And now I'm stuck here forever thanks to you and that stupid drink. I was an idiot for believing either of you—" she gestured to him and Lucifer, "could be trusted."

God interrupted their impasse. "I revoke the bond to hell formed by your consumption of that cursed wine. Fawn you may leave with no fear of my son retaliating."

She turned to him and inspected his expression, searching for any sign of an overt lie or omission, but she came up empty. "Then I would like to go home."

God nodded once and flicked his wrist toward her. A cloud of white smoke surrounded her, then the ground disappeared.

LUCIFER SIGHED. THOUGH HE HAD HOPED TO HAVE her ruling by his side, it occurred to him now a better plan would be to eliminate her. There was no use in keeping her, the only person who could defeat him, alive.

He stared down at his visitor, who was of stocky build with a muscle mass to rival any human body builder. "Do we have a deal?"

"We act as executioner for you, and we get what in return? The opportunity to kill one measly witch?" The man scoffed. "We can find our own prey, thank you very much."

Lucifer's eyes and temper flared and the fires rose to mirror his emotional landscape. "You know this one is special. Your nephew must have told you all about the power she has. You will *never* have an opportunity like this again. Perhaps I will ask another clan of your kind."

His guest's pride kicked in and the man stood even straighter, almost like a stone statue of a soldier. Lucifer briefly entertained turning him into just that, but dismissed the notion.

"That won't be necessary. We will take the job and it will be our honor to fulfill this task." He paused. "And what of her relations?"

Lucifer waved his hand in the air. "Irrelevant, though you may do whatever you want with them. Consider them a bonus for you. I would be remiss in not telling you they are a strong unit and will not go down without a fight. I expect there will be casualties on both sides."

"How many on each?"

"That depends on your clan's talents," Lucifer replied. "Should you succeed, I will gladly resurrect your fallen men."

The man hesitated, a wariness stealing over his features. "At what price, sir?"

"None, whatsoever. This will be your final reward for working in my service and joining my campaign against God."

"He has certainly done no favors to my kind since our creation. How will I collect on what you have promised?"

"Do not get ahead of yourself. I will find you when it is time. I'm glad we've come to an agreement. You may go now."

CHAPTER 14

CALEB WOKE SUDDENLY WITH A SENSE OF TERROR gripping his heart in a vice-like grip and knotted his stomach until it felt as heavy as a stone.

He was still staying in God's castle because Fawn hadn't forgiven him. He hadn't expected her to, but it hurt she still hated him so much. Wasn't the soulmate bond designed to push them together? Why wasn't it working on Fawn?

He quickly got dressed and hurried into the throne room where he found God frowning as he looked out one of the large windows.

"My errant son has just dispatched a team to kill Fawn. I'm afraid you have less time than planned to reunite with your soulmate."

"Did you not see this coming?" he asked, tilting his head down and keeping any accusatory note deep inside.

"Go to Earth first thing tomorrow. Even if she will not see you, she must be made aware of what's happened. You must protect her."

Caleb halted and replied over his shoulder, "I would die for her." He spent the rest of the night wide awake.

FAWN WAS BUSY REORGANIZING HER ROOM WHEN IVY came in. Though she thought she had only been in Hell for a few days, it turned out it was almost a month. When she saw her room hadn't changed, she felt a strong urge to redecorate.

When her friend didn't say anything, Fawn could sense something was wrong. Looking at Ivy, her friend's anxiety was evident in her features. Fawn paused in her chore. "What's wrong?"

Ivy's hands fidgeted, twisting each other until Fawn worried she would strain a muscle or sprain her wrist, and her eyes darted around the room before finally landing on Fawn. "Caleb wants to speak to you."

Fawn crossed her arms. "Since when are you in contact with him enough to become his messenger?"

"Since he came to me for help while you were in Hell. He *does* love you, Fawn."

"He's told me so before." Fawn shrugged. "I just don't believe him anymore. If you had your heart broken by the one person who isn't supposed to be like that, you'd understand," she added when she saw Ivy gearing up for a rebuttal.

"I'm not saying you have to have another relationship with him if you don't want to, but I *know* he wasn't lying. I can see the bond between you being stretched thin, but it's really strong on his end. It's your side tapering out. It's common knowledge emotionally separated soulmates suffer. You can fix it. Why won't you?"

Fawn didn't answer immediately. "Because he hurt me. And you can call it stubbornness, pride, or whatever, but I call it self-preservation, and I'm not putting myself in harm's way again."

"I think you should hear him out."

Fawn closed her eyes and silently counted back from ten. "All right. But this is the last time unless *I* decide otherwise."

Her friend nodded. "Absolutely." Ivy paused. "He's here waiting for you in the main room, by the way." Before she could reply, her friend had already left.

Fawn didn't know whether she was mad at her friend or him for being so persistent, but she definitely felt frustrated over the indisputable fact that he had been eavesdropping on her conversation.

CALEB ROSE FROM HIS SEAT ON THE COUCH when he heard Fawn walking quickly towards him.

"Ivy said you had something to tell me."

He swallowed. She probably expected him to make some sort of excuse, but he decided this visit was more about trusting *her* than demanding she trust him. "I wanted to clear the air between us. I haven't yet fully apologized to you for everything I've done and, if you'll allow me, I wish to remedy that oversight."

"Before you start—"

He waited for her to finish.

She stood up and wrapped her hands around both sides of his head. A burning sensation seared through his mind and he cried out, much like he had when Lucifer had forcibly revealed his wings.

She released him and he stared at her in confused resentment. "What did you do to me?"

"I broke down your mental barriers. I want you to show me your aura when you're talking."

"And you couldn't have asked?"

"I couldn't trust that. You already somehow evaded me during two Readings. How would I know you wouldn't do it again?"

He bristled at the accusation, but made no reply because he knew she was right. "I concede. But a warning would have been appreciated."

She shrugged, and he could tell she still harbored anger toward him, though it now seemed to burn cold rather than hot like it had before.

Now that the mental pain had abated, Caleb began. "I've been a dark angel since 1854 when the Broad Street cholera outbreak killed my sister. I was twenty-two at the time." Her eyes flared with recognition and he added, "I didn't lie about that. My father had died back when I was fifteen in 1847 during the Seventh Xhosa War."

He cleared his throat. "I was not so honest about my mother's death. I had tried to get medicine for both her and my sister, but failed. We were too poor so I tried to steal from the nearest apothecary. I was caught by none other than Lucifer and he said I could take enough medicine for only one dose. When I asked for a way to save both my relatives, he said he would immortalize whoever I did not give the medicine in return for my service."

"And?" she asked in a deadpan tone.

Her mental link to him was still closed and her aura was securely hidden, leaving him completely unable to gauge her reaction.

107

She caught him examining her and her eyes flared with irritation. "Are you going to continue, or are you done?" She started to rise from her seat when he didn't immediately answer.

Panicked she was about to kick him out, he jumped back into his story. "I was desperate to get the medicine for my sister, so I agreed. By the time I gave her the medicine, she was too sick for it to save her. And because there was only enough for one dose, I had not only failed to save my sister, but also doomed my mother to die."

He heard Ivy sniffle, but Fawn remained impassive.

"I didn't know what to do and was completely distraught. In the middle of my mourning over my sister, Lucifer came and instead of granting my mom immortal life as I thought he would, he turned her into a marble statue. He had taken a loophole, and I was stuck doing whatever he ordered me to."

"And your job was to seduce women." She did little to disguise the utter disgust in her voice.

"Yes." There was no use in denying the truth. "And you were to be my last—you *were* my last," Caleb clarified. "But Lucifer had offered me my freedom if I converted you to his cause. Thankfully, God took me under his care after you rightfully removed me from your life."

He saw her surprise at his last statement and added, "I can't make you take me back, but I do hope you will someday forgive me. You can't know how much I regret hurting you."

Fawn stood to retreat back into her room, but he grabbed her hand as she passed. She didn't turn to face him and her posture straightened so much it seemed as if a pole had been sewn into her spine.

He didn't try to make her face him, knowing it would only make her fight him more. "I want you to know I consider us being soulmates the most important part of my life. I had to get that off my chest first because I needed you to hear me out, but the most *urgent* piece of news I have is a clan of Hunters has been tasked to kill you."

There was a gasp. Both he and Fawn turned their heads to see Ivy holding her hands over her mouth.

Fawn, however, didn't seem so surprised. In fact, she had almost no reaction at all. "I think one of them is following me. I've run into him on campus and during our movie date."

Caleb remembered and mentally kicked himself for not pursuing the subject further back then. He had sensed something was wrong with the guy at the movie, but he hadn't known he was a Hunter. He should have known Lucifer was having them tailed. He was probably responsible for the cloaking spell.

Ivy asked, "Are you sure it was a Hunter? Supernaturals normally can't sense them until it's too late."

Fawn shrugged. "I don't know how to explain it, really. It was like I could feel the hate emanating off him and attacking me."

The siren blanched. "If one *is* after you, your life just got a whole lot more complicated. And if it's an experienced one, you might even have to go underground. For your sake, I hope it's a stupid newbie."

Caleb could feel Fawn's alarm. He reached out and pulled her into a hug. Her hands automatically came up between them to maintain a buffer zone. It didn't work. One hand pressed into her lower back, closing any distance between them, while the other tucked her head into his chest under his chin. "Please just let me hold you."

Her body was still tense, but she didn't push him away. The moment he had touched her, he felt her resistance melt and he was grateful that, despite her anger at him, she was still listening to the influence of their soulmate bond.

"If you thought you were in danger, why are you still here? You should be halfway across the country."

She disengaged his arms. "I'm not dropping everything to leave."

"Even if it means you get to live?" he prodded.

"My home is with my friends and family. I'm not going anywhere without them."

"It's too conspicuous for you all to leave at once."

"Then I guess I'm not leaving at all."

He threw his hands up in the air. "I'm asking you to save yourself."

"And I'm refusing that request."

He took a step back and ran his fingers through his hair. "If you won't leave, I'll remain by your side until the danger is gone."

Fawn started pacing and didn't answer.

He sat back down on the couch. He saw Ivy stay in the doorjamb, her arms crossed as her eyes anxiously following Fawn's movements.

His soulmate suddenly stopped her movements and turned to him with a determined expression. "All right. But *just* as my teacher. You deceived me on everything else, but I did learn legitimate magic during our time together."

Ivy piped up with unusual caution. "Are you sure?"

Fawn walked closer to Caleb, who had been scrutinizing her actions. "I inexplicably still trust you with my life, but nothing more. And if you betray me again, I swear—supernatural soulmate bond be damned—I will destroy you."

He knew she wasn't joking and nodded solemnly. "I understand. But will you give me permission to still hope you will change your mind?"

"I can't control your thoughts, but you know what they say about hope: It breeds eternal misery."

CHAPTER 15

"You did what?" Alec shouted into his phone. He closed his eyes and focused on not wanting to maim his sister's best friend. "Ivy, why would you meddle in her life like this? I thought we agreed to leave it alone?"

"Well, she was miserable and Caleb wanted to talk to her."

"Who are you to encourage her to talk to someone she clearly doesn't like? She would have gotten over it, Ivy. My sister is strong enough to withstand the heartbreak and move on. And now thanks to you, she's right back in the middle of it."

"Of course I know that, but you have to remember this isn't a normal post-break up funk. You know that, right? Not all girls fall into a depression just because a guy broke her heart."

"Of course I know that! I'm not stupid, Ivy."

"I have a good feeling about Fawn and Caleb this time around."

"And if this goes south again? How do you think that will hurt Fawn? And affect both of us. You pushed her toward him before, but you didn't know his true nature back then. You don't have that excuse anymore. You should know better."

"It won't go wrong this time."

"How are you so sure?"

"They're soulmates."

"That didn't stop him from betraying her last time."

"You're such a pessimist. I know you'll change your opinion one day when you find your own soulmate."

"I don't know why you believe him. What if he's lying again?"

"He's not. God told him they were soulmates."

Alec scoffed.

"What?"

"I just don't really put much stock in what *he* says anymore."

"Caleb or God?"

"Both. I don't take kindly to anyone who messes with my family. You know that."

"You're mad at God?"

"He certainly didn't do my sister any favors. Are you telling me you're *not* angry?"

"Of course I am! But not really at any specific person, or I guess 'entity' is the right word for God..."

He couldn't help but smile at her rambling, despite his aggravation. Knowing her, she had all but set them up on the date. That made him frown again.

"Stop scowling," she said.

He could picture her standing with a hand perched on her hip in that haughty and annoyingly hot way she normally did during their arguments. "How did you know?" he muttered.

"Because you always do when you know I'm right."

He lowered his voice. "Ivy, if this goes south again..."

"I'm responsible. Got it, Captain Jackass. Talk to you later."

The next thing he heard was the call cutting off. He stared at the device. If his upgrade date wasn't months away, he probably would have thrown it at the wall. No one else had ever gotten under his skin like Ivy did. Not even his sister.

Fawn waited for Ivy to speak. Her friend gripped her phone tightly. "I know he's your brother, but he can be so frustrating at times."

"I've grown used to it. What did he do to piss you off this time?"

"And to think he's trying to lecture *me*, his soulmate!"

Fawn stared at her friend. "You're each other's—That's amazing! Does he know yet? How long have you known?"

Ivy shrugged. "I've known since the beginning of high school. Right after I fully adjusted to being a siren, I started feeling this weird pull toward him. And I thought he started feeling something for me, too, but he never did anything. I never ended up telling him because I couldn't find a right time to do it. Besides, he thinks I'm a slut for sleeping with so many guys."

Fawn released her friend's hands and crossed her arms as her anger toward Alec rose. "Did he tell you that?"

Ivy shook her head. "Well, no. Not specifically, but I can see it in his eyes whenever I mention a date or fling."

Fawn immediately calmed and shook her head, a knowing smile playing on her lips. "Thank goodness. I was about to lecture *him* about being a misogynistic, hypocritical jerk. He's as many flings as you do." She saw Ivy flinch and regretted her last sentence. "Sometimes you're just as unobservant as my brother..."

Ivy's gaze sharpened. "What are you talking about?"

Fawn could hear the near indignant tone and quickly explained, "He doesn't know you're each other's soulmates, but he *does* really like you. Oh, come on, Ivy," Fawn added when her friend's expression morphed into one of disbelief. "You and he have been attracted to each other for years. I'm surprised the sexual tension hasn't set a room on fire already. I bet it could spark flames if it did." She smiled, but Ivy didn't. She turned serious again. "I never knew you were both so scared to enter a relationship. Neither of you have any reason to be afraid."

"Why hasn't he said anything?"

"He was intimidated by your list of past boyfriends."

"Flings," Ivy corrected.

"You know that doesn't matter to a jealous person. And you *know* how hotheaded he can get."

"Does he know you're telling me this? Did he put you up to this?" Ivy's voice was strained.

"I'm not doing his dirty work. I'm helping two of my favorite people in the world get over their mutual fear." She paused before adding, "I think you should tell him soon. And that you're a siren. I'm sure he'd understand your extensive relationship past once he knows you're just trying to survive."

"I hope so. Maybe I should just give him more time. If I need you to play magical matchmaker, I'll let you know. But don't think you can escape your troubles by helping me."

"Believe me, I know."

"I don't want to be wrong on the timing..." Ivy paused before nodding in agreement with some internal decision and added, "Okay, I'll tell him. Wish me luck." Her friend quickly grabbed her jacket and phone. "I'm going to call him back now."

"My fingers are crossed for both of you."

The door closed and a voice sounded behind her. "So you'll happily play matchmaker, but deny your own soulmate of the same pleasure?"

She whirled around and saw Caleb standing in the doorway. His arms were crossed and his eyes were boring into her, demanding an answer. She tried to step around him, but he mirrored her movements. "Move out of the way."

He didn't budge. "It's been two weeks, Fawn. I'm waiting for you to tell me my efforts are enough, but I'm not the only one who needs to put in effort. It's a two-way street."

"Then you haven't been listening to me at all. I don't *want* this relationship. It's been shoved down my throat along with this stupid prophecy. I want choices, Caleb! And if you're so upset about not having me in love with you, you should have come clean sooner."

He took a step towards her, and she fought the urge to back up. She refused to be intimidated anymore. "I've taken responsibility. As to choices, we don't have the luxury. The only thing to do is make the best of it."

She stalked up to him so they were almost touching, and lifted her chin. "I deserve better than this, and so do you. No one should be in a loveless relationship."

"I *do* love you."

"But I still don't know if I do. I can't be in a relationship with someone I don't love with all my heart."

"Before you said you didn't and now it's 'I don't know.' I think that means my chances are improving." She shot him a warning look. "I get what you're saying, but indulge me for a moment. Hypothetically, *if* you didn't come back to me, what would you do?"

"Stay single and away from you, since I unfortunately can't find satisfaction with anyone else."

His gaze hardened. "You remember what happened last time you tried that."

"It was *fine* until you showed up again."

"You're being stubborn and you know it. You were deteriorating." He grasped her shoulders in a gentle but strong hold. "I understand you're not ready to fully forgive me and return to our relationship, but if you're being threatened again we need to be a united front. I'm not leaving your side until these Hunters are dealt with. I won't force you to interact with me more than necessary, but that doesn't mean I won't keep trying to change your mind."

His words were both comforting and irritatingly bossy. She retreated a step and said quietly, "This is still hard for me to adjust to."

His eyes flashed to the brightest shade of violet she had ever seen them. Fawn couldn't tell whether it was with pain or irritation. She watched him stride toward her. When he stopped mere inches away, she noticed a muscle ticking in his jaw.

"Why do you always make me the villain? I am your soulmate—the one man in this world who is wholly dedicated to your happiness."

She rolled her eyes. "I really should find a replacement, then. Because you've failed—multiple times."

Suddenly, Caleb surged forward, knocking her on her back. He held her down with an iron grip and seemed to be working something out in his mind. Instead of fighting like she normally would, she waited, curious to know what he was thinking. He shook his head once then released her, retreating just enough so she could move out from under him.

She did, watching him warily.

He didn't turn around.

Should I try to calm him? She shook her head. She wouldn't know where to start. "I'll be in the other room."

CALEB WAITED TO MOVE UNTIL THE DOOR HAD closed. Only then did he unclench his fists. He was in trouble. When he gave her space, the more she pushed him away, but each time he tried to close the gap, she declared he was suffocating her. There was no way to win with her.

He should let her go. She clearly didn't want him, and had a better chance of happiness without his constant hovering. Even so, he couldn't tolerate the distance between them.

His phone rang and he answered despite knowing the number.

"What are you doing with my sister?" he heard Alec demand.

Caleb sighed. Great—yet another angry Belgrave sibling he needed to deal with. Bracing himself for their angry tirade, he answered, "Teaching her how to protect herself against Hunters."

"I know I said I'd give you a chance, and I will, but I hope you know you will *never* deserve Fawn."

"Don't you think I know that? I would be concerned if she forgave me immediately, *but* is it too much to ask she keep an open mind?"

"After all the shit you put her through? Yes, I would say you're reaching a bit too far with that request." He made a frustrated sound on the other end. "I didn't say this earlier in respect to Ivy and my mom, but I don't trust you. At all. But I promised myself I wouldn't interfere like Ivy unless I need to. Don't push my sister or you won't like what follows."

Caleb refused to take the bait. "I will *not* abandon her again."

Somehow, that appeased Alec. "Maybe you're changing after all..."

CHAPTER 16

FAWN WAS LEAVING HER LAST MORNING CLASS AND was on her way to lunch with Ivy when her phone rang.

She checked the number and answered, "Hello?"

"Fawn! Hey, do you have a minute to chat?"

She glanced around, making sure no one was following her. She may have chosen to stay where she was, but she knew Caleb's warning about the Hunters was real—not just some stupid ploy he had used to make her depend on him. When she was certain she was safe, she focused back on the call and held her cellphone in place with her shoulder. "Sure, Dylan. What's up?"

The last time she had talked to him, they had both been applying to colleges during the summer between junior and senior year of high school. She smiled. Apparently, they were making a rule about a three-year call.

She was not prepared for his next words.

"I need some relationship advice."

If she had been a clumsy person, she would likely have dropped her phone. Luckily for her and her phone contract, she wasn't in the habit of dropping her cellphone.

She laughed without humor. "Normally I would be happy to help you out with anything, but given some recent events, I don't know if I'm the best person to ask about this anymore. There seems to be a lot I'm still figuring out in this area." She laughed softly. "And we thought dating in middle school was hard. If only we knew how easy we had it back then, right?"

"Uh oh, is there something you need to tell me?"

She smiled at his levity. An outsider would assume it meant he didn't care, but she knew he was only acting like that to cheer her up. He had done it whenever she had had a bad day at school. "Yeah, but I don't know if I can tell you. I feel a bit strange telling you... no offense. I just find it weird we're each helping our ex with their current relationships. What does that say about our relationship?"

"I don't think it's weird at all. And if it does say anything about our past relationship it's we trust each other enough to confide in each other and ask for advice. And, remember, before we ever started dating, we were friends. We still are. We parted amicably, right?"

She could imagine him leaning forward with interest just like Ivy did whenever she was fishing for information. "Of course we did, it just—I don't know. Sorry, I've been feeling out of sorts ever since this whole debacle went to Hell." He didn't know she meant it literally, but she knew he would understand all the same. "I also wasn't expecting you to call about this. Honestly, I thought it would be the last topic you wanted to discuss with me."

He sighed. "Fawn, I know you. I can tell when you're trying to dissuade me from pursuing a conversation."

"It's not that—"

"If it makes you too uncomfortable, I *suppose* I could ask my cousin, but she'll never let me hear the end of it. And she lives in my neighborhood so there really is *no* escaping her." He paused for dramatic effect. "You wouldn't do that to me, would you?"

She closed her eyes and smiled, missing how easy their friendship and subsequent relationship had been. They had never argued and always had a good time together. "Fine. What do you need help with?"

"My three-year anniversary is coming up in a few weeks."

Fawn lay a hand over her heart and gasped overdramatically. "You got married and you didn't invite me? And I thought we were friends..."

"Dating anniversary. I need to get her something, right?"

"Do you want me to be honest?"

He sighed. "Always."

"Well, if you've been dating for three years, she *might* be expecting an engagement ring."

"Fuck."

The curse was muffled. "Not a keeper, then?"

"No, well, maybe? I don't know. That's okay, right? To still be figuring it out years into a relationship?" She heard him exhale violently. "Shit, I should have called you sooner."

"Why?"

"Our anniversary is in three days."

"Well... at least we're talking now. And to answer your question, I wouldn't know from experience, but if you're really not sure, then I think it's okay. But I will say if you're even *considering* breaking up with her, I suggest you do it in advance of your anniversary. Definitely don't do it the same day or the day right before or after. She'll probably want to kill you if you pull a stunt like that."

She reached her lunch spot and saw Ivy and Caleb already sitting in the booth. Luckily, his back was to her. Not wanting to draw the angel's attention, she pointed to her phone and immediately got on the food line without dropping off her things.

"And she probably could. She can be vicious. She could give you a run for your money even when you're pissed."

"Hey! I'm not that bad." She remembered how awful she had been to Caleb after she learned of his deception and again in Hell, and cringed. Okay, she wasn't a saint, but she never claimed to be. And Dylan didn't even know about those instances. "But I get your point."

"You know I'm only kidding, Fawn—mostly."

"Of course. Anyway, I'm just giving you some tips that could save your life—or, you know, at least your manhood." She snickered.

"It's not funny."

Fawn could practically hear him scowling through the phone.

"Oh, come on. It is. Just a little bit."

"What do I do if I don't want to give her that commitment?"

"I don't know. You know I'm not someone who ever needed gifts. Get her a bracelet, maybe?"

"She won't chuck it at me when she realizes it's not the jewelry she is expecting?"

"Is she really that high-maintenance?" She couldn't keep the judgment out of her voice. Dylan didn't deserve someone who was egocentric in a relationship.

"No. I'm just freaking out over here because I don't have a lot of time to get this all figured out. Does it have to be fancy?"

"If it means something to both of you, no. It's the thought that counts, and if she's a good person, she'll recognize that."

"Okay, I think I have an idea."

"Great, I actually have to go..."

"Oh, no. You're not getting off that easily. You helped me, now we talk about your troubles so I can return the favor."

"You're as bad as Ivy." That was one perk of having him in another state. They could no longer tag-team, or even worse, gang up with Alec to interrogate her anymore.

"I'm your friend, as well as your ex, as you've so often pointed out. I want to be there for you, but I can't if you won't open up to me."

Fawn finally reached the front of the line and paid. She grabbed her food and ID, and pointed to the door so Ivy could see she had to go.

Her friend nodded.

"Hold on a second." Fawn closed her eyes and magically transported herself back to her dorm. Once inside, she placed her food on the small table next to her bag.

"You still there?" Dylan's voice sounded as she unlocked the door.

She inwardly sighed. He was relentless. "Yeah, sorry. I was in the middle of buying lunch."

"You're going to make me drag it out of you, aren't you?"

"No, but let me finish before you weigh in, okay? I'll lose my nerve otherwise."

"Okay..."

"This ended only a few weeks ago and I'd be lying if I said I wasn't still licking my wounds."

"I didn't realize how recent this was. If it's too painful for you, I don't want to force you anymore."

"No." She took a deep breath. "I want to tell you. I met someone, and we fell in love really fast," she started when Dylan didn't answer. "And it was great, for a time. But then I learned he had lied about who he was and now he wants to try again, and I don't want to forgive him..." She trailed off, at a loss of how to continue.

"Are you done?" he asked after a beat.

"Yes, that's the end of it." She couldn't go into more details because Dylan wasn't part of the Supernatural world.

"I don't really get what the problem is. If you don't want to give him another chance, you don't have to."

"But he won't go away. And everyone around me keeps saying we're *perfect* for each other." Dylan didn't need to know the list included God. "Well, except my brother."

"Then tell Alec. I'm sure he'll chase the bastard away."

Fawn tapped her fingers on the table, her nervous tick from high school returning. "It's... more complicated than that."

"You're stuck with him for one reason or another. I get it. Do you still have feelings for him?"

"I don't know." She sighed. "What a pair we are. So indecisive."

"I think confused is a better adjective, and that's okay. But if you *think* there's a chance there's still something between you two, I wouldn't let it go." He paused. "Hope that helps. I need to go help my dad with something. We should chat again soon."

"Definitely. Thanks for your advice. Hope mine was useful."

"It was. Thanks, Fawn. Bye, stay golden."

"You, too." She hung up and stared out the window.

Her phone buzzed again, this time with a text from Ivy: *Incoming. Careful, he's pissed.*

Just what she needed right now. She slumped into the chair and began eating as quickly as she could in preparation for the argument that was no doubt about to ensue between her and Caleb. She rubbed her temples in frustration. That's all they seemed to do these days.

DESPITE IVY'S ATTEMPTS AT DISTRACTING HIM, CALEB HAD known the moment Fawn walked into the dining hall by the sound of her footsteps, and heard the distinctly male voice coming from her phone.

When he'd heard the mystery guy say he was her ex, he had temporarily been blind-sighted by a red envy that made his chest and head burn so hot he had wondered if he had been magically transported into one of Lucifer's bonfires.

Everyone always said green was the color of the horrid emotion, but they were wrong. *Red* better captured the anger and resentment that often accompanied the simple jealousy, but no one ever talked about that—too ashamed to admit how affected they were by other's luck and good fortune.

But he had stopped lying to himself about his emotions the moment he realized doing so had allowed him to continue with Lucifer's plan and hurt the woman he loved. He now knew honesty was the best policy, even with himself.

Yes, he had known Fawn had had a boyfriend before him. It had been in her file, after all. But hearing how comfortable and easy-going she was with the man after all these years rubbed him the wrong way and made him irrational.

Ivy must have noticed because she stared at him until he met her gaze and shook her head once. "Caleb—"

But he was already getting out of the booth. When he was at the door, he heard her whisper, "Don't mess this up."

He would certainly try, but he couldn't make any guarantees to anyone. Not to himself, and certainly not to the well-meaning siren who had done nothing but root for his and Fawn's relationship.

He stretched his hearing out and found his soulmate in her dorm. Not wasting any time, he switched to angel speed and shot down the hill until he stopped outside her door.

Before he even knocked, she was standing in the threshold and pulled him inside. The door shut behind with a bang, startling him.

"Before you start yelling at me, I knew you were coming because Ivy warned me. Yes, Dylan is my ex. Yes, I loved him. No, he didn't break my heart, and no, I don't still pine for him. And yes, we've remained friends. Did I get them all?"

What could he say without sounding like the controlling, jealous boyfriend he currently felt like? He didn't want her to hate him more than she already did. "I wanted to know why you couldn't join us."

"He was asking me what to get for his girlfriend for their three-year dating anniversary. He's clearly moved on, and so have I."

Did she really not hear the wistfulness in *Dylan's* voice when they had been talking just now? Or was she right and maybe it was his mind playing tricks on him?

"And if you haven't noticed," she continued, "I've been trying to avoid you. So of course I couldn't have eaten with my friend even if I hadn't been on the phone because *you* were there."

"You're right," he forced out. "I'm sorry. I'll go now." He fled before she could add anything else.

F AWN WATCHED HIS HASTY DEPARTURE AND SIGHED. THAT had gone much better than she had expected, but for some reason, she still felt dissatisfied with what just transpired. Would they never figure out their relationship? She shook her head. It didn't matter. It's not that she even wanted one... least of all with *him*... right?

Frustrated with her wayward thoughts, Fawn tossed the now empty plastic container into the trash. She had had barely enough time to finish it before Caleb had arrived.

She was washing her hands when her cell phone rang again. Well, wasn't she just Miss Popular today? Grabbing a small towel, she dried off while inching closer to her device and saw her brother's number flash across the screen.

Not in the mood to talk to him, she let it ring in the kitchen as she walked into her room and swapped out the materials for her morning classes for the ones she needed for the evening. Once her phone stopped making noise, she grabbed it and slipped it into her pocket and left her dorm once again.

CHAPTER 17

Fawn's doorbell buzzed. She approached the door slowly and stared at it before asking loudly. "Who is it?"

"Hey sis, let me in."

She opened her door and saw her brother standing outside with a smile. She hugged him tightly before pulling back and asking, "What are you doing here?"

"You stopped answering my calls and I wanted to check on you. You're lucky Mom makes us wear these necklaces or I would have been worried something *really* bad had happened." He looked around and asked, "Where's your precious angel, anyway? Isn't he supposed to be glued to your side at all times? What if I wasn't me, but a demon impersonating me?"

"No one can pretend to be you without me noticing."

"Really?"

"They wouldn't be able to capture your signature, strange combination of lovable yet frustrating personality."

He rolled his eyes. "Thanks for that. Do me a favor and actually answer my question about Caleb."

"He's coming in a few minutes. *He* keeps asking to stay here over night, but I said no. Luckily, Ivy hasn't fought me on it."

Her brother shook his head. "As much as I dislike the guy, I agree with him."

Fawn blinked. "The world must really be ending. I never thought I'd hear the day when you *agreed* with Caleb."

"Under any other circumstances, I'd say you're an idiot for keeping him around."

"Thanks, Alec." It came out sharper than she intended, but she didn't apologize. "This is exactly why I stopped answering when you called. I don't need your lectures."

"I'm just trying to look out for you."

"I know you mean well, but it's patronizing. You act as if you think I'm falling back into his arms just because he said 'I'm sorry.' You don't give me enough credit here. Ivy thinks us being soulmates will fix everything, but I'm not so sure. Like you, I'm being careful around him."

"But how is having him near you so much *not* affecting your mind? If the soulmate bond really *is* as powerful as Ivy constantly claims it is, how can I trust you're fully thinking this through?"

"You should trust I know what I'm doing because I'm your *sister*. And honestly? I have reason to doubt the extent of the power of this bond because *you* don't seem to be affected by it at all. You're still the lovable, but slightly overbearing brother I grew up with."

"What are you talking about?"

Fawn stared at him and realized her best friend must have chickened out. "Ivy didn't tell you."

"Tell me what?" he demanded.

"That you're soulmates." She sighed. "Look, what I'm trying to say is until your relationship is absolutely perfect, you have no right to tell me how to deal with my own." He looked as if she'd slapped him and she instantly felt bad. She took a step forward. "Alec—"

"Don't." He paused, took a deep breath, and asked, "Where is she?"

"At class. She'll be back within the hour. Alec, please forgive me. I didn't mean to be so harsh."

He nodded and began walking aimlessly around the room. "I'm sorry, sis," he whispered. "I just don't want to see you hurt again."

She pulled him into a hug and closed her eyes. "I know. Thank you."

A small noise caught her attention and she reopened her eyes to see Caleb standing in the doorway, a hurt expression on his face. "So, I'm still untrustworthy, am I?"

She immediately released her brother and walked up to her angel. "Caleb, wait—"

But he was already gone.

She turned to her brother, ready to make an excuse to follow Caleb, but he beat her to it and said, "You should go after him."

Once she reached the exit and was sure no one was paying attention, she repeated his name three times in her head and couldn't fight the feeling she was in the movie *Beetlejuice*. She turned, and was met with empty air.

He hadn't come. He must be really upset.

Determined to make things right, she closed her eyes and imagined herself wherever he was. Fawn felt a small cyclone encase her and felt the ground disappear before she was dropped onto solid earth again. She opened her eyes and saw she was under the big tree on the Great Lawn.

A few feet away, Caleb stood with his back to her.

She approached him, coming to stand directly in front of him so he couldn't ignore her, and shot off, "Why did you leave?"

"There's only so much rejection a guy can take, Fawn. I heard you telling your brother you wouldn't 'fall back into my arms' just because I apologized. And I don't expect you to have no problems with me, but I *had* hoped you would at least do me the kindness of keeping an open mind."

"Does that mean you're leaving?"

He shook his head. "I told you I would protect you. I know you don't believe me to be honorable, but I *do* keep my promises."

"Caleb, what you heard..."

"Is how you feel. Don't apologize for speaking the truth."

"I want to apologize for hurting you." His expression stayed unreadable. "And I didn't tell my brother this, but I *do* want this to work between us. I can't jump right back to where we were, but I have hope for us."

CALEB'S HEART SOARED AT FAWN'S CONFESSION. HE *HAD* been genuinely hurt and was ready to take Alec's advice in leaving Fawn alone once the danger had passed, even if it pained him. He hadn't been fishing for compliments, but her words reignited the fire in him that drove him to win her back. And maybe it was because they were destined, but he didn't care about anyone's plan but his own and Fawn's happiness.

He was done being a pawn in Lucifer's or God's plans.

They had never truly been helping him out of the goodness of their hearts but merely to push an agenda surrounding his fantastically gifted soulmate. His heart swelled at the thought of how much she had endured at the hands of the two most powerful beings in the universe, how fast she picked up new concepts in magic and self-defense, and most of all, her openness to give him a second chance.

Only yesterday he wouldn't have dared wish for as much as he had now. All he had left to do was make her never doubt his love again and hope they both made it out alive of the Hunter attack.

Their complete silence had him worried. Though Ivy was correct that most Supernaturals except Fawn couldn't sense them in advance, angels were the only species who were able to track the Hunters' movements. It had never been his duty to do so under Lucifer, but he had always heard whispers around the castle when a big attack was coming. It was the other demons' version of sports season and even at his most depraved, he was unable to stomach witnessing the many slaughters.

Fawn was staring at him, waiting for his answer, and he smiled at her. "I'm sorry. I was distracted."

She shrugged. "It's okay. I wasn't expecting another declaration of love from you immediately. I think you've given more than anyone would ever expect."

He heard the disappointment in her voice and assured her, "I've meant each one. And I fully intend to make sure you never question how I feel again."

She smiled at him, but her eyes belied her concern. "What were you thinking of just now?"

"How lucky I am to have you. And I'm concerned I haven't heard anything else about the Hunters," he added when she rolled her eyes. "It's not like them to be this secretive."

Her face paled, but she rallied. "Then we'll just have to be ready for them, won't we?"

He nodded. "And we will. Shall we return?"

She took his arm and he transported them back to the dorm.

"Can someone please explain to me exactly what we're up against?" Alec asked, exasperation coloring his voice.

"They're Supernatural beings who were created by God as bounty-hunters to track down and re-imprison any of the allies and creations of Lucifer who may have escaped to Earth."

"But witches aren't created by the Devil, right? Why are they coming after Fawn?"

Ivy interrupted before Caleb could answer. "They may have been created to do good things, mainly protect humans, but they're a lot like people who use patriotism or 'the greater good' as an excuse to eliminate anyone they don't like. And I wouldn't be surprised if Lucifer corrupted them even before hiring them to kill Fawn."

"Great. So, we have some hotheads to thank for an ancient feud that created a group of people who are inclined to hate witches and therefore were happy to make a deal with Lucifer to kill me. Am I missing anything?" Fawn asked.

Their grim expressions were answer enough.

"Didn't think so," she muttered and walked away, her bravado now gone along with her hope of winning. A single tear fell from her eye, leaving a wet path down her face. She didn't bother to wipe it away.

Caleb came over and said, "Hey, don't let this discourage you."

She turned to him. "How can I not? Caleb, no matter how much I 'own my power,' I'm not a fighter." She put a hand on his chest to stop his rapid-fire reply. "And before you bring up the Black-Eyed Beings, that was a *fluke*. I have no guarantee this will end the same way."

"You're not alone, Fawn. You have your best friend, brother, and me here to protect you."

Ivy stood up. "If you don't mind, I'm going to call my mom and let her know we may be under threat again." With that, her friend left for her bedroom.

CHAPTER 18

T HE NEXT DAY, IVY DIDN'T COME BACK FROM her last class. At first, Fawn assumed her friend had forgotten to text her, but it seemed improbable. She knew Ivy wasn't with a hookup because Alec had finally talked to his soulmate about their relationship.

When she had been missing for over an hour, Fawn called her, but it went to voicemail. She hung up and tried again and someone picked up, but it wasn't Ivy.

"Hello, witch."

Fawn didn't recognize the voice, but said, "Who are you and why do you have my friend's phone?"

"She's a little *tied up* at the moment. Will be for some time, too, but we're willing to negotiate with you."

Fawn saw Caleb stiffen beside her and Alec's level of agitation grew, his gaze bouncing between her and Caleb. "What's happening?" he silently mouthed at her.

Fawn shook her head and closed her eyes to calm herself down, not wanting her voice to betray fear or eagerness. "Really?"

"Usually we'd wipe this piece of scum off the Earth, but we're willing to make an exception just this once."

"So you can kill me instead," she replied.

Caleb started forward, but Fawn blocked him so she could hear the man sneer, "Do you want your friend or not?"

Fawn paled and silently mouthed to Alec that Ivy had been taken.

When Alec grabbed for the cell, she let him take it and put the call on speaker. "We're listening," he said.

"Give us the young witch in return for the siren."

Fawn was about to accept his terms when Caleb clapped a hand over her mouth.

"No. I won't let you," he whispered in her ear.

She struggled against his hold, frustrated he was so much stronger than her, even without using his angel abilities. She finally gave up and instead tried to verbally plead with him. "She's my best friend and my brother's soulmate. I have to."

"I was in your position two hundred years ago," he whispered. "Believe me, I know you want to do all you can, but if you go without knowing magic, this situation will go from bad to worse."

While he was distracted with talking, Fawn pushed on his arm extra hard and broke free. Before he could stop her, she spoke into the phone and said "Give us a minute," before putting the call on mute. "I'll go and then the rest of you can plan a way to get me out."

She looked up to see a pissed off angel. "Why are you even considering this insane trade? You know we can't sacrifice you."

"Ivy can probably last for a few days, giving us enough time to get her out. She wouldn't want you going in for her," Alec reasoned, though it clearly pained him to say it.

"How can you say that? If my destiny is to save the world, maybe I'm supposed to infiltrate the Hunters and bring them down from the inside." She was grasping at straws, but she hoped they wouldn't call her out. Surprisingly, no one did.

"Fine," Caleb conceded, earning an incredulous look from Alec. "You go, but I'll shadow you the whole time."

"Fuck no!" Fawn's brother exclaimed. "Are you two insane?" He turned on Caleb. "I thought you promised to protect her in this whole scenario. That's the only reason she let you within ten feet of her."

"And that's what I intend to do," Caleb said. "But I'm not looking to take away Fawn's choices in the situation."

"What good are you if you let her waltz right into danger?" her brother shot back, his voice growing louder.

She put the phone back on. "All right. Where do I meet you?"

"The closest entrance to the Boston Commons at midnight. If there's any fight on your end, I can easily give orders to have your friend killed. Do not test us, little girl."

She bristled at his condescending tone. "Understood."

"Good."

The call clicked off, and she turned to see Alec frowning at her, his eyes burning with worry.

"It had to happen," she defended herself before her brother could yell at her for losing her head.

"Doesn't mean I have to like it," he grumbled.

THE SIDEWALKS WERE DARK BY THE TIME FAWN waited at the corner. Though he was invisible, she felt Caleb standing nearby.

You'll be fine, she heard in the back of her head.

She answered without turning around to face him, not wanting to accidentally reveal his location to anyone who could be watching. *I know you'll take good care of me.*

Finally, a group of people emerged from the park, Ivy trapped in the middle. The men were large and wore all black. Using her powers, she could see they had bulletproof vests and gun holsters.

Caleb gave her shoulder a quick squeeze before stepping back. Unfortunately, being invisible didn't change the fact that he was still a solid being. If someone bumped into him, they would be found out.

"Grab the witch," the leader commanded.

One of the men grabbed her and she began to fight. Another one grabbed her from behind, forcing her into submission. They blindfolded her, but Fawn was still silently following their movements in her head.

"We're here," a man growled in her ear before she was shoved forward, almost tripping on a small step in front of her.

After a few more moments, she was pushed into a seat and the blindfold was removed. She blinked, taking in the windowless room. In front of her was a large metal vault door. *An abandoned bank?*

As if on cue, it slowly swung inward, grating on the tile floor. She winced at the sound. A Hunter walked in. She gasped when she recognized him as Viktor, the guy she had seen around campus.

"You can quit trying to find an escape route."

She turned her head to look at him and scowled.

"The feeling's mutual," he said. "I can't stand looking at you."

"Why? Because you're jealous of our powers?" she baited him.

Be smart, Caleb mentally chastised her. Fawn saw him shake his head at her.

They had tied her hands behind her back, but left her feet free. For that, she was grateful. She considered kicking the Hunter, but didn't think she would survive his no doubt violent retribution.

"No, it's because you're all monsters."

She couldn't help but wince at his harsh tone. "That's not true," she whispered. Why was she arguing with this maniac?

"Yes it is," he scoffed. "What decent person murders a family for their own entertainment?"

"You, apparently."

"You don't know what you're talking about," he snarled. He crossed his arms and slowly examined her. "There are more important things to be taken care of."

"Like what?"

He surged forward and grabbed her, tipping her chair backwards at a dangerous angle so that if he let go, she would fall and her head would most likely split open on impact. "None of your business."

In a moment, Caleb was hovering behind the man. Fawn stared at her attacker, who looked like he was about to blow a fuse. Luckily, another Hunter appeared in the hallway.

"This isn't over," her captor threatened before he walked out and locked the door behind him.

Still invisible, Caleb knelt in front of her. *You don't know how much I wanted to kill him for that stunt just now.*

She smiled. *It's better this way. Do you know where they're keeping Ivy?*

He shook his head and she sighed. *I can find out*, he said. *But, really, Fawn. You have to be smart and not provoke them.*

Fawn mentally told Caleb, *I wish I could hold you.*

He smiled at her. *Me too.* They heard noise outside and he took a step back.

The door opened and the leader slapped Fawn, whipping her head to the side. She ground her teeth and glared up at him, hatred darkening her blue eyes. Behind him stood two younger Hunters. One of them was Viktor. She didn't know who the other was, but judging from their appearance, the two were somehow related.

"Go on! Fight back," said the stranger. When she stayed silent, he jeered, "Not so powerful all alone, are you?"

Fawn turned her gaze onto Viktor, who looked positively fierce, but dissatisfied. He chose that moment to speak up. "It's not worth it, Uncle," he said, addressing the leader of their group. "She won't fight back and can't escape, let's leave her."

She narrowed her eyes and imagined a fire while staring at the one who had just taunted her, who was the easiest target.

Moments passed before anything happened, but then the young Hunter cursed. "The bitch burned me."

Viktor snickered. "I guess I was wrong. She knows the fight against stupidity demands attention all the time."

"Shut up," her victim snapped, patting out the flame on the cuff of his pants.

"Children," the leader scolded. He motioned his nephews to leave the room. He approached her and hissed, "Stupid girls who play with fire get burned." With that, he left her cell, too.

Caleb held a finger to his ear.

She took the hint and extended her hearing to the hallway.

"You two will stay here and guard the little monster until further notice," she heard the leader say. "Don't underestimate her."

Then she heard the older man's footsteps retreating. *Go, find Ivy*, Fawn told Caleb.

He kissed her forehead. *I'll be back before you know it.*

Fawn watched him melt through the metal door and hoped she hadn't made a grave mistake in meeting the Hunters' demands.

STILL INVISIBLE, CALEB WOVE THROUGH THE HALLWAYS, CONSTANTLY readjusting his angle to avoid accidentally touching any of the brawny Hunters roaming the halls. There were so many of them, it was as difficult as avoiding ants at a picnic.

Where are they keeping you, Ivy? Caleb wondered, stretching his hearing out as far as it would go. He heard someone shout a curse and Ivy mutter, "Weak bastard" a floor above. Not wanting to chance bumping into someone's feet by moving through the ceiling, Caleb used his angel speed to climb to the next level and continued walking until he was outside Ivy's holding cell. Unlike Fawn's, hers was smaller and had bars on it like in a police station. Like her friend, she was tied down to a chair, facing out. A Hunter was blocking his full view of the siren.

"You won't be laughing when you're dead," the man threatened before opening the door.

Once the oaf had locked the door, Caleb used his angel speed and snatched the key from the man's belt. He then walked through the bars and untied Ivy, whispering in her ear, "Don't move," as he did so. "Are there cameras in here?" he asked. He couldn't see any, but that didn't mean they were in the clear.

"No," she murmured.

He placed the keys into her hands. "When I give the signal, can you reach your hand through the bars and free yourself?"

She nodded. "What are you planning?" she whispered.

"An escape. Still figuring out the details. Are you good? I need to go back to Fawn."

"When are we leaving?"

"Tonight."

T HE DOOR OPENED AND AN EXTREMELY TIRED AND pissed-off Hunter entered. He grabbed her and pulled Fawn up. "We're leaving," he growled. He plunged a syringe into her forearm. She yelped and glared at him.

Caleb walked backwards in front of the Hunter, his eyes narrowed to slits, his violet irises darkening.

Has Alec contacted you? She asked her soulmate, distracting him from his murderous thoughts.

His step almost faltered, practically making the vicious Hunter bump into him. Luckily, he recovered and started moving again before that could happen. *He's here. That's why you're being moved.*

I thought I felt him in the building.

I didn't realize how accurate that twin connection of yours was, he commented. Without giving her a moment to think, her soulmate punched the Hunter, throwing the man to the ground.

Caleb grabbed Fawn and broke into a run. They rounded a corner, and she stopped him.

"What are you doing?" he asked, frantically scanning the hall for any wandering Hunters.

"Just wait." She closed her eyes. After a few moments, her appearance shimmered before changing to look like her incapacitated guard.

"Good thinking."

She smiled briefly, before inhaling deeply, drained by the effort. "I think they poisoned me. It's blocking my magic. That took longer than it should have."

"Let's hope we can take care of that soon. Can you feel where Alec is right now? Maybe he can heal you faster."

"He's barreling towards us. Let's keep moving. I don't want to be here any longer than I have to."

After five more minutes of running through the maze that was the Hunters' headquarters, they met Ivy and Alec. Her brother thought Fawn was a Hunter and moved to strike her right as she changed back, letting the disguise disappear instantaneously and reveal herself.

He pulled back and cursed. "I almost knocked you out! You should've told me earlier."

"I'm sorry, I was a little preoccupied fighting for my life to slip you a message."

The siblings turned back to back and each clasped one hand together while holding the other out to ward off the armored men. The contact revitalized Fawn immediately, and she began blasting them with balls of magic. When there remained no others on her side, she turned and began attacking the one's on her brother's. Soon, they were surrounded by bodies, all knocked out, and they stepped over them toward the exit.

Caleb turned to Alec, "She's been poisoned. We need to get her out of here."

"I'm not strong enough," Fawn's brother said. "And our mother has a protective spell against all strangers trying to enter our home."

All three of them looked at Fawn.

She was breathing heavily, the poison beginning to take a heavier toll on her. "I can try, but I need to channel all of you."

They formed a square and linked their hands. Fawn closed her eyes, and they immediately landed with a thud in the living room of the Belgrave apartment.

CHAPTER 19

THE MOMENT HIS FEET TOUCH THE GROUND, CALEB lifted his soulmate's limp body into his arms and walked toward Stella. "They injected her with some poison before they tried to move her. I don't know what it is, but it's blocking her magic. She passed out as we were landing."

"Put her on the couch. Alec, grab water and a washcloth. Ivy, please get her some lighter clothes."

"And what about me?" Caleb asked, briefly glancing up from Fawn's weak and now limp body.

"Stay with her while I get the Grimoire." The witch quickly left the room and returned the same time as the others.

The two men looked away while Stella and Ivy changed Fawn's clothes. She groaned as they repositioned her, but didn't open her eyes.

"Did you see what they poisoned her with?"

Caleb shook his head, wishing he had killed the Hunters the moment they reached the compound.

Stella nodded to Alec and he began dabbing his sister's forehead as it began to break out in sweat. As he did so, their mother began leafing through the pages of the precious tome. She had been at it no more than three minutes when she suddenly closed the tome and sighed. "I can't heal her with magic. If I were to do that, it would only accelerate the poison in her body and likely kill her."

Caleb sucked in a sharp breath. "Is there nothing you can do to heal her? Or at the very least slow down its progress?"

"There is nothing in here worth trying if it could harm my daughter. The poison they used is probably witchroot." They all gave her blank looks. "Have you ever heard of wolfsbane?"

"Of course we have, what's the point?" Caleb asked, his tone sharp. "I'm sorry."

Stella offered an understanding smile. "This is equivalent for witches, a very potent poison that targets the magic in our blood. The more we use our power, the worse it gets. A battle with this in one's system would have killed a less powerful witch." She put the book aside and moved closer to the angel. "She needs a blood transfusion. Neither Alec or I can be the donors because we're also witches, and I'm pretty sure Ivy's blood may also be attacked by the virus given she is a siren and a target for Hunters. They are notoriously known for creating compound poisons for situations such as these. But there may be hope." Stella met Caleb's gaze. "Hunters don't attack angels so they don't have poison to harm you. Your blood may be safe."

"What do you mean *may*? It's not that I don't trust you, but I refuse to do anything that could hurt her."

"Putting your blood in her veins is the best shot we have at saving her, Caleb. We have to try this, and soon or we may lose her to the poison so much that even this would not work."

He hesitated. "What will that do to Fawn? I don't want her to become a dark angel like me, under Lucifer's influence. I wouldn't condemn anyone to a fate like mine."

"Heal her and nothing more. She will return to her natural state as a witch. I can foresee no bad consequences."

He sighed and held out his arm.

She waved it away and said, "I can magically transfer your blood, but it will take time."

"As long as it takes," Caleb assured.

The transfusion itself only took twenty minutes, but as soon as they finished, Fawn began to shiver, and sweat formed on her forehead.

Caleb lifted Fawn in his arms again and she curled towards his chest. Then he took off with her towards her bedroom.

"Please get better," he whispered to her as he placed her gently on the bed. Caleb stripped Fawn. When he was done, he said, "I'm going to get some things for you, then I'll be back." She nodded once. He filled a bowl of warm water and a glass too, just in case she got thirsty, and a washcloth.

He dunked it into the bowl and began dabbing her forehead. "How are you feeling?" he asked, moving hair away from her forehead and stroking her cheek with his knuckles.

"Like death warmed over."

She closed her eyes, and he moved closer to her, worried that if she fell asleep, she might not wake up. "Try and stay alert, love." He stroked her cheek with the back of his hand, the other still moving the washcloth over her arms. "I know it's hard. Do it for me? I don't know what will happen if you fall asleep and I don't want to take any chances with your life in the balance."

She yawned. "Only if you hold me."

He shook his head. "I'll make you overheat."

"I'm cold right now. Please?" she asked. How could he refuse when she seemed so small and vulnerable?

He dunked the cloth in water again before crawling into the bed, pulling her back against him. Propping himself up with one arm, he continued to cool Fawn down. "Better?"

"Yes, thank you." She gave him a grateful smile that made his heart swell with pride.

He redressed and went into the kitchen to make her some soup. She was in no condition to leave her room anytime soon.

As she ate dinner, Caleb left again to find Alec. "She doesn't know she killed the Hunters."

"We can't tell her now," her brother said. "It'll devastate her."

Caleb followed his advice and didn't tell Fawn until she was ready to go to sleep. She appeared shocked, but didn't break down like he had feared. He tucked her in and left her room.

A WEEK LATER, ALEC, IVY, CALEB, AND A RECOVERED Fawn were in the living room. After three days of being bedridden, Fawn began feeling like her normal self again, and she resisted everyone's—mainly her brother and Caleb's—suggestion she continue sleeping until she was fully recovered. They had finally acquiesced, as long as she promised to stayed in the apartment and didn't overexert herself.

Now, fully healed, she, Caleb, Alec, and Ivy were playing Pandemic. Just as they lost the cooperative game, Ivy got a phone call. She answered and walked into Alec's room for privacy. After fifteen minutes, she reappeared, a strange expression on her face.

They all waited in suspense, no one willing to break the silence and voice their curiosity.

Ivy dropped her cellphone, dropped to her knees, and began weeping. Alec wrapped her up in his arms and held her close.

Fawn walked across the room with Caleb following close behind her. "What's going on? Is something wrong?"

Ivy nodded. "The rest of my family was attacked by Hunters."

"Did any of them survive?" Caleb asked.

Fawn turned to him and shook her head. *How insensitive can you be? Now is not the time to ask something like that.*

But it's important to know, he countered.

Ivy shook her head and Fawn felt as though her heart was being torn apart. She knelt by her friend and held her hand.

"I have no one left," the siren sobbed.

"That's not true," Alec countered. "You have us."

"We won't abandon you," Fawn added.

A few more minutes passed before Ivy calmed enough to disentangle herself from the Belgrave twins' embrace. "We need to start training a lot more."

Both twins shared a concerned look.

"Yes, but you should probably rest," Alec interjected. "You've just had a really large shock and need to recover."

Ivy shook her head and grabbed Fawn's hands tightly. "You'll spar with me right?"

Seeing the need in her friend's eyes and her own increasing rage toward the Hunters. She noticed her brother and Caleb exchange an uneasy glance, but ignored it and pulled Ivy up. Her friend needed a distraction, and if the Hunters had been able to ambush a siren who had escaped them once, they *really* needed more protection.

They walked into the living room and took their places ten feet apart from each other.

"I'm afraid I'm too wound up to go easy on you," Ivy warned.

"Likewise. But I won't use magic." She wasn't in *nearly* enough control for that.

The two of them charged at each other and they began grappling immediately, using what they had both learned in their Krav Maga class. After a few moments, Fawn was able to push her best friend away.

Ivy returned with a vengeance and her left hand struck out.

Fawn came up with a block and attacked Ivy's other side. Luckily, her friend was protected and it seemed neither of them was making any progress against the other.

Although she had initially felt guilty for annihilating the Hunter clan, she now wished she had taken her time and drawn out their suffering. Another clan killing Ivy's family as retaliation, who wasn't even their main target, was so sadistic it made her sick.

Perhaps Lucifer had been right in noting the similarities between him and her. When he had first said it, she had obviously refuted such a ridiculous claim, but he was still an angel with greater insight than she could ever hope to have. And what did that say about her?

CALEB HEARD THEM FIGHTING AND BEGAN TO FOLLOW their example and move into the next room, but felt Alec's hand on his shoulder. He turned and began to brush him off, but stopped once he saw his serious and grave expression.

"I'm concerned about them."

"I am too. Fawn hasn't responded like I thought she would. She seems almost numb to it." He didn't bother mentioning her most recent, dark and violent thoughts to Alec, not wanting to alarm him even more than he already was.

"I'll bet she's less upset about fighting back now." His smile slipped. "I can't imagine what Ivy must be feeling right now. Or Fawn. They're both so sensitive to injustice. Though I think Ivy is more jaded. I hope Fawn doesn't follow her example."

Caleb agreed. He had already seen his soulmate transform once, right after she had learned of his betrayal, and seeing her so cold had broken his heart as much as her utter rejection had. "I just don't want her to lose her kindness by stooping to their level."

And if God forbid she did, then Lucifer will have succeeded in his original object, which was arguably worse than killing all of them. If he *did* corrupt Fawn's goodness, who knew what she would end up doing with her magic?

"She does what she needs to survive, but I agree with you." A crash sounded and he quickly added, "We should probably supervise them before they break something even my mom's magic can't repair."

The two of them entered the room and Alec replaced Ivy as his sister's opponent. The siblings began fighting with magic once the siren was safely out of the way. Caleb stood in the threshold and watched.

Twenty minutes in, Fawn threw her hands up with a frustrated shout when another splash of water hit her upraised arm. The same thing had been happening since he had entered the room. "I get it okay? You were right. I'm not ready to take them on. Stop attacking me!"

Alec kept advancing, throwing fireballs and water streams at her. He had clearly been practicing when Fawn had been in Hell.

"Dammit! Didn't you hear me?" She turned to see Caleb watching with an intent expression. "Do something!"

Caleb shook his head and reprimanded, "Stay focused." He turned to her brother. "Again." Perhaps her new motivation to fight wasn't as bad as he originally feared.

By the end of the duel, it was clear Fawn was ready to rip someone's head off.

He approached her, offering a water bottle and towel to clean up. She pushed it away. "Come on, Fawn, you need to stay hydrated."

"I'm not thirsty."

"Take it anyway."

He frowned down at her. "You're being unreasonable."

"No!"

Suddenly a fireball was flying at him. He dodged and stared at her.

"If I'm supposed to have any chance at fulfilling this prophecy, I need to get better, I just don't know *how*." During her rant, Fawn gestured with her hands. The more worked up she got, the faster she released fireballs—now aimed at the rest of the group.

Caleb was behind her immediately, restraining her arms behind her back. "Fawn, you need to *calm down*."

She struggled against him. "Let go of me!"

"Not until you stop trying to burn us all alive."

They were at an impasse, the deafening silence stretching uncomfortably long. She was breathing heavily, unable to meet the worried and betrayed gazes of Alec and Ivy.

Stella walked in and said, "Well, I think that's enough training for today. Why don't you all go clean up and prepare for lunch?"

The four nodded, and Caleb finally let go of Fawn. She ran to her room without another word and locked the door, leaving him outside.

He materialized beside her. "You know this isn't meant to hurt you."

"But it *does*—" She hated the pathetic tone of her voice.

He sighed and pulled her against his chest, lacing their hands together. "I'm sorry you're upset. If I could prevent you from ever feeling bad again, I would."

When she stopped shaking, he released her. "We should get you something to eat."

Lunch was uneventful and seeing Fawn was still not herself, he suggested she go take a nap. She didn't even argue, and he knew things were worse than she was letting on.

Later, he walked in and saw her side rising and falling with her breath. He sat next to her and gently shook her awake.

She turned onto her back and rubbed her eyes. "What time is it?"

"Dinner's ready," he said.

She threw off the covers and followed him into the dining room.

"How are you doing?" he asked.

"I was just tired. I'm fine." She finished her meal and pushed back from the table.

"Where are you going?" her brother asked.

"Back to sleep," she called back.

Fawn felt her arms being bound behind her back. She struggled in vain and was forced to accept she would not get free. In front of her stood her brother, mother, friend, and lastly, her soulmate tied together in a rope as if they were around the mast of a ship.

The leader of the Hunters and the one she saw on campus multiple times approached the group. The former said, with a sick smile on his face, "They shall be killed as you killed us. *Slaughtered.*"

Instantly, the two men drew double swords and simultaneously stabbed all four of her loved ones in the stomach. She screamed and they pulled out their bloody weapons. She watched as the blood stains grew and her mom, brother, Caleb and Ivy's bodies dropped to the ground, dead.

Fawn sat up sharply and saw she was in her own darkened childhood room. She pulled her blankets back up from the foot of the bed where she had kicked them into a lumpy pile. She had the sickening feeling she was being watched, as if the ghosts of the dead Hunters surrounded her, wishing her harm. Deciding she'd rather sleep with someone in the same room as her, she kicked back her covers again, and walked into the living room. Even in the dim light, Fawn could see the silhouette of Caleb's sleeping form on the comfortable fold out bed.

"Caleb?" she whispered. He didn't stir. She slowly approached him, her feet padding across the carpeted floor as she did so. Kneeling near his head, she took in his peaceful expression and couldn't help but brush his dirty blond hair out of his eyes. "Caleb, can you hear me?"

Still no answer. Sighing, she looked around and saw no one who would be able to see her next actions. Quickly, but carefully, she crawled onto the foam platform bed and lay down with her back up against him before pulling the covers over them both.

Warmed by his natural body heat and comfort of his presence, Fawn fell asleep. In her sleep, she felt Caleb move and wrap his arm around her waist, holding her close to him until morning.

CHAPTER 20

F AWN WOKE TO THE SAME AWFUL FEELING SHE was being encircled, except this time, it was real. Her brother, her mom, and Ivy stood near the bed, facing out at a new group of Hunters. Instead of black, they wore blood red outfits that caused a shiver to run through her body.

She moved to shake Caleb awake, but he was already alert and protectively covering her. She saw he was leaving his back open and she feared what would happen if a Hunter got through her family's line of defense. She pushed Caleb off despite his protests and magically moved the bed away, clearing the floor so everyone had room to fight.

For a few moments, no one made a single movement. And then, as if a leash snapped, the Hunters stormed forward.

"Watch out!" Alec yelled just as one lunged at Ivy.

She moved out of the way, causing the man to hit the ground hard. She wasted no time in kicking his gun out of reach and taking it for herself, aiming at his head like a professional killer.

Another Hunter aimed his gun at Fawn's stomach. She stared at it, stunned. Instantly, a white wing shot out, causing the bullet to ricochet and hit the attacker in the thigh instead. "Where's your head?" Caleb hissed at her.

"I'm sorry," she whispered.

His voice softened immediately. "Hold in there, okay? We'll get out of this all right."

Fawn nodded and saw a man coming to attack Caleb from behind. She reached up as if to hug her soulmate from behind, but extended her hands to blast the Hunter in the stomach. He dropped immediately. A gray mist rose out of the body before dissipating into the air.

Caleb saw her watching. "That was his soul leaving."

"I—I killed him?" Fawn stammered, staring at her hands. This time she knew her awful power and felt sick to her stomach.

"I know you're upset, but right now, that talent is an advantage."

Stella had been holding her own against two Hunters, but when a third joined his brothers in arms in fighting her, she began to falter.

Fawn and Caleb arrived just in time. Caleb whipped his wings against two of them, causing them to bang into each other, allowing Stella to finish off the remaining man. When he fell, no other Hunters remained standing.

A moment of relief cleared the sweaty air, but then the window shattered and three new Hunters climbed in. These men wore not the usual solid red uniform of the others, but black with red accents. Fawn took them to be the leaders and knew they would be incensed at seeing their fallen comrades.

The one on the right aimed his gun at Fawn. Caleb was in front of her, in a second. He grit his teeth as the bullet entered his side.

Fawn watched as the tide turned in the Hunters' favor.

The one fighting Caleb roughly grabbed her soulmate. Holding him in a deadly headlock, he said, "Let me go now or he dies."

Fawn froze. She didn't know if angels could ever die.

"It's now or never," the man threatened. "One... two... three." Before she could react, he snapped Caleb's neck.

Time stood still before fury bubbled up inside her to the point where her body felt as if fire was searing through her veins. Fawn could see the two Hunters were now gaining the upper hand. She needed to help her friend and family. And the only action that came to mind was to annihilate the threat. She closed her eyes and screamed until her throat burned as much as the rest of her. She felt the energy suddenly release and opened her eyes.

All the Hunters were lying on the ground and everyone else was staring at her. When she realized Caleb was alive, she dropped to the ground beside him and began to sob.

"Shh," Caleb comforted her. "It's over. You can let it all out."

"I—I thought you were dead..." Even though it had been a shock the first time, which had only been a few minutes ago, the reality now came roaring back to her. "I'm a monster," she declared, horrified by the frighteningly true revelation. "I've killed two clans of Hunters."

"You are *not* a monster," her soulmate insisted in a calm, but firm tone. "Don't ever think such a thing."

"It was the only thing to do," her brother interjected. She turned to look at him, surprised at his ruthless statement.

Caleb groaned, regaining her attention. Fawn lifted Caleb's shirt and saw his wound had stopped leaking. At first she was elated, then felt his pulse and her panic returned. He was no longer bleeding but not because he was healing—his heart was slowing down. She turned to her mother, "What's happening?"

"They must have found a way to harm angels."

"Fix him!"

"I can't. He doesn't have a link to enough people here for us to successfully heal him through channeling."

"Then what do I have to do to *make* it enough? I can't lose him now." She leaned over him. "Don't leave me, Caleb. You have to come back. Stay with me."

"You alone may be able to heal him, but—"

"Just tell me how to save him. Please."

"Visualize your soul revitalizing his body, and his life force strengthening as you transfer some of yours to his."

Fawn closed her eyes and calmed her breath to as steady a beat as was possible given her emotional state. The world faded away to just her and Caleb. She squeezed her eyes shut tighter, trying to focus on doing what her mom had instructed, but nothing happened. Caleb was still lying too still on the ground and she didn't know how to make him better. Panic rose inside of her. What if she didn't figure it out in time and lost him? And so soon after she had been reunited with him?

He groaned again and she tried to make herself to snap out of her panic. She knew the more she worried about failing, the less chance she had of succeeding, but that knowledge only aggravated her anxiety.

Think! How does one visualize their soul saving someone else? Did her mother mean blood by life force—?

Her line of fruitless questions was cut off when she felt a cold liquid on her hands. She looked down and saw a liquid gold flowing out from her palms and fingertips. Not knowing what else to do, she massaged it into him like a moisturizing cream. The salve sank beneath his skin, glowing brighter before completely fading. She repeated the process until he opened his eyes. They were back in the living room. Stella, Ivy, and Alec were staring at her.

"You saved me," Caleb croaked, sitting up slowly in bed. "Why?"

"I wasn't ready to let you go," she said quietly. "I forgive you, Caleb. I wanted you to know that. I should have told you sooner, and I apologize for not properly absolving you, but after what just happened..." she trailed off. "I didn't want you to have any doubts about how I feel."

He smiled up at her. "Thank you, love. Do you mind helping me up? This floor isn't that comfortable."

Fawn helped him into her room with the help of her brother, though he complained at first of having the angel in his sister's room at all.

"Well, I'll leave you two alone now," Stella said. "Both of you should drink water and eat soon to keep up your strength. It would not be a good idea for either of you to test your limits right now." She walked to the door. Alec and Ivy joined her.

After the door was safely closed behind her, Fawn turned to Caleb. "Are you staying tonight?"

"I should probably go back to my bed in the living room."

Fawn blushed. "I meant here—in my room."

"Are you sure? Today was a big day, and you were injured, and are probably in shock... And I almost died. Maybe we should give ourselves a break tonight."

"Please stay." She whispered before pulling his lips down to hers.

He stopped her. "What are you thinking?"

"That I'm really glad you're alive."

When she didn't say anymore, he hesitantly asked, "Where does to-night leave us?"

"I'm not completely sure. Maybe I *should* sleep on it." She turned over, leaning her back against his front. "Good night." A calm silence fell over them. The only sound in the dark room was their slow breathing.

C ALEB GLANCED AT FAWN'S SLEEPING FIGURE BEFORE GENTLY disentangling himself from her embrace. He had been sleeping too, but God had invaded his dreams and asked him to go meet him.

"You asked for me."

God nodded from his seat. "I wanted you to know you have pleased me greatly. And to reward you, I will now grant you the ability to see your family."

Caleb felt his heart flutter, but then had the sinking feeling this was more complicated than God was making it seem. "At what cost?"

"You can move on from this world and join them in the afterlife, or you can return to Earth and be with your soulmate as an angel until her lifetime comes to an end."

He already knew his choice, but still asked, "And when she dies?"

"You can either choose to remain an angel for eternity, or stop existing. There is nothing after this life for angels."

Caleb replied, "I choose her."

God nodded. "Very well." He waved his hand and a cylinder of white smoke surrounded Caleb, sending him back to Fawn's bedroom.

CHAPTER 21

F AWN'S ALARM SOUNDED. SHE UNLOCKED HER PHONE AND shut it off before turning to her left to apologize to Caleb, but his side of the bed was empty. Curious, she felt the sheets on his side and found them cold. As if absorbing their temperature, Fawn felt the coldness seep into her heart as her excitement sunk into disappointment. They were only beginning to repair their broken relationship, but did he regret—or worse, resent—her decision to go to sleep rather than stay up and confess the true depth of her changing feelings toward him? Or was it that he had wanted something more physical from her last night? Either way, she had most likely denied him something and she could understand frustration on his end, but that didn't lessen the chill her worrying had settled over her.

She shook her head free of the doubts and got up to get dressed. No sooner had she finished pulling on her clothes than she saw Caleb in the mirror as he quietly opened her door, in a vain attempt at sneaking back in without calling attention to himself.

"Where have you been?" Fawn asked calmly, despite the tumultuous fears that were now taking root. She picked up a brush and started working through the knots of her long, dark hair.

"I was summoned."

"And what did he say?" Half of her was clamoring to hear the answer, and the other part wanted to forget he had been missing at all.

"As I've fully redeemed myself, I can now return to see my family in Heaven."

She couldn't tell what he was thinking from his tone, but she could feel an inexplicable surge in excitement from their soulmate bond. She felt her heart sink. Had she been duped again? Believed he had chosen her only to come in second?

"So that's it? You got me to say I forgive you, and now you're leaving me? I thought we were past the lies!"

He passed his hand over his face and made an exasperated sound. "See, this is why I didn't want you to know I'd left in the first place." He knelt on the floor next to her chair and took her hand in his. "I chose to stay here."

"I—But wasn't that the whole reason you met me? Don't you want to see your family again?"

He waved his hand in the air as if easily brushing the topic aside. "I've already made the mistake of choosing the dead over the living once. I don't care to repeat it."

"If you turned down Heaven, will you still be an angel?"

"Yes." He unfurled his great white wings, filling her room. "See? Definitely still an angel."

She reached out and gently touch the feathers like she had the night before. "I have a question for you."

"Ask away."

"Does being an angel make you immortal?"

"Yes, but we're not eternal. If I were to 'die,' I would cease to exist. Which makes me all the more eager to cherish every *moment* I share with you."

"For the record, I'm glad you're still an angel. That way you're stronger than humans and able to fight better against Lucifer's army."

He stroked her newly untangled hair. "Nothing, not even being a true mortal, would stop me from fighting beside you."

CALEB WOKE AGAIN TO FAWN'S SHIFTING IN BED. She was sitting up and facing away from him, pulling her hair back into a French-braid.

He glanced at the clock and saw two more hours had passed as they had dreamed peacefully. "Good morning again," he said. He saw her jump slightly in surprise at his voice in the otherwise silent room. "Can we finish our conversation from last night?"

He cleared his throat and reached out to her, letting his fingers trail down her braid and spine. "I was under the impression you were starting to trust me more... and maybe feel something more for me?"

She smiled again. "I've decided that I miss you."

"I don't understand." He tilted his head. "I'm right here."

She rolled her eyes. "I'm ready to move forward."

Excitement burst through him and he pulled her in for a kiss, glad to finally have the privilege again. Stopping her last night had been painful, but necessary. He was glad he had exercised self-control and allowed her to fully come to her own conclusion without being influenced by the stressful events of yesterday or her own hormones.

She kissed him back with equal enthusiasm and they were still entangled when she suddenly jerked away from him with a yelp.

Her right hand flew to her necklace and he saw the pendant was now emitting an almost blinding light. He went to hold her again when the door burst open revealing Alec, who wore a matching expression of terror. Fawn shot up from the bed, grabbed her brother's hand, and together, they disappeared into the hall.

Caleb followed them to the Reading room. Ivy soon joined the group and followed the twins too. What he saw was enough to freeze the blood in his veins.

FAWN STARED AT HER MOTHER'S UNCONSCIOUS BODY IN the center of a bloodied pentacle drawn on the wooden floor and suppressed a shudder. She turned to her brother, and though she could tell he was trying to remain calm, she still sensed his fear as though it were her own.

Suddenly, Stella sat up with a glazed look in her eyes. "You may have won the battle, but you will not win the war," Lucifer's voice said through Stella. "And you," she addressed her daughter, "my father's champion, a murderess in cold blood. You've corrupted yourself beyond repair. How do you expect to defeat *me* when you're no better?"

Fawn stood still, unable to move as the harsh words assaulted her. A hand landed on her shoulder and she turned to see Caleb.

"Don't listen to him. He's just trying to upset you."

It's working, she silently admitted to him.

"If you can get rid of the pentacle, she should return to normal. I have seen enough possessions, and that has almost always worked."

Suddenly, Alec began speaking in God's voice. "She has beat you once and saved her family twice. You will lose, Lucifer."

A silence followed before both mother and brother collapsed to the ground on which they stood. Ivy prevented her soulmate from hitting the floor, and Caleb and Fawn caught Stella as she fell backwards. The three of them immediately began cleaning up the pentacle—or at least trying to with little success. No matter how hard she scrubbed, the bloody marks wouldn't go away.

After a few moments, Alec woke up as if still in a daze, but Stella wasn't moving. "What happened?"

"God and Lucifer possessed both of you to have a nice, threatening conversation," Fawn said flatly. She stood up and found the Grimoire.

"What are you looking for?" Ivy asked.

"How to perform an exorcism."

Her friend paled. "Are you sure?" the siren asked.

"I have to."

Caleb's hand grabbed hers and she looked up at him. "Please, think this through, Fawn. You're still learning magic. What if something goes wrong? Even non-Supernaturals know how dangerous it is to perform this ritual."

"I'm more powerful than them and the average witch. You said so yourself. I'll be careful. But this is my mother we're talking about. I need to try to save her." Fawn found a section dedicated to crystal magic and listed the properties of each beside a hand-sketched depiction.

She read until she found aquamarine and saw one that helped clear the mind. Her eyes sought her brother's across the room. "Alec, find mom's bag of aquamarine? And a mortar and pestle?"

He started rummaging in the cabinets.

"Ivy, can you get salt and a cup of water from the kitchen?"

Her friend didn't answer before leaving to do just that.

Alec and returned. She motioned for them to place the objects next to her angel on the floor.

"Can you crush some of the aquamarine, mix it with the salt and water until it's a paste?" Fawn asked Caleb.

He did as she asked and held the stone bowl up to her when he was done. She dipped her fingers in it until her middle and index fingers were coated with it. Fawn then painted a rune combination of healing, strength, and protection on her mother's forehead.

"Ivy, can you get five candles?"

Fawn told her to place each candle on the points of the pentacle. She magically lit all the candles and channeled the fire to clear her mother's mind. But every time she did it, she came up against a wall of fire inside her mother's mind.

"This isn't working." Fawn magically shut the book in frustration before putting more paste on her fingers. She put her hands on either side of her mother's head, and closed her eyes to search for how to perform an exorcism, silently asking her ancestors to help save her mother—their kin. She got no response from them and decided to plow on without them, this time diving into herself for the answer.

How many times had Caleb said she was more powerful than she was conscious of? She finally found her answer and began chanting the words that came to her, but as the first word barely left her mouth, she saw a white light and then nothing else.

CALEB WATCHED IN AWE AS FAWN WALKED TOWARD her mother with such purpose and held Stella's head in her hands. She began to chant.

"*Vade, Satana, inventor et magister omnis fallaciae, hostis humanae salutis.*" She got louder as she continued, "*Cecidit angelus, resistimus vestris malis tactus. Hanc animam purgare. Tenebris filium dei, quas eieci te ad domum inferni.*"

Caleb watched carefully. Then, he saw bloody tears begin to fall from both mother and daughter, and he surged forward, wrapping his arms around Fawn's waist and pulling his soulmate away from Stella, breaking the spell as he severed their physical contact.

Alec ran to his mother's side and Ivy went to the bathroom to retrieve two clean, wet washcloths. When she came back, Caleb took one and attended to his soulmate alone while the other two did the same to the still unconscious Stella.

part three

We do not need magic to change the world.
We carry all the power we need
Inside ourselves already:
We have the power to imagine better.

J.K. ROWLING

CHAPTER 22

Aᴜ FTER LUNCH, FAWN WAS EAGER TO RESUME TRAINING. Since defeating the Hunters, she had been less zealous in her sparring sessions with Ivy, Alec, and Caleb, but having her mother possessed by the Devil reinvigorated the fire in her to defeat Lucifer and save her family.

Caleb reached out to her and squeezed her hand. "Love, are you sure you want to jump back into your magic lessons? You've been through a lot of stuff recently, and I'd hate for you to burn yourself out."

"I'm fine." She pulled away from him. "I really am," she added when Alec and Ivy watched her as though she might explode. "I'm going to make space in the living room for us to train."

"Fawn—" Caleb started to follow her, but Alec grabbed his arm.

"The worst that happens is she messes up the furniture."

"I've seen Fawn wired, but I've never seen her like this," Ivy said.

"That's what I'm worried about," Caleb said. He stepped up first, and asked, "Ready?"

She nodded and he sent a blast of magic fire toward her. She stared at it and willed her hands to do the same, but to no avail. She tried conjuring a magical shield instead, but had the same result.

She kept focusing and mentally shouted at herself to perform until at the last second a transparent, concave wall of magic appeared. Luckily, despite its weak strength, it was enough to withstand Caleb's attack. Before the flames fully dissipated, he was suddenly at her side.

He grabbed her shoulders and made her face him, a deep frown dominating his face. "What just happened? Why didn't you move out of the way? I know you were trying, but keeping yourself in the line of fire is dangerous, not to mention incredibly reckless."

"I don't know. I can't do magic."

Stella walked into the living room and said, "It's because you're close to burning out. Witches are born with magic, but when one of our kind uses our powers so extensively and consistently as you have been recently, it becomes harder to perform magic until our body eventually shuts down that ability. It's a temporary handicap imposed as a self-defense mechanism. It safeguards a small amount of magic so it can regenerate, but given the circumstances, being stuck in such a state now would be *extremely* dangerous for you."

"If it happens to her, do I automatically burn out, too?" Alec asked.

"No, thankfully, it is not something that can transfer through your twin bond."

"Could I give her some of my magic? Like something similar to a mystical blood transfusion?"

Stella shook her head. "Unfortunately, no. At least, not to my knowledge. I can't imagine it would be possible, or dark witches would likely try to steal others' magic."

"If there is nothing we can do and Fawn has to wait until she recovers, what can she do in the meantime?" Caleb asked, the anxiety clear in his voice. "How is she supposed to protect herself and prepare to fulfill the prophecy if she can't practice using her powers?"

"I don't know. Unfortunately, there is no immediate remedy. I suppose it was created as a way to humble us, to prevent any of us from exercising our power too long unchecked. I believe it would be best if she took a break from all of this."

"Now is not the time to be going on a vacation!" Fawn objected. "I need to prepare for what's coming."

"None of that will matter if you can't use your magic," Caleb solemnly interjected.

"We're about to fight the Devil. I doubt a change of scenery will stop him from coming after me."

"Caleb will perform the same wards that are here," Stella answered.

"Where are we going?" Fawn asked.

"My townhouse in London," Caleb suggested.

"You still have a home there?"

He nodded, but didn't add anything else on the subject. "I'll go pack for both of us. You should stay here and say your goodbyes. I don't know how long we'll be away."

"I'm going to go prepare some salves for you and herbs for your protection." Stella turned and walked toward the Reading room. The wooden door closed and Fawn turned to Alec and Ivy.

They each hugged Fawn. Alec looked grim when they parted and she did all she could to assure them, but doubted her own words as she considered the next, unknown chapter before them.

"What do you think is going to happen?" the siren asked.

Fawn glanced toward where her mother was no doubt busy preparing who knew how many special concoctions that could do who knew what. She secretly hoped they would fix her, but she also was afraid of getting her hopes up only to be disappointed.

"I don't know. But I'll stay in touch, okay?"

"Hourly check-ins," her brother clarified.

"He's over-exaggerating," Ivy cut in, looping her arm through his. "You only need to text me every few hours."

Fawn shook her head. "You're both being ridiculous. Everything is going to be fine. We're just going on a short vacation. I'll be back in no time. Maybe even with my magic back."

INSIDE FAWN'S ROOM, CALEB LISTENED TO HIS SOULMATE'S conversation with the others as he flitted about. Though he dared not say it, and he had suspicions Stella felt the same, he feared something awful was about to happen, making their plan to leave all the more urgent. As he pondered, he continued packing, grabbing enough clothes from Fawn's closet and drawers to last for a month.

He doubted they would need to stay away for so long, but it was better to be prepared. He noticed they had stopped talking and re-entered the living room and took Fawn's hand. "Ready?" He wished he could ease her mind fully, but saying any more than he already had would be filling her head with false hopes and he had vowed to never again keep another secret or utter another lie where his soulmate was concerned.

Using his angel magic, he opened a portal and guided her forward. They landed on the sidewalk in front of his childhood home.

She looked over the garden of trees wrapped in lights and walked closer. "This is beautiful. Can you show me around?"

He held out his arm to her. "It would be my pleasure." He ushered her through the gate and pointed off to the left, on the side of the house. "My mother and sister used to work for hours in this garden." He could practically see them there, now. He blinked back the tears and squeezed Fawn's hand, grounding himself in the present moment.

"I'm sure it must have been beautiful."

"It was." He sighed, remembering how it used to bloom with rosebay willowherbs, poppies, and roses. "I suppose I should have taken better care of this place between my past missions." He tensed, anticipating Fawn's negative reaction and likely rebuke concerning his past employment. To his surprise, she didn't say a word.

He could sense there was so much happiness in her aura there wasn't even a ripple of her usual judgement on the topic.

He led her through the back door, away from prying eyes, where they entered a small hallway with blue-gray walls. He ushered her past the kitchen on the right and pointed her attention to the simple family room on the left.

It was much smaller than his other apartment and had an old rug in the center under a small, hand-made wooden table. "I used to play with my little sister in there when I was little. After my father died, I didn't have as much time, but she loved our sibling time."

"That's beautiful."

He nodded before turning and walking up the stairs to the master bedroom. It was about the half the size as the living room below and only had space for the medium-sized bed and one cabinet. The walls were the same color as the front entry way and felt incredibly cozy.

Now at the end of the tour, He placed their bags on the floor beside the small closet and finished with, "Well, that's it. I know it's nothing much, but it's home."

Fawn walked around the room once, turned toward him, and launched herself at him, her arms latching around his neck as she kissed him deeply. "Thank you."

He returned her attentions, pulling her closer and moved them until he sat on the bed with her straddling him. He tugged lightly on her hair, making her temporarily pull back. "For what?" he asked.

She smiled, though the expression in her eyes told him it was a sad one. "For being you, and making me temporarily forget what a mess my life has become."

THAT NIGHT, FAWN HAD ANOTHER NIGHTMARE. IT WAS similar, but much worse than the one with the Hunters. In *this* dream, while fighting off the second crimson-clothed Hunters, she lost control of her power and killed her loved ones before realizing what she'd done. Whenever she had previously wished for Hercules' strength, she hadn't wanted the Greek demigod's curse too.

"It's your fault they're dead."

She looked up to see Lucifer grinning at her. "What do you want?" she spat. "Haven't you already done enough?"

He surveyed the carnage around her then knelt in front of her. He grabbed her jaw in his bloody hand and said, "Had you taken my side, they would have thrived under my rule."

She woke up in a panic, her hair sticking to her face and her breaths coming fast and heavy.

"Fawn?" Caleb asked, groggily. "Are you okay?"

"I just had a nightmare. I'll be fine."

Silence engulfed the room.

The next morning, they had breakfast in bed. When they were done, Caleb moved the tray to the floor. "I need to run out and grab a few more things. Why don't you go take a bath? I promise I'll be back within twenty minutes."

Fawn did as he suggested and sighed as she soaked, letting the hot water loosen her tight shoulder muscles. She didn't remember falling asleep, or being tired to begin with, but woke up to Caleb watching her silently from the bathroom's threshold.

He walked towards her. "You could've drowned, you know."

She pulled the plug and sat up. "I didn't mean to doze off."

"Doesn't make it any less dangerous."

"You don't have to worry about me all the time, Caleb. I can take care of myself. When did you get back?"

"Just a few minutes ago. I got everything I needed."

"Are you going to tell me?"

He smiled. "Maybe later." Then he was kissing her.

Fawn pulled away. Even though they had been intimate with each other many times before, she felt exposed. "Can I put pajamas on first?"

His eyes flitted over her face, an unreadable expression in place. "If that's what you want." Suddenly she was wrapped in a towel and being carried bridal style into the adjoining bedroom. He set her down in front of the dresser and turned away from her.

She changed quickly, wrapping her arms around his middle when she was done. He faced her and kissed her nose. "May I continue?"

She pressed her lips to his in silent answer and walked backwards until the bed was behind her. He hovered over her and started kissing her neck. She could feel the beginning of a headache and closed her eyes. Shouting and the loss of heat brought her back to the present.

Caleb was holding—*Caleb*—by the front of his shirt.

"Get away from my soulmate, you fucking asshole."

She sat up on the bed and instantly regretted it, her head spinning.

The one being threatened chuckled. "Careful, there. You're going to feel a bit sick for the next hour or so, but it'll go away eventually."

"What... did you do... to me? And why am I seeing double?"

The other, angry Caleb demanded, "What did you do to her?"

A red cloud engulfed the first one, revealing a smug Lucifer. "You should have taken better care of your soulmate, Caleb. What will God do now that his Chosen One has no magic? He can't win a war without a weapon." He disappeared, his laughter still rattling inside her head.

Unable to stay alert, she lay back down and closed her eyes.

CHAPTER 23

CALEB RAN TO HER AND PULLED HER CLOSE. He had felt something was off while he was in town, but it hadn't been the usual danger warning he received. The guilt of not being able to protect Fawn reared its ugly head. Would she forgive him? And what would happen now she didn't have *any* magic?

Her eyes fluttered open. "Caleb..." she croaked. "I'm so sorry. I should have known it wasn't you."

"I'm the one who should be apologizing. I shouldn't have left you alone, especially when I knew Lucifer was plotting against us."

"You don't have an excuse to blame yourself. It's not like you *knew* what he was planning. I, on the other hand, should have seen the signs. He was acting more aggressive and cold than you do. I didn't feel relieved to see him like I do you..."

"Of course not, but I should have been here to protect you. Then none of this would have happened."

She didn't answer for a moment. "Can we test something?" He nodded. "Show me your aura."

Caleb dropped his mental walls immediately and watched Fawn's forehead crease with concern. "What's wrong?"

"I can't see it."

Any hope that Lucifer had been bluffing disappeared. She looked so small and vulnerable. It was a ridiculous notion because she was still the woman he loved, his soulmate—and nothing besides her magic had been taken away. "Magic doesn't define you, love."

"That's a lie and you know it. My entire life has revolved around my magic and this prophecy."

"While that's true, you're still a whole person without your powers."

She turned away from him, but his angel hearing told him she was quietly crying.

He lay down on the bed next to Fawn and stroked her hair. "We'll find a way to fix this." When she calmed, he called her brother.

"Hello?" Alec asked.

"We have a problem."

"What happened?"

Caleb could hear the tension in the male witch's voice and wondered if he had perhaps felt something through the twin bond.

"Lucifer stole Fawn's magic while pretending to be me."

"And where were you? You were supposed to protect her."

Caleb hung his head in shame, even though he knew Alec couldn't see the gesture. "I was in town, buying things to surprise your sister."

"You couldn't have magically conjured them?" the brother spat. "Maybe then Fawn wouldn't be defenseless without her magic."

"If I had known anything was wrong, believe me, I never would have left. And I'll regret I did until we find a way to fix this."

"Oh, don't worry. I'll make sure you remember this fuck-up long after that," Alec muttered. "Can you put her on the phone?"

Caleb looked over at his soulmate, who looked more scared and quite frankly pathetic than he had ever seen her—more so even than when she had been suffering from denying their Bond. "I don't think she's in the position to explain what happened just now."

"Bullshit. Hand her the phone."

"Are you going to yell at her?"

"No, you idiot. I have tact."

Caleb reluctantly held the phone out to Fawn, but she made no move to take it. Instead, he placed it beside her head on the pillow.

He stood to leave. "I'll give you some privacy."

She grabbed his wrist and gently tugged him back down beside her. Turning to the phone she said, "Hi."

"How are you doing?" her brother asked.

"I don't want to talk about it, Alec. I'll see you tomorrow, okay?"

"You're coming back?"

"Well, Lucifer already found us, so I think we'd be safer in numbers. I'm sure Caleb can organize a way home for us." She turned to him for confirmation and he nodded. "Can you... tell Ivy and Mom what happened for me?"

"Of course. What are you going to do now?"

"I don't know..." her voice cracked. "Probably wallow in despair for a bit longer."

"Fawn..."

"I'll be okay," she assured him as much as Caleb and herself. "I love you." She hung up before he could add anything else.

ALEC THREW HIS PHONE ONTO THE BED WITH more force than necessary. It landed an inch away from Ivy's head. He felt guilty when she flinched, but he was too mad to care. "Our twin bond broke, you know. I felt it snap before Caleb even called." He paused. "I keep expecting to feel her pain about this all, and then I remember I can't anymore." He tensed when he felt her hand on his shoulder.

"I know you're upset. I am too. I don't want you to think I'm not, because I really am, but what can we do about it?"

He spun to face her. "I've never heard you sound so defeated. Where's the headstrong siren who pushed my sister into way too many college parties and encouraged her to date her soulmate? You never let something discourage you."

"My best friend just lost her fighting chance to survive a war against Hell, her twin bond, and possibly her soulmate bond, too."

"We really do need to consult my mom, though, and see if she knows of any ways Fawn can regain her magic."

"When are Caleb and Fawn coming back?"

"He said late tonight, early tomorrow. She's apparently devastated and he doesn't want her any more stressed than she already is. She never wanted this destiny, but I think her magic powers have become such a huge part of her she doesn't know what to do without them." He yawned and pulled the covers over them. "It's late. We should go to sleep. The problems will still be there in the morning." He draped his arm over her waist and turned out the bedside light.

"Goodnight. I love you."

He kissed her shoulder. "Me too."

The next morning, Ivy had jokingly suggested they Google the solution to their problem, and they were now sitting hunched over his laptop as they sat on the living room couch.

Alec heard footsteps and heard his mother's voice, "Any luck?"

"Possibly..." Ivy started.

"It's unlikely," Alec interrupted, ignoring his soulmate's small protest. "We found some stuff, but it could be bogus, for all we know."

She sat down across from them. "May I see?"

They slid the computer across the coffee table. Stella waved her hand and a cup of warm tea appeared. She took a slow sip and scrolled for a few moments before closing the screen.

"How do you feel about it, Alec?"

"Will it work?"

"Answer the question first."

"If it's going to help Fawn, of course I'll do it."

"Ivy, what do you think?"

"Why does it matter what she says? It's my decision."

Stella fixed her son with a chastising stare. "Because she is your other half and will have strong feelings about such drastic measures."

Ivy cleared her throat. "No disrespect, Stella, but I don't want Alec to give up his magic if there's another way to help Fawn get hers back. I know it's selfish of me, but I want to know he can defend himself." The siren sighed. "I bet you hate me now."

"Why would you say, dear?"

"Because I'm practically asking you to sacrifice one child for the other. No parent should ever have to decide something like that."

Stella offered her a warm smile. "While you are correct, I have always known that my children would be placed in dire circumstances that required difficult action. And I could never think ill of you, Ivy. This *may* work, and there might be an alternative."

"And what would that be?"

"Caleb could sacrifice his magic for her," Ivy supplied.

"Why didn't you mention anything before?"

"Because filling up a half-full tank of gas with another type of fuel can cause a disastrous combustion. It would have been too risky when Fawn still had some of her own magic."

"Did you know this would happen, Mom?"

She shook her head. "But before we jump to conclusions, we need to think about the consequences of going through with this, regardless of who becomes the donor."

"What do you mean?" her son asked.

"Caleb is over two hundred years old. Without angel immortality, he'll die," Stella clarified.

"So, I'm as good as dead if *I* save her..." Alec clarified, "and Caleb *is* dead if he's the one to restore her magic?"

"I'm afraid so," Stella answered.

"Why is nothing ever simple?" Alec muttered.

F AWN WATCHED CALEB ADJUST THE SHOWER KNOBS. HE had *refused* to let her out of his sight for more than a second ever since the debacle.

"We were going to have to talk about it again eventually."

She leaned against the glass door, hesitating. "I don't know how I feel." He opened his mouth to interrupt, but she continued, "Part of me is relieved I don't have the responsibility anymore. If I don't have my magic, *maybe* the Prophecy isn't about me. And then I remember if it *is*, I have no chance of winning this war without them."

Her stomach knotted when Caleb didn't immediately reassure her. She undressed and stepped under the stream.

He did the same and joined her. After pressing a kiss to her forehead, he sighed. "I can't tell you which it is. For your sake, I would love it to be someone else."

They finished their shower in silence.

Fawn pulled on a summer dress and took out a comb. Caleb took it and gently worked it through the tangles. "What else do you feel?"

She shrugged, watching him in the vanity mirror. "What else *can* I feel about it?"

He didn't answer. A few moments passed before he placed the comb down and turned her toward him. "Done."

She rubbed her eyes and nodded. "All right, you've had your chance to psychoanalyze me. Can we talk about something else now?"

"That barely scratched the surface, and you know it." He saw her tense and added, "but I'm done probing for now."

It pained him to ever be the cause of his soulmate's discomfort, but with such an important destiny, they couldn't sweep her sudden loss of magic under the rug, no matter how much any of them wanted to.

CHAPTER 24

WHEN FAWN AND CALEB EMERGED FROM THEIR ROOM, she was bombarded with questions, all with the same answer: "Yes, I'm okay. No, I don't know how to fix this."

If Caleb hadn't had his arm protectively around her, she may have collapsed under Alec and Ivy's interrogation. Losing her magic hadn't only left her normal, but made her feel even weaker than she used to when she wasn't using magic.

Once they had satisfied their curiosity and collectively decided she *was* indeed telling the truth, they filled them in on their progress.

"We've been researching the problem," Ivy explained. "And we haven't found anything definitive."

Alec came out of the living room. "Yes we have." His tone was sharp and exasperated, as if they had had this argument many times before. "There's a ceremony we could do that would—" Ivy's broken expression made him halt. "I'm sorry, Ivy, but you know I have to do this."

"No, you don't. There have to be other options. Even if there aren't, it doesn't have to be you."

Fawn looked between them and changed the subject. "Well, until someone figures out how to restore my magic, and everyone agrees to go through with it, I think it's best if I continue my defense training."

Her brother cleared his throat. "Are you strong enough for that? I mean," he continued when she gave him an offended look. "You did just spend most of yesterday out of commission and two nights ago. Shouldn't you give yourself a break?"

"I'm fine. I can't sit around and wait for them to come after us again."

"We can protect you," Caleb said.

"I can't have you always running into save me. I know it distracts you—don't try to deny it. We both know it's true. And if Alec isn't focusing on protecting himself, he could die. And you said you're not eternal, so one of these days, it could cost you *your* life."

He nodded in agreement. "Perhaps, but I also know it would be well worth it."

She gaped at him. *Was he serious?* When he didn't blink, she admonished, "Don't say that."

"Why not?" He took a step towards her. "It's true."

She took one back as if that would distance her from the awful idea. It wasn't even a possibility, but she saw her brother growing more interested in their conversation, and had a sinking feeling he was in on it. "Don't. No one is sacrificing themselves for me."

"Even if it means you get your magic back?" her brother interjected.

"Alec!"

Fawn saw Ivy shoot her brother a glare mixed with pain, anger, and a deep sadness which she had never seen her friend express.

"What are you two talking about? Was this the plan you were mentioning earlier?" *Why are you even asking? They'll just take it as encouragement*, she scolded herself. "You know what? It doesn't matter because it's not going to happen." She stared meaningfully at both guys. They both met her gaze head-on, determination shining in their eyes.

"Don't let your stubbornness get you killed. Even you have to admit this makes logical sense. We found a way for you to reclaim your magic. Mom, Caleb, or me, can give our magic to you. But the transfer would leave the donor completely mortal."

"No. *No* way. You're both completely insane for even considering this. I can't accept this twisted form of generosity if it means I could lose any one of you when it could have been prevented. I won't be responsible for your deaths, and you can't use me as an excuse to sign your death warrants."

"We want to help you. Why won't you let us?" her soulmate demanded. "None of us want you to die, and here we are offering you an opportunity at restoring your magic." His voice rose as he spoke. "We're *willingly* doing this for you. Because we love you. And we're not asking you to sacrifice both of us. The spell only requires one donor. I know how much you value free choice. You have options."

"I'm not letting someone else die in my stead. I'm happy this way. I swear."

"I don't mind, Fawn," her soulmate argued. "If you can still save the world, I'll help you any way I can."

"If this is some perverted way you think you can prove your devotion to me, you've proved more than your point, Caleb. Now, *please* drop the crazy idea so we can move forward with real, practical ways to prepare for the upcoming battle."

"It's not an empty offer, Fawn. Yes, it is arguably the grandest gesture I've made to prove my allegiance to you, but I do not intend to withdraw my candidacy because I've 'made my point,' as you so crudely put it."

Fawn closed her eyes. She didn't think the good news of possibly getting her magic back could make things *more* complicated than her unexpected defenseless state.

Ivy stepped forward. "All right. They're not going to let this go, so we might as well start sparring."

Fawn nodded and brought her arms up to prepare to defend herself against an attack.

An hour later, the doorbell rang. Fawn sprinted to the foyer and opened the door. Marcus, Dylan, and a girl she had never met were standing on the other side. "Come in. It's so nice to see you again, Marcus, Dylan." She turned to the stranger. "I'm Fawn. And you are?"

"Bailey. I'm Dylan's girlfriend."

She held out her hand. "It's nice to meet you."

After a moment, the girl returned the gesture. "Likewise."

Fawn turned to see Caleb and Dylan watching each other with wary eyes. "This is Caleb. He's my soulmate."

The guys nodded at each other.

Dylan hugged her and whispered, "I assume this is the guy?"

She nodded.

"Congratulations," he murmured before pulling away.

Alec stepped in to say hello. "Hey, man. Long time no see."

"Come into the kitchen," Stella invited. "I'll make everyone something to eat."

Soon after everyone had gotten a plate, Stella called Marcus away into the Reading Room.

"Can you fight?" Caleb asked Dylan.

Her old friend nodded. "I learned right after we moved. Dad started my Alpha training once we had more space and fewer prying eyes."

Fawn stared at him. "You're a werewolf?"

He nodded slowly. "You couldn't tell?"

"I wasn't exactly in the habit of using my magic back then. Why didn't you tell me?"

Dylan shrugged. "It never came up."

"What are you talking about 'away from prying eyes'?" Alec interjected. "Isn't the French Quarter as crowded as it gets in Louisiana?"

"Yes, but we live near the Bayou. We also have an apartment in the Quarter for non-wolves to visit us. It's safer that way for everyone—human and werewolf alike."

"I still can't believe you kept that a secret," Alec said, awe and admiration clear in his tone.

Dylan shrugged.

"When did you two meet?" Fawn looked between Dylan and Bailey.

"A month after we started freshman year in college," she answered.

Fawn didn't miss the underlying possessiveness in her tone. Luckily, Stella and Marcus came out of the Reading Room, both with a serious expression in place.

"We have decided we need to recruit allies," Marcus began. "Everyone will stay with their significant other."

"I've been speaking with many covens, and since most have suffered from witch hunts instigated by Lucifer, many have already pledged their allegiance to us. The others are leaning towards doing the same, but only request they meet Fawn in person first."

"If they were hoping to see a magic show, they'll be disappointed," Fawn said.

"What use are you if you don't have any magic?" Bailey asked, eyeing her with barely concealed contempt.

"Watch it, dog," Ivy snapped from across the table. "That's my best friend you're insulting."

"Girls," Stella intervened, giving them both stern looks. "Unity is key if this is going to work. Am I being clear?"

Ivy glared at the wooden table and mumbled, "Yes, Stella."

Bailey had the good sense to keep her mouth shut.

Marcus spoke up, eyeing his group. "I expect you both to give Stella, her children, and their soulmates the utmost respect. We are guests here, and grateful for it. Represent our pack well."

"Apologies, Alpha," Bailey muttered, not meeting his gaze.

"Where are we going?" Fawn asked, changing the subject.

"You and Caleb will be staying in the North East for the aforementioned reasons," Stella answered. "You should start in Salem. They are one of the most powerful covens in the country and if you persuade them, others may follow." She turned to Alec and Ivy. "You will be tackling California. Be careful on your travels." Finally, she addressed the young werewolves. "You will go to the states near the Great Lakes."

"Stella and I will be going to Las Vegas, then Florida, and back home," Marcus added. "Everyone has their assignments. Meeting dismissed."

Bailey stood up, then sat back down when she noticed no one else had moved.

"You may go get ready," Stella affirmed.

They retreated to their rooms, leaving the wolves and Stella in the living room.

"You didn't tell me he was coming," he whispered.

"I told you before. There's nothing there. Why are you so upset?"

"I underestimated my capacity for jealousy when it comes to you."

Fawn gave him a sweet smile. "There's *nothing* to worry about. Can you pack? I'm going to make us food."

Dylan was sitting alone in the living room. "Hey, can I talk to you?" he asked.

"Sure." She entered the kitchen.

He followed her. "I wanted to apologize about Bailey. She doesn't trust non-wolves. I think she also was on edge with meeting you."

She opened the refrigerator and pulled out cheese, lettuce, tomato, and honey mustard. "Did she know about us?"

"Yes. Did Caleb?"

Fawn pulled out a board and knife, and began preparing some sandwiches. "Yes. He was upset at first, but calmed down pretty quickly."

"Really? Because I think he hates my guts for ever being romantically associated with you."

"I'll admit, he surprised me with his jealous streak, but I hope that will go away with time once he realizes you're not a threat to his relationship with me."

"Right..."

Sensing he wanted to say more, Fawn set the knife down and looked up. "Dylan, things ended before you moved."

"They ended *because* I moved," he corrected. "I still have feelings for you, Fawn."

She took a step back. "Dylan... What are you saying? You can't say things to me like that. You have a soulmate, for—" she cut herself off. She had been about to say "God's sake." When she saw he was still waiting for her to finish her statement, she said in a calmer voice, "The point is, you have a soulmate now. We *both* do."

"Bailey's not my soulmate. We're dating, but she's not my destined soulmate. Hers was killed in a bar fight with a gang."

"And yours?"

"Normally, male wolves leave home when they turn eighteen to find their mate, but I never felt that urge. I think it means she's dead."

"That's awful." He took a step forward and she retreated. "This still doesn't change the fact that I have a soulmate, whom I love very much."

As if on cue, Caleb walked in, kissed the top of her head, and wrapped his arm around her waist. "The bags are ready. Are you almost done here? It's best if we can get to Salem while there's still sunlight."

She smiled and kissed him on the cheek. "I'll meet you outside."

"Don't be too long."

"I won't." When he left, she said. "I love you Dylan, but only as a very close friend." She stepped back. "Good luck on your trip." With that, she left.

CHAPTER 25

"You're speeding," Fawn chastised. Caleb checked the speedometer and eased up on the gas. They arrived at the Coach House Inn right as the sun was setting. He barely put down the bags before Fawn was kissing him. She moved forward, straddling his hips, changing her target to his neck. He groaned and scooted back until his head hit the pillow, letting her continue her exploration. When he couldn't take it any longer, he rolled on top and they continued deep into the night.

The next morning, they dressed quickly and ate a short breakfast before getting back in the car. When they arrived, they walked to the top of the hill and waited.

Soon, Caleb could hear people surrounding them, still hidden in the woods at the base of the mound. "They're here," he whispered, squeezing her hand.

An elderly woman, no younger than eighty, stepped out first and stopped in front of her. Two other women, one Fawn's age, another her mother's, followed. They stood on either side of the first.

"Are you the one who put an end to the two clans of Hunters?"

Fawn nodded jerkily. "I am."

"Hm. Good riddance to those abominations of nature," the old woman said. "Can you demonstrate your powers for us?"

Fawn shook her head and held her chin high. "I'm not in a habit of making a spectacle of myself."

He inwardly applauded her audacity to refuse such a powerful witch with her followers in attendance. A weaker person would have caved, but not his Fawn.

The crone scrutinized his soulmate a bit longer before turning to him. "And you are the redeemed angel? Her soulmate?"

He kept his face devoid of emotion. "I am."

The two younger women stepped forward. "Please come with us."

"I'm not leaving her."

He suddenly felt as though he were being torn in two and sank to his knees. He ground his teeth, determined to not cry out in pain.

"Stop! What are you doing to him?" he heard Fawn ask.

"A customary precautionary check to make sure he will not tell Lucifer what we say."

"I'm telling you, he's not working for the Devil anymore. He's working for God now."

The pain stopped. He heaved a sigh of relief and stood behind Fawn, wrapping his arms around her waist.

"He has not done my coven many favors in the past."

"Same here," Fawn said, "but I hate Lucifer more than Him. God doesn't make me suffer, he just doesn't step in to stop it either."

The old woman seemed to mull over his soulmate's words. "Prove to me you are no longer working for the eternal bastard."

Taking a deep breath, Caleb unfurled his wings.

The crone took a step forward to touch his feathers, but Fawn stepped forward, blocking the path.

"I only need one," the leader explained. "Angel feathers are extremely rare and can make spells exponentially more powerful."

Fawn nodded. "You may have one—but I will pluck it—" she didn't trust the woman to not hurt Caleb again, "and you must promise to join our side and use the feather in a spell against Lucifer and his army."

"Make it two and we have a deal."

"One for now," Fawn insisted. "If we win this war, then you can have your second."

"In that case, it would be our honor to fight alongside you. It's about time the King of Hell got a bitter taste of his own medicine."

The leader turned around, facing away from them. "Sisters, come out into the open and take a blood oath." About a hundred cloaked women emerged from the tree line and began closing in on them.

"Blood oath for what?" Fawn whispered.

The crone sliced her palm open with a silver athame and let the blood fall onto the hill. "Upon the grave of my ancestors, I pledge my fealty to the Belgrave coven until this battle is over."

The others followed suit, pulling out their own daggers and repeating the process.

Fawn's body stiffened as the air filled with their words. "Do you feel that tingling?" she whispered.

He shook his head. "I don't feel anything."

"Does this mean I have my powers back?" He was surprised to hear the optimism in her voice. Perhaps she had changed her mind about how she felt about her magic?

"It may just be because they're binding themselves to your coven." He regretted stifling her hope, but it was better she didn't have any illusions and assume she had magic, only to find herself in a dangerous situation falsely confident about her self-defense abilities.

He glanced up at the crowd. Now that the oaths had been made and the noise had died down.

"We will await your call," the old woman said before bowing.

"I—Thank you."

She tried to walk away, but the witches came closer.

"Ah, ah, ah. Remember our deal, dearie. A feather before, one after."

Fawn turned to face him with an apologetic expression on her face. He nodded in confirmation and folded a wing closer to her. He bit back a curse when she pulled a feather from the end.

"Sorry." She turned back to the old woman who was waiting with an equally eager and impatient expression on her face.

"A gesture of good faith," Fawn said, as she handed over his feather, keeping eye contact with the elder witch.

"Yes, of course," the woman said absent-mindedly, caressing the feather with disconcerting glee.

"We will call on you soon," Fawn said, her tone sounding more imperious than he had ever heard it before.

This time, when she moved to leave, the witches let her pass. He followed close behind her. Once they were back in the car and a mile away from the meeting spot, Caleb briefly turned away from the road to check in on Fawn, who hadn't said a word since they left. "What are you thinking?" he asked.

"Can they hear us?" she whispered.

He shook his head.

"I don't trust them," she said after a pause. "They seemed too eager to let us fight this battle on our own. And only when they saw your wings did they care about helping us."

"Most people are selfish, Fawn. You can't hold it against everyone or there would be very few people left to trust. Why don't you call your mom and Alec to check in so they know Salem is on our side?"

She pulled out her phone.

"Yeah, they agreed. They just wanted one of Caleb's feathers. ... I made them promise to use it towards our cause."

He heard Stella say, "And the other?"

"I didn't specify."

"Fawn, I don't know if you understand how powerful those feathers are. They have the power to magnify a spell to affect a whole civilization if a single witch uses it. Imagine a whole coven equipped with one focusing their energy at once."

"It was the only way they were going to agree to help us."

Stella was silent. "I am not blaming you. But in the future, avoid such deals with the other covens."

"Okay, Mom. Would you mind telling Alec for me? We're going to Gettysburg now."

"Be careful. They're very suspicious of outsiders."

"We'll remain vigilant," Caleb said loud enough for Stella to hear him from the driver's seat. "Talk to you again when we're on our way to Sleepy Hollow."

Fawn said goodbye and then ended the call.

CHAPTER 26

Out of the corner of his eye, Caleb watched Fawn as he continued to drive. Two hours ago, she had plugged her headphones into her phone and was now sleeping even though they were still in her ears. Not wanting her to damage her hearing, he magically lowered the volume until not even he could no longer hear the strains of her favorite female singer-songwriter.

After three more hours of travelling, he pulled into a shopping center and gently nudged her awake.

At first, she didn't budge, but a moment passed and she opened her eyes. "Where are we?" She sat up and looked out the window, taking in the small gas station.

"A quick stop. We're only two hours away. We should arrive by twilight. I thought we could get some food, and then if you want to take a turn at the wheel, you can."

"Sounds good. I'm heading to the bathroom. Can you get food?"

"I'm not leaving you alone."

She rolled her eyes. "You have angel hearing and speed. I'm perfectly safe with you nearby. You don't have to be glued to my hip at all times." She rubbed her thumb over his knuckles. "I'll be fine, promise."

"You can't guarantee that. You know I'm right. I could make a list of times you've said something similar and been proven wrong." He waited her out.

"Fine," she sighed. "But you have to wait outside."

He nodded, knowing that would be as far as she would concede, and followed her to the restroom. Once she was back outside, he wrapped his arm around her waist and held her close as they bought their food and refreshments like a normal, mortal couple.

Once they were back at the car, he had the driver's door open when Fawn coughed. "Aren't you forgetting something?" His eyes rose to hers and she held her hand out for the keys. He dropped them into her palm and she smiled as they passed each other and switched sides.

"Remember," he said, making her turn to him. "Don't speed."

"Haha," she deadpanned. "If we get pulled over, I'm blaming you."

"You'll be in the driver's seat."

"Bastard." She turned the key in the ignition and started the car.

66WHY DO YOU KEEP TURNING OFF THE RADIO?" Fawn asked, thoroughly annoyed when Caleb turned the volume off for the third time in a row.

"Because you like to sing along to the music."

"Are you insulting my talent?"

He smiled. "Hardly. But without your magic, you need all your attention for driving. I'm positive your mother would not appreciate it if her cost of insurance suddenly spikes if the car gets totaled because you are a distracted — even if it's because of the amazing soundtrack to an award-winning musical."

She adjusted her grip on the steering wheel. "I'll have you know I drove just fine before I was using my magic regularly, and unlike *you*, I never used my special abilities to skirt highway laws." She saw him smile and asked, "What now?"

"Nothing. I just like you like this."

"Annoyed? Or in charge?"

"Both." He held up his hands in surrender when she glared. "What? It turns me on seeing you like that, but I was thinking more of how much I enjoy when you are relaxed."

"I think you need a dictionary because fearing for the safety of the ones I love and not having magic does *not* qualify as 'relaxed.'"

"Are you always so snarky?"

She rolled her eyes. "Like you don't already know the answer to that. But you know you love it. It's all part of my charm."

He leaned back. "Yes it is," he said appreciatively.

Fawn spared a quick glance at him. "Are you sure you're okay about Dylan? I'm sure you heard his confession to me in the kitchen."

"Guilty. I fully intended to give you privacy..."

"But?" she prompted. She couldn't even get mad about him eavesdropping. If it had been her in his position, she would have likely done the same—a shameful, but true confession she had no problem admitting to herself.

"I couldn't when I saw how much he still loves you."

"Just so you know, I was surprised as you were. I swear what I told you before was the truth."

He sighed. "Believe me, I know. I just can't seem to get rid of the last of my lingering jealousy."

"Caleb, there is no competition—"

He waved her off. "There's nothing you can do or say about it that will change how I feel. I need to get over it on my own."

She swallowed her protest and nodded. The conversation lulled, and they finished the drive in silence.

CALEB FELT BAD FOR SHUTTING FAWN DOWN, BUT he didn't know how the conversation could have continued without leading to another argument. Once they reached the small hotel, he unloaded their two bags and refused to let Fawn take hers. It was a small gesture in his mind, but he hoped she would take it as an apology.

They checked in and were walking into the room when his guilt reached its suffocating level and he blurted, "I'm sorry."

She sat on the bed and shook her head. "You don't have to be."

He searched for another topic. "Do you want to talk about the plan for tomorrow?"

She shrugged. "What is there to talk about? It's going to be like today, right?"

"Well, almost—"

"I won't give any more of your feathers out. I learned my lesson."

"No one is mad at you for making the trade. It was an honest mistake neither your mom nor God warned us about."

"Do they ever?"

He knelt in front of her and took her hands in his. "Hey, don't be negative. We'll need to stay motivated if we're going to convince all these covens to join our cause."

She lay down and covered her eyes with her arms. "I don't know how missionaries stand all this."

Caleb laughed. "Neither do I. They don't have anyone nearly as charming as you to keep them company."

She uncovered her eyes to look at him with suppressed amusement. "Do you ever turn off your charm?"

"Nope. Don't think there's an off switch." He pulled off his t-shirt and turned around. "You're welcome to search for it, though."

She shook her head. "I'm not in the mood tonight."

He lay down next to her on the covers and any arousal he had felt disappeared. He wasn't mad, but he would be lying if he claimed to not be even the slightest bit disappointed.

She turned onto her side, toward him, and said, "Can you hold me?"

His arms were around her in an instant. Whatever she needed, he was glad to provide it. And right now, it seemed she needed comfort. He pulled her closer. "Everything is going to be fine," he assured her.

She didn't answer, but merely snuggled closer into his chest.

"I've got you," he promised. "I'll always take care of you."

CHAPTER 27

THREE DAYS LATER, EVERYONE WAS REUNITED BACK AT the Belgrave apartment around the sizable dining room table, enjoying a large, homemade meal by Stella.

"Did anyone run into any problems?" she asked, placing more mashed potatoes on her plate before passing it to Alec on her right.

Fawn poured herself more ginger ale and took a quick sip before replying, "You would have heard from us if we had."

"Or wouldn't have," her brother countered between chewing, earning a silent chastising glance from his mother.

"That sounds like a story," she prompted her brother.

She saw Ivy glaring at Alec, but he either didn't notice or didn't care as he began talking. "Things were going fine on our trip until we reached our second to last vampire coven. Miss Feminist over here didn't listen to me when I asked her to let me do the talking—"

"And why would I?" Ivy interrupted. "That was the most sexist thing you could have asked me to do. I'm not an animal who is meant to be 'seen, but not heard.'"

Alec continued, speaking louder than before, "If you had listened to me, you wouldn't have gone on a feminist rant when the leader of the coven made a sexist comment—which pissed me off as much as it did you—and made him angry. Thankfully they had already agreed to join our cause, but we were chased out of there within inches of our life."

Fawn failed to hold in the laugh she had been struggling with since her brother had started.

"It wasn't funny," Ivy grumbled.

"Yeah, sis, we almost died!"

She took a bite of food, a sip of water, and swallowed. When she could talk, she pointed her fork at both of them and said, "But you didn't. You survived and are still here for me to tease when you two do something silly and mess up."

"It's not like you don't do the same thing."

"I never said I was perfect. Besides, what type of brother would you be if you were always nice to me? I'd start suspecting you were pulling a prank on me if you acted like that."

Alec made a faux gasp. "Like I would ever stoop to such infantile methods. I'm much more sophisticated than that."

Fawn rolled her eyes. "Yeah, right. Remember that time you—"

"Well, I'm glad you made it out okay," Stella said, putting an end to the brewing sibling argument.

"All the packs we met with immediately agreed," Dylan said.

Stella nodded. "That's good to hear. When will they start making their way here?"

"In a few days at maximum. They needed to set a few affairs in order first."

She continued her inquiry, glancing around the table. "Did anyone encounter plain refusal?"

"Good." Stella stood up. "Alec, Caleb, if I could speak to you for a moment in the Reading Room."

They stood to clear their plates.

"You can leave those for later."

They both put down their dinnerware and followed her.

CALEB CLOSED THE DOOR AND LEANED AGAINST IT with his arms crossed. Stella leaned on the small table with a crystal ball and ornate rosewood box which he assumed housed her tarot deck.

"What are we doing in here?" Alec asked, pacing. "For all we know, we could be attacked any minute and if I'm going to die, I want as much time with my sister as possible."

"Who says it's going to be you?" Caleb asked. "If it should be anyone, it should be me. I'm her soulmate. I don't know much about the ceremony, but if there's any chance of our special bond amplifying my donation, that would be our best bet."

"Are you kidding? Fawn would never forgive us for letting you die."

"Like she'd forgive me for letting one of her own *family* take on the job? She'd hate me as much if not more."

Stella said, "Calm down boys. For tactical reasons, having an angel and a witch surviving is the best choice. Therefore, I will sacrifice myself so neither of you need to."

"No, Mom! You know more about magic than I do. Fawn needs you to teach her."

"But when I eventually die in the future, she will need you, her brother, to comfort her." Though she did not raise her voice, Caleb recognized Stella's steel resolve.

Alec must have recognized it too, because his shoulders sagged.

However, Caleb could not allow Fawn, his soulmate, to go through the same pain he had experienced of losing a mother—least of all because of Lucifer. He said as much, finishing with, "No more arguing. I will be her donor. I will hope for the best, but at worst, she will still have her family intact."

F AWN FELT THE REMAINING PEOPLE AT THE TABLE watching her. "What?" she asked They all looked down at their plates and began eating again.

Fawn suddenly felt sick. Because of her, countless people were putting their lives in danger to save her. Some strangers, others close friends, and most importantly, her family and Caleb. It wasn't fair it was the one time she was supposed to help *them*—not the other way around—and here she was rendered as useless as a newborn baby.

"Excuse me," she said, pushing back from the table, taking her plate with her into the kitchen.

Without her powers, she couldn't overhear what they were saying in the Reading Room, but she would have to be an idiot to not guess it had to do with her current situation.

Life was so unfair.

"Fawn?"

She turned to see Ivy standing next to her. When had her friend even come in? Now that she peeked into the dining room, she noticed the werewolves had left too and she hadn't even heard them go. "Yeah?" she asked, her throat unusually tight.

"I'm sorry," she said.

A crease formed between Ivy's brows. "If anyone should apologize, it's me."

"For what?" Fawn echoed.

"I'm being selfish with Alec. He keeps making the point Stella is the best versed in magic, Caleb knows Lucifer better than the rest of us, and you're the foretold savior in the Prophecy. He said he's the only one who could die without altering destiny. And I haven't wanted him to sacrifice himself—even if it means the rest of us can live. Which is terrible, but true."

"I don't blame you. You just started being real soulmates. I would never ask you to give that up. We'll find another way, I promise."

"We're running out of time. And they're making the decision now as we speak, so I don't think it matters to them that you're objecting."

Fawn threw her hands up. "They're being ridiculous."

"Practical," Caleb corrected from behind her. He wore a grim expression and his arms were crossed over his chest. His eyes were hard, daring her to argue.

Fawn saw her mother enter the master bedroom and followed. "Please tell me you didn't make an executive decision behind my back."

Her mother smiled at her, but it didn't reach her eyes. Even her jewelry's shine seemed duller than usual as if reflecting its wearer's somber mood. "It's for the best, dear."

"That's not for you to decide."

"As your mother—"

"Okay, fine. Yes, you have a say, but it shouldn't discount my opinion on the matter. This isn't just about me. Otherwise it'd be a simple decision." Her mother raised her eyebrows, but Fawn continued without pausing, "I'd fight the best I could, and if I died, that'd be it. But having someone give me their magic permanently affects whoever is that person's soulmate and family."

"If you die, we all suffer a loss."

"War always leaves casualties."

"This is our best fighting chance. I know you do not like it, but believe me when I say we have exhausted our sources to find another way to restore your magic."

"What do you mean?"

"The other teams were not only asking for alliances, but also any knowledge to help your situation."

"Of course they were."

This time, she heard Caleb enter. "Do not get angry at your mom. She is doing what she thinks is the best way to save her children."

"I'm assuming it's one of you who decided to take on this insane suicide mission?" The pause was all she needed for confirmation. "Which one of you?"

Caleb wouldn't look at her, and she could only stare at her soulmate whom she had only recently begun to love unconditionally. "Were you ever going to tell me?"

He wouldn't look at her. "Not before the spell, no."

Fawn fled the room. She found her best friend sitting quietly in the living room. "Congratulations, Ivy. Alec will survive this."

Her brother emerged from the kitchen with a glass of water and handed it to her. "I'm sorry," he said.

Dylan walked in and came towards her. Should she let him talk to her, or leave?

He moved faster than she expected, stopping in front of her while she was still pondering her choices. "Are you okay? You look like someone has died."

"They haven't yet, but they will."

His eyebrows furrowed. "I don't understand."

"If you're done insinuating yourself into my relationship, I'd like to speak to my soulmate now," Caleb said.

She refused to be baited again, choosing instead to smile sweetly at Dylan. "Thank you for your concern, but I'll be okay."

"If you need anyone to talk to—"

"She has me and her family," Caleb interrupted again.

"Thank you," she said, trying to soften the antagonism.

Dylan looked between her and the angel before nodding once, his eyes on the floor, and leaving the way he came.

"I never thought he'd leave."

She pulled away from her soulmate and stormed into her room, slamming the door and locking it before sinking onto the bed and rubbing her eyes with both hands.

"Fawn," a voice said.

Fawn sat up immediately, and came face-to-face with Evelyn.

"I don't know what you can say right now," she growled. "But I'm not exactly in the mood for another cryptic warning."

Her ancestor had the decency to lower her head in acknowledgement. "I apologize for not being more clear with you, but I was forbidden. I did the best I could to guide you."

Fawn exhaled loudly. "It's not your fault."

"I am here now to help you better than I could before."

"How?"

"By helping you find another way to save the ones you love."

"You couldn't have shown up ten minutes ago and stopped the three people I love most from going behind my back and choosing who to offer up as a sacrificial lamb?"

"There is still no other way to restore your magic," the angel stated, "However, if you ask the correct questions, I will give you information that will put your mind at ease."

"Does everyone from Heaven speak in riddles, or is it just you and God? Because it is immensely irritating when you offer help, but don't actually give it! And I don't know what to ask."

"Fawn?" Caleb's alarmed voice sounded through the door. "Are you okay? Let me in."

She quickly turned to Evelyn. "Don't let him in," she whispered.

Her ancestor nodded after a moment and waved her hand. "No one can enter until you open the door."

She sighed in relief. "Thank you."

"I must insist that you continue asking questions."

She rolled her eyes. "Caleb will become mortal once his angel magic leaves his body and jumpstarts my own powers." She paused and saw Evelyn smile. "Is that a false assumption?"

"That depends on how much he transfers."

"How would he stay an angel?"

"If you shared the magic instead of a full transfer."

"What would happen if I died while we're sharing the magic?"

"All of your magic will revert back to him." Evelyn bowed. "And now I must leave you. I hope you know how proud I am of you—we all are. I wish you the best of luck in the future, my dear. I will see you again when the time comes." With that, she disappeared.

Fawn sat back down as she digested the new information. Now that she knew Caleb would live and could survive this war even if she didn't... She smiled. It changed everything.

CALEB KNOCKED ON THE DOOR AGAIN, NOW THOROUGHLY exasperated with his stubborn soulmate. He had tried to magically enter multiple times, but to no avail. What was she doing in there? And how had she blocked him without her powers? He was about to try and break the door down the old fashioned way when he heard the lock turn.

Fawn stood before him with an unreadable expression on her face. She began walking towards the living room and he followed. When they arrived, she asked, "Can we do the transfer now?"

If he argued, he would sound like he didn't care about saving everyone's lives, but something told him they should wait until he knew what had changed his soulmate's mind.

"Caleb?" Fawn asked. "Are you ready?"

He closed his eyes and counted to ten, praying that he wasn't making a mistake. "Yes."

"Give me your hands," Stella instructed both of them, producing an athame from thin air. They both obeyed and Stella sliced their offered palms. "Hold hands," Stella said. They did.

"The point of this is?" Alec asked from his observational perch on the couch.

"As their blood combines, their lives and magic will temporarily be joined," Stella explained. "And then we'll transfer his magic to Fawn."

"No."

"What do you mean, 'no'?" her brother asked. "Isn't that the whole point of this?"

"It won't be a transfer. We'll just be sharing the magic. Evelyn told me this will work," she added before anyone could object.

So *that's* what had turned her around.

"We'll both have magic at full capacity," Fawn assured them.

"Does anyone object?" Stella asked.

Everyone was silent. Taking this as confirmation, she said, "When you feel your hands burning, start chanting with me." That was the only preamble she gave before beginning herself. "*Cum sanguine coniunctos in hasce formas: mente, anima, et magia.*"

Stella repeated it three times and the fire in his veins grew hotter until it felt as if he were being boiled alive. His eyelids grew heavy and closed of their own accord. Then he felt a cool ocean washing over the lava in his veins, leaving only a tingling sensation in its wake.

He opened his eyes. Fawn was beaming at him with more love than he remembered ever seeing on her face, but he was too busy staring at his soulmate's forehead.

She noticed his attention. "Why are you looking at me like that?"

"There's a symbol on your forehead."

As if just realizing the same thing, Stella leaned forward and gently turned her daughter's face upward for inspection. "It's runic. Ivy, please hand me the Grimoire again." Once she had it again, she flipped open to the back cover page. "I've seen this before."

"It's the same rune that was supposedly on Excalibur's hilt," Caleb explained. "And Moses' staff. And Perseus' shield. Any past legend has had that rune secretly inscribed on their object of power. Some people call it the 'Savior Rune.'"

"So what does it mean that it's on *me* and not on one of my possessions?" Fawn asked.

"You're a weapon," Ivy answered, putting the pieces together first. She looked around the room. "She's not the wielder—God is."

CHAPTER 28

Fawn opened her eyes and murmured, "They're here." She was rising from the bed when Caleb reached out and touched her arm.

"Who is, love?" Caleb asked.

She didn't answer, and he must have understood because he went still for a moment before saying, "Go. I'll be with you in a moment."

She magically dressed and entered the living room. Her mother and the others were just coming out of their rooms, too.

"What is going on?" Alec asked.

"The demons are coming," Fawn and Stella answered together. "They've opened a portal in Central Park. We need to close it." Having delivered their message, they blinked and took in their surroundings.

"How did you know that?" her brother asked.

"God possessed them," Caleb answered, finally entering the room, wearing jeans and a simple black t-shirt. "There's no other way for them to *both* have the same message without divine intervention."

"Should we start calling our allies?" Ivy asked. "I know it's early..."

"They know what they signed up for," Marcus gruffly interjected. "I'll help contact them. We will meet you there soon, Stella."

She nodded and the Belgraves, Caleb, and Ivy joined hands before Stella magically transported them to Cleopatra's Needle.

On the side of the stone obelisk was a round portal resembling a black hole. From the infinite depths emerged an unending of stream of demons of all sorts. Some looked like the ones Fawn had already encountered, ones Caleb was familiar with from his time in Hell, and ones he had never seen before. He'd never thought he'd been particularly sheltered in Hell, but apparently, there had been a lot kept from him.

"We need to contain them," Stella said, reaching out to her children's hands. "Our allies will be able to enter, but they won't be able to get out to spread their malefic influence, either."

They took her hands and began chanting.

Caleb saw a filmy light shoot up from between the trio and it began to spread and fall in a dome shape. He watched the progress and saw the demons attempting to break the protective shield without success, but he was paying more attention to his soulmate's state of mind. She was hiding something from him, but he still hadn't figured out what.

He cupped her face. *You can trust me.*

She nodded. "I know I try to put on a brave face, but the truth is, I'm terrified. The entire Supernatural community is depending on me to succeed. I don't think I can handle this."

"Remember all the good you've done with your powers. If I could eradicate all your insecurities, I would, but this has to come from you."

"Everyone has been alerted," Marcus said, entering the protected area, Dylan and Bailey flanking him. "They are all on call, awaiting your orders," he finished.

The demons had begun circling them and suddenly surged forward. Then he felt Fawn lunge away from him. He turned just in time to apprehend a demon hurtling through the air toward him. Seeing red, he trapped the offender in a headlock before breaking its neck. He let the body drop and crouched into a more defensive position, ready for when the next two who came at him. He bent low and launched the one over his shoulder, smashing into other. For good measure, he broke both of the passed out demons' necks.

He rose just in time to see three more charge him.

How are you holding up?

Fine. Killed two and seem to have strengthened the protection ward by funneling their life energies back into it.

That's my girl. Incoming—They turned in time to counter-attack four demons charging at them.

You don't know how turned on I am, watching you defend yourself against these bastards, he said.

Save it for later, she said, turning back to the battle at hand.

Caleb quickly surveyed the fighting ground and saw they were equally spread out in pairs. Ivy and Alec were fighting off a hoard of demons in one corner while the werewolves were also working as a team to defend themselves. Stella and Marcus handled another section while Dylan and Bailey covered the remaining area.

Caleb loosed the beast inside him and plowed through the demons' ranks, killing any and all that were within his reach. After a while, when he had lost count of his kills, Caleb felt his energy draining. Looking around, he saw everyone on their team hunched over, breathing hard amidst the scattered corpses of the demons of all types.

From the corner of his eye, he saw a bloodied monster rise from the carnage into a crouching position. The creature's gaze was set on Fawn, who wasn't looking in the right direction to see what was happening.

"Fawn!" he shouted, running between her and the creature. He felt pain shoot down his spine and turned to see the monster had implanted its tail between his shoulders. Determined to not let the monster attack Fawn, he pulled the sharp end out of himself and, using the tail as a leash, pulled the demon closer to him before launching himself up into the sky, taking the demon with him.

He heard his soulmate call his name, but resisted the temptation to look down. His opponent rabidly clawed against him, landing a good swipe on his chest, shredding the top layer of skin into ribbons. Caleb groaned in pain and thrust the hellion away from him, and still gripping the tail, began to spin it in circles around him as if he were preparing to throw a hammer. He finally let go, sending the creature far away. Caleb saw it disappear in a puff of red smoke, then felt the demon on his back again, its hands grasping his head.

And then everything went dark.

FAWN SCREAMED AS CALEB'S BODY BEGAN TO FALL from the sky. Her entire vision went black for less than a second before she felt a bolt of electricity shoot through her as though she were a telephone poll in a storm. Once she regained her vision, her eyes tracked him for a few moments before she was successful in slowing his descent. By the time he was no more than five feet from the ground, she had brought him to a complete stop and gently lowered him the rest of the way.

She turned to see the demon land, standing victorious over her beloved's body. Furious and empowered by the unexpected surge of new power, she took a single step forward before she heard her brother.

"You can't avenge Caleb's death if you die the same way he did."

Her breathing was labored, but she calmed herself until she could see with deadly clarity. Fixing her gaze on the creature, she imagined his body incinerating: his skin dissolving like flash paper, and then his muscles being flayed from his bones. As she saw the demon's life about to snap away, she imagined harnessing its life force and funneled it back into Caleb.

She heard one last screech before the monster disappeared into the air like a flicker of dark smoke from a candle. Then she ran over to Caleb's body. She glanced around to confirm no other demons remained to attack. "Are they gone?"

Stella nodded. "It is over."

Her brother, Ivy, Stella, and even Dylan approached. "Is he okay?"

Are you there? she silently asked him. There wasn't an answer, and she gave herself over to the tears which had been threatening to fall ever since his neck had been snapped.

A puff of red smoke bloomed in the center of the field like something out of the Wizard of Oz. Lucifer stood in an immaculate black suit, his eyes blazing red. "I hate to break the party, but I have unfinished business with your little savior."

CHAPTER 29

Fawn stepped toward the Devil before anyone could stop her. "You
don't need to make a show of this." She cleared her throat, realizing she sounded like a weak beggar. In a stronger voice, she added,
"We can settle this privately."

He flashed a brilliant smile, sending goose bumps multiplying
across her skin. "Unfortunately, the only way I can trust you to com-
ply with my demands is if we have an audience." Lucifer advanced
toward her and she closed her mind from everyone but Alec. She
heard her brother curse under his breath, probably realizing she had
her own agenda. "Don't do anything stupid," he warned.

"You should listen to your brother, dear," the Devil sneered, stopping mere inches away. "After all, you don't want to render Caleb's
sacrifice moot, do you? It would be a shame if his death were in vain."

"I don't need to listen to my brother. I know what I'm doing." Fawn
tilted her head up to maintain eye contact. "You're going to kill me
anyway. I might as well try and fight back."

Her defiance prompted another unnerving smile to spread across
Lucifer's face. "I must say, I have enjoyed our little dance, but it's grown
tiresome and the time has come for you to say goodbye." His hands
closed around her neck and he lifted her into the air, above his head.

Unbearable burning flared from the base of her head and seared
through her head, chest, and spine until she felt as though she were

being burned alive like the Salem witches. Her hands came up and tried to pry his fingers off, but his grasp was unbreakable and she found herself gasping for air.

Closing her eyes, she focused on burning him—and not dying.

He only squeezed tighter. "I don't consider myself a violent man. In fact, I hate wasting talent, but you, my dear, have caused me more trouble than you're worth."

Fawn wanted to spit at him, or preferably claw his eyes out, but she was trapped in her own head with darkness quickly closing in on her vision. For a moment, everything was completely dark before she saw a white light and felt herself lift out of her body.

Floating above the entire scene, she saw her mother, brother, Ivy, Marcus, Dylan, and Bailey surround Lucifer. They charged forward, only to be blasted backward by the Devil's magic. They fell on the ground. One by one they rose, but Lucifer snapped his fingers and they were instantly immobilized.

A burst of energy shot through Fawn and she was suddenly back inside her skin. As if electrocuted, Lucifer dropped his hands from her, his eyes widening as fear, confusion, and anger swirled in his black eyes.

She took advantage of the distraction and blasted him with her magic, channeling all her hate and anger at him as payback for threatening her loved ones' safety and peace of mind.

Back to his usual, confident self, Lucifer turned to face her head-on with his hands in front of him like a catcher in a baseball game. She watched as her magic gathered in his hand, but didn't hurt him. Then it disappeared as he covered it with his other hand. He seemed to absorb the energy, his eyes glowing hotter as he did so. "Thank you for that. I needed a little pick-me-up."

She sent another wave of magic—this time a fight to survive and save those she loved, not a vengeful retribution—just as he blasted her stolen magic back at her.

The magic collided, sending them both flying backwards into opposite sides of the field. Using her magic to give her hyper-speed, she ran over to him before he could rise. "This is all your fault," she snarled at Lucifer before placing both hands on his chest and, using Caleb's magic and her own, she stilled Lucifer's heart and retreated.

"Is that all you can do?" the fallen angel taunted.

Fawn shook her head. "Not even the start, but I don't want to drag this out. I have other things to do with my life besides living under your poisonous influence."

"You know you can't kill me."

She took a deep breath and channeled all the magic around her, siphoning everything she could from her twin bond and the protective wards around the park. She need all the help she could get. "True, but I can immortalize your defeat."

Understanding dawned on her adversary's face just as she blasted a grey stream of magic at him, turning him to stone like he had done to Caleb's mother centuries ago. His face was frozen into an expression of shock, his mouth agape with a silent shout he had never had the chance to release.

Staring at her handiwork, she created a titanium baseball bat and held it out to the others. "If anyone needs to take out their frustration."

"Won't that set him free?" Alec asked.

"No." Somehow, she was positive of the fact, and that was enough to satisfy her. "He will never be a problem again."

His fear now gone, Alec grabbed the piece of metal and began smashing the statue with all his might. Ivy went next. Stella declined the offer, as did the werewolves.

Fawn took it from her best friend and finished off what was left until there was a pile of dust where Lucifer once stood.

The adrenaline of staying alive and her anger at the author of so much of her misery now out of her system, she returned, suddenly exhausted, to Caleb's dead body. She grasped his ripped shirt and shouted. "I told you I didn't want you to sacrifice yourself for me!" She lay her head on his chest. The lack of a heartbeat made the tears she had been fighting finally fall. "Why would you do this to me?"

"Fawn—" Her mother touched her shoulder, but she didn't loosen her hold on Caleb.

Suddenly, she and her soulmate were on the living room floor. They must have transported while she was distracted.

"Fawn."

"I fulfilled your stupid Prophecy, after suffering so much for your cause—one I didn't even sign up for. You owe me big time."

The old man nodded. "I do."

"Bring him back. And don't you dare say you can't—or won't. It's the least you could do for me after everything I've suffered."

"As you wish."

A transparent version of Caleb, his ghost, appeared by God's side. He smiled contentedly at Fawn. She felt as though her heart was going to burst if she couldn't ever hold him again. She whirled on the deity and snapped, "Is this some kind of sick joke?"

"What do you mean?" God asked.

"You've manipulated me my whole life, and Caleb's, too, by making that deal with Lucifer in the first place, and now we don't get to be with each other? You're not only going to let him be ripped away from me, but also taunt me with a ghost?"

God shook his head. "I admit I have not done right by you in many ways, but I am not cruel. Look at him," he said, gesturing to her ghost soulmate.

Caleb walked toward his body. He lay down in corporeal form until his ghostly essence was completely inside. Fawn watched as his wounds healed and felt his heart begin to slowly beat once more. She waited until he had opened his eyes before wrapping her arms around him and giving him the strongest hug she had ever given.

"You're alive!"

He smiled at her. "I told you everything would be okay."

"You didn't know that. I thought I had lost you." Before he could answer, she kissed him. She savored the sensation of his warm lips against hers and strong hands at her back and in her hair, pulling her closer to him. She ended the kiss when she needed air and looked over her shoulder at God. "Thank you."

"If that is all you require of me..." the deity started.

"Will we be safe?" Fawn asked.

"Yes," God said. "The whole world will be."

"Does that mean there won't be Evil anymore?"

He shook his head. "No. You defeated my son, not Evil in its entirety. Don't worry, that is not your responsibility," he added quickly.

"Thank God," she sighed.

He laughed. "You're welcome."

"Do I have my magic back from Lucifer? I don't want to put Caleb in danger again by sharing his powers."

"You are back to your original state before my son meddled with your abilities," God explained. "You have fulfilled the final part of the prophecy: *United, together as one, through love, darkness shall be overcome.* I'm proud of you both." He pointed to her forehead and she felt a small tug as he pulled white light from where her mark had been back into his hand. Without any further explanation, God bowed to her and disappeared in a cloud of white smoke.

She finally released Caleb and he beamed at her, completing her in a way she previously thought impossible.

Stella, Alec, Ivy, and the three werewolves moved forward to greet the resurrected Caleb. Fawn saw her mother wave a hand, and suddenly flutes of champagne appeared in all of their hands. Stella raised her glass of and said, "To our victory."

"It was a long time coming," Alec added.

They clinked their glasses and drank.

"Where will we go from here?" Fawn asked.

"Wherever you want," Stella said. "After you finish college."

Alec rolled his eyes. "Yes, Mom."

"I'm sure God will help in organizing that," Caleb said. "At least you only have to make up two years instead of four."

"But it's Junior and Senior year—there's so much work involved," Ivy muttered.

The conversation moved toward saying good byes to Dylan, Marcus, and Bailey.

Dylan said goodbye to Alec first, and saved Fawn for second-to-last. She embraced him in a hug and said, "It was good to see you again."

"Same here," he said, not quite meeting her gaze.

Caleb stepped forward and she tensed, hoping there wouldn't be a confrontation between them. Her soulmate surprised her when he held out his hand and said, "Thank you for helping protect her."

Dylan returned the gesture and they shook hands. "Of course. It was nice meeting you. I'm glad she's happy with you."

The three guests had left, and Fawn was glad to have the apartment back to only family and soulmates. She let out a small yelp of surprise when Caleb lifted her into his arms and whisked her into their room and locked the door behind them.

He deposited her on the bed and she propped herself up on her shoulders to look at him. "I love you, Caleb. You know that right?"

He nodded and joined her on the bed, lying beside her. "And I love you with my whole existence." His hand went to her hip, turning her toward him. "I can show you now, if you like."

"Maybe later," she mumbled, taking his wandering hand in hers and resting her head against his chest. She sighed, letting herself revel in the sensation of him holding her in his arms. They lay in silence for maybe an hour before Fawn was confident this wasn't a dream—that Caleb really had come back—and was relaxed enough to fall asleep.

A week later, Fawn's bags were packed again, ready to leave home. She and Alec were heading back to school at their mother's insistence. She didn't care that much, but he wasn't too pleased about it.

She watched him say goodbye to their mother in the foyer.

"See you for Summer Break," he finished.

"Unless we do summer school," Fawn added, stepping up beside him, earning a look of mock horror from him.

"Be safe," Stella said.

"That's easy now," Ivy said.

"Still, take care of yourselves."

"Alright, Mom," the twins said, smiling.

Once inside the car, Caleb put it in drive and turned toward her with a conspiratorial smile. "Ready to have your first taste of freedom?"

"I would hardly call returning to college freedom," she remarked, smiling in spite of herself.

"Who says we're going back now? I have a surprise for you."

CHAPTER 30

C ALEB PARKED THE CAR AND LOOKED OVER AT the still-sleeping form of
Fawn. She hadn't stirred once since the start of their trip and it
warmed his heart to see her peaceful enough to fully let go and rest
without worrying when and where the next attack would be coming.

Not wanting to wake her, he silently opened his door and walked
to the other side where he carefully lifted her out of the seat and into
his arms. He waited for the bellhop to unload the car before he magically locked the vehicle when the man wasn't looking.

"You can check in at the concierge desk on the left," the man said.
"I'll bring these up to your room."

"Thank you." Caleb walked into the five-star hotel and checked in.

He ignored the way the receptionist ogled him and practically
snatched the key cards from her hand when she finally offered them
and left with a curt "Thank you."

Inside the elevator, he readjusted Fawn in his arms and pressed
the button for the penthouse suite.

He opened the door, laid her on the bed, and started unpacking.
When he was done, he saw her just waking up. "Hello. Nice sleep?"

"Very." She stretched. "Where are we?"

"The West End. We have tickets to see *Les Misérables* tonight—I
know it's one of your favorites."

"Thank you, but I would've been fine with a simple dinner at home."

"We can still do that if you want..." he said, sitting next to her on the bed.

She shook her head. "No, this is fantastic, but in the future, you don't have to go through such lengths to impress me. Spending time with you is more than enough."

"I'm very glad to hear that. You should start getting ready."

Her eyes lit up. "Shower with me?"

"We'll never get there in time if I did."

"What are you talking about? We can just flash there."

He pecked her on the cheek and chuckled. "You're not going to tempt me now."

She pouted, but didn't press the issue further.

"Get ready, love. I brought a few dresses for you to choose from. They're hanging in the closet."

Fawn lay back down. "I don't want to move..."

"Up and at it, love. The show starts in two hours and we have a reservation for dinner in an hour."

She stood up and smiled. "I'll get ready. See you when I'm done."

Caleb pulled her down for one more kiss. "Hurry."

FAWN PUT THE HAIR DRYER DOWN ON THE sink and stared in the mirror, pulling her locks up on one side of her head, the other, and directly on top of her crown. She let the drop and decided on Dutch braiding it in a headband.

When she was done putting in the final bobby pin, she walked back into the bedroom, still wearing her towel, and found it empty. Caleb was sitting in the other room watching the TV.

Quickly, she rifled through the five dresses and wound up picking the floor-length purple dress. She finished zipping up and called Caleb. He poked his head into the bathroom and groaned.

"Do you like it?" she asked.

He pulled her against him as a silent answer, kissing the top of her head. "What do you think?" He retrieved their coats and escorted her down the hall, into the elevator, and waiting car outside.

When they reached the theater, it was buzzing with excitement. Looking around, Fawn could see people of all ages in the red velvet seats, even some small children. She doubted they would last long, but smiled as she remembered going to her first musical at the age of five.

The lights turned down and she leaned forward in her seat. They sat in the first row of the mezzanine, giving her a full view of the stage. She felt Caleb hold her hand in the dark and turned to smile at him briefly before refocusing on the show. She cried during Fantine's death and was moved by the chorus of "Do You Hear the People Sing?"

When the house lights came back on for intermission, she could feel the dried tears on her cheeks that never failed to appear whenever she listened to the show's soundtrack. Caleb pulled her in for a kiss and she smiled as his lips met hers.

He pulled away and suddenly knelt down on the ground.

"What are you doing?" she asked, stunned. She looked around to see if anyone was watching them. He couldn't be... could he? They hadn't really talked about their relationship status again after she had decided to forgive him after she learned he had been working for Lucifer.

He held out his hand for her left one and she tentatively took it. He kissed her ring finger and produced a small black velvet box from his jacket pocket. "Caleb—" Fawn choked on his name, unable to fully convey her confused anticipation.

He opened the box and took out a silver ring with two stones in it, one topaz and the other aquamarine. "This," he turned the piece of jewelry so it caught the light, "is a promise ring."

"And what are you promising me?" she asked, unable to take her eyes away from him.

"To love and cherish you for the rest of my existence. I say that because death will never do us part." Caleb winked. "Will you do me the biggest honor and marry me, Fawn Belgrave? Say you'll let me always be by your side."

An elderly woman from a few rows behind them said, "Say yes, dearie! He's clearly a keeper!"

Fawn smiled, gave up on fighting the tears, and kissed him, letting him feel her love in its rawest form. When he pulled back to look at her, she smiled and breathed, "Yes."

He lifted her by the waist and spun around. "You have made me the happiest angel alive," he whispered in her ear. He placed her feet on the ground again and beamed at her.

Fawn placed a hand on his cheek and said, "You've done the same for me, so I'll promise to do all you just said, too."

The bells chimed, signaling the show was about to resume. They took their seats again, clasping each other's hand tightly.

When the show finally let out, they magically returned back to their room, discarded their clothes, and got tangled in the sheets, not emerging from their bed until early afternoon the next day.

EPILOGUE

THREE YEARS LATER

CALEB WATCHED WITH TEARY EYES AS FAWN DRIFT toward him in a white lace sheath. Despite the veil, he could see her face as clearly as if it were hovering over him like it did each morning.

He had objected her wearing it, but she had insisted on it.

"Why?" he had asked.

"Because it's traditional."

"And since when have we adhered to any convention?" He had approached her, leaning down to kiss her as he finished his question, but she had taken a step back and fixed him with a stern expression.

With a hand on his chest to maintain the small distance between them, she had said, "Caleb, I've dreamed of my wedding since I was a little girl."

He smirked. "I never realized how romantic you were. I always took you for one who didn't care about this kind of thing."

"Well, I am, all right? I care about what our special day will look like. I want it to be perfect, and after all the stuff we've gone through, we deserve it."

He smiled. "Absolutely."

"I did stop thinking about marriage in middle school." She shrugged. "I didn't know I still cared about these clichés until I met you."

"I'm a cliché?"

"You know that's not what I meant. You bring out the romantic in me again," she had clarified.

He never would have been able to predict he would be marrying Fawn Belgrave when he first received the assignment from Lucifer. How could he have known his ticket to freedom was just that?

I love you, he mentally told her.

I love you, too, her voice echoed in his head. She lifted her head and, using his angel sight, he saw her blue eyes sparkle with joy. She stopped in front of him. He held out his hand, nodding his thanks to Stella, as she released her daughter's arm and took her seat in the front row of the audience.

Ready? Fawn asked, drawing his attention back to his beloved.

He nodded and turned to the Justice of the Peace. Despite not having gone with a lavish wedding, they had instead decided to only have Fawn's family and closest friends present, it seemed inappropriate to say vows that omitted God and any mention of death in front of a religious man of any kind.

Though there were very few seats, the whole space was filled with the ghosts of Fawn's ancestors. Evelyn stood closest to the front, near Stella and Alec. Her expression was one of peace and pride, and Caleb was glad she approved of their relationship.

"You may now kiss the bride," the Justice said.

Finally! He pulled Fawn close and planted a deep, yet chaste, kiss on her lips before releasing her and turning to their friends and family with a triumphant smile.

Only close friends of the Belgrave family had been invited, much to Fawn's college friends' disappointment, but he was glad they had kept it to an intimate party. It meant less schmoozing and more time to be with the people he cared about.

Next to Stella, he saw his mother, father, and sister rise and clap with the small audience. He stared in shock and startled when Fawn touched his arm.

"When did they arrive? *How* are they here?"

"I asked God to let you see them on this special day." His new wife whispered. "I know they're the reason we even met and you weren't able to reunite with them. I wanted you to get your happy ending."

"How can I thank you enough?"

She smiled. "You don't have to. It's my wedding gift to you."

He kissed her again. "It's perfect, love. Thank you."

"Go say hello to them. I'll give you some privacy."

He wrapped his arm around her waist. " Come with me. I want them to meet my better half."

Together, they approached his family. They embraced them in a ghostly hug, whispering their well wishes before they disappeared back to Heaven.

Alec and Ivy came forward and congratulated them as a couple before hugging each of them separately.

Alec hadn't been too pleased with his decision to move forward without asking him first, but the brother got over the small transgression when he saw how happy Fawn was when they announced it to the family. Ivy and Stella were almost as ecstatic as his fiancé when they learned the news.

"Take care of my sister," his brother-in-law warned in a low voice before releasing him from the tightest, and most threatening, hug he had ever received.

"I plan on it," he answered. "When can I expect to return the favor of being best man?"

He saw Alec cast a surreptitious glance toward the siren. "If you didn't mind, I was planning to propose to her at the reception. Normally, I wouldn't even think about detracting attention from you and my sister, but I can't wait any longer."

Caleb nodded. "I have no problem with it. I'm sure Fawn won't either, but you should ask her."

Ivy came toward him with a determined look on her face. "I'm sure Alec already threatened your life if you hurt our girl, but I'll add that I'll torture you before her brother finishes you off."

Fawn looped her arm through his as Alec did the same with Ivy. She looked at her brother and best friend. "Stop threatening my husband and go get something to eat."

At the reception, Alec proposed to Ivy and the entire audience awed as they witnessed the other Belgrave twin move toward wedded bliss.

The rest was a blur to Caleb. He only cared about his wife, and stuck by her through the entire evening. When they finally left their guests downstairs, he was thankful for more individual time with Fawn and showed her just how much he loved her in that moment— and would continue to do so for the rest of his existence.

THE PROPHECY

A sorceress with blood laced in gold sevenfold shall
determine the fate of the world.

Love misled shall betray her and destruction shall reign
until forgiveness won.

United together as one, darkness shall be overcome.

OTHER BOOKS

SHORT STORY
COLLECTION

UNMOORED

TAMING
THE ALPHA

ACKNOWLEDGMENTS

I would like to first thank my friends, family, and most importantly my *readers* for supporting my writing. I don't know what I'd do without any of you.

Special shout outs to Jessica Elliott, my brilliant critique partner, Jennifer Munswami (JM Rising Horse Creations), my magical cover artist, and Danielle Lincoln Hanna, my awesome editor.

Important note: authors live on reviews. And so, I ask you, my wonderful reader, to leave a review on your favorite retailer, and recommend this book to your friends.

If you want to be kept in the loop about all my future publishing endeavors, subscribe now at zarahoffman. com/subscribe, and you'll receive the first three chapters of the sequel, *Unmoored*, Alec and Ivy's story.

ABOUT THE AUTHOR

Zara Hoffman is a college student and has been writing since she was eight years old. She spends most of her time doing homework and writing new stories because if she didn't, her head would likely explode. Her books are for young adults or the young at heart. After all, growing up is overrated.

www.zarahoffman.com
zarahoffman@zarahoffman.com